Praise for *Sophie's World*

'A marvellously rich book. Its success boils down to something quite simple – Gaarder's gift for communicating ideas' *Guardian*

'An *Alice in Wonderland* for the 90s . . . *Sophie's World* is being talked up as philosophy's answer to Stephen Hawking's *A Brief History of Time* . . . this is a simply wonderful, irresistible book' *Daily Telegraph*

'An extraordinary achievement' *Sunday Times*

'Challenging, informative and packed with easily grasped, and imitable, ways of thinking about difficult ideas' *Independent on Sunday*

'A terrifically entertaining and imaginative story wrapped around its tough, thought-provoking philosophical heart' *Daily Mail*

'A unique popular classic' *The Times*

'Seductive and original . . . *Sophie's World* is, as it dares to congratulate itself "a strange and wonderful book"' *TLS*

An Unreliable Man

Jostein Gaarder was born in Oslo in 1952. *Sophie's World*, the first of his books to be translated into English, has been translated into 60 languages and has sold over 40 million copies. He is the author of many other bestselling, beloved novels and children's books, including *The Orange Girl*, *The Christmas Mystery* and *The Ringmaster's Daughter*. He lives in Oslo with his family.

Also by Jostein Gaarder

Sophie's World
The Solitaire Mystery
The Christmas Mystery
Vita Brevis
Hello? Is Anybody There?
Through a Glass Darkly
Maya
The Ringmaster's Daughter
The Orange Girl
The Castle in the Pyrenees
The World According to Anna

An Unreliable Man

JOSTEIN GAARDER

Translated from the Norwegian by Nichola Smalley

WEIDENFELD & NICOLSON

First published in Great Britain in 2018
by Weidenfeld & Nicolson
an imprint of The Orion Publishing Group Ltd
Carmelite House, 50 Victoria Embankment
London EC4Y 0DZ

An Hachette UK Company

1 3 5 7 9 10 8 6 4 2

This translation has been published with the financial support of NORLA.

Extract on p37: p.4 'The Seeress's Prophecy' from *The Poetic Edda* by
Carolyne Larrington 2E (OWC 2014) by Permission of Oxford University Press.

A CIP catalogue record for this book is
available from the British Library.

ISBN (Hardback) 978 1 4746 0582 3
ISBN (eBook) 978 1 4746 0584 7

Typeset by Input Data Services Ltd, Somerset

Printed in Great Britain by Clays Ltd, Elcograf S.p.A.

www.orionbooks.co.uk

Gotland, May 2013

Dear Agnes. I was going to write to you. Remember? Or at least, I was going to try.

I'm sitting on an island in the Baltic Sea with a laptop in front of me. To the right of the laptop I've placed a large cigar box. It contains everything I need in the way of memory aids.

The hotel room is large enough for me to get up and take nine steps to and fro on the pinewood floor as I consider how to begin my tale. All I have to do is make my way past a three-piece suite, and I alternate between passing the slim teak table and pair of red armchairs, and moving down a similarly narrow corridor between the table and a red sofa.

I've been given a corner room, and have a view in two directions. From one window, to the north, I look down on a cobbled street in the old Hanseatic town, and from the other, to the west, I gaze out over Almedalen and far out across the sea. It's warm, and both windows are open wide.

I've been standing here half an hour, looking down at the people passing on the street below me, most of them in dresses or shorts and loose, short-sleeved tops. Whitsun tourists. Many are walking along in pairs, often hand in hand, but others pour forth in great rowdy groups.

I can put to bed the myth that young people make more noise than people of my own age. As soon as they form crowds, especially if they've been enjoying a drink, middle-aged people can be just as boisterous as teenagers. Or just as human: *Look at me! Come on, listen to me! Aren't we having a wild time together?*

We don't grow out of our human nature. We grow with it. And we let it grow on us.

I like the perspective I have on the street life below me; at such a short distance I get quite close to the passers-by. Some scents find their way up to me too, because people do give off aromas, particularly in narrow alleyways on windless summer days. There is someone walking along with a lit cigarette in their hand, and I can feel the smoke irritating my nose. But at the same time, I am just high enough over the cobblestones that the objects of my scrutiny do not, as a rule, look up and catch sight of me. I am half hidden behind a blue curtain, which occasionally blows out through the window when a sudden gust of wind takes hold of it.

From one and a half floors above the hill I can enjoy my privilege: observing without being observed.

And I've been keeping an eye out for sailing boats far out on the water's glittering surface; it's the mild breeze through that window that on occasion makes the curtains of the street-facing window move.

In the course of the last half hour I've counted three white sails. It has been a beautiful day, almost completely calm. The sailing conditions have not been the best.

Today is not just Whitsun. It's also 17 May, Norway's very own national day. It makes me a little melancholic to think of it, almost like having one's birthday in perfect secrecy among strangers: no one makes you feel special, and no one sings you 'Happy Birthday'.

Here, no one has sung the national anthem either. I haven't seen so much as a Norwegian flag, but I have noticed that there is a crocheted blanket on the hotel bed, and it's as white as the snow on Mount Glittertind.

I mean: a red room, white bedclothes and bright

blue curtains. That will do as a token of the Norwegian colours.

While noting down the date I realised that, at the time of writing, a month has passed since we saw one another in Arendal.

And a few hours after that you met Pelle. And you really hit it off, I must say.

We'd only met one another once, just over a year previously, a few days before Christmas 2011, and it's the background to that first meeting I want to try and sketch. You've asked me to explain why I behaved the way I did. I shall attempt, to the best of my ability, to respond to that request. And I think too that now is an appropriate time to send you a question in return:

I had made a fool of myself at our first meeting, but you still kept me from giving up and leaving. It's a little mystery I'm still pondering. I wasn't the only one surprised by your response. I think everyone sitting.round the table would have been in agreement. And many of them probably thought as I did: Why did you hold me back? Why didn't you just let me head for the door?

Where should I begin?

I could take a chronological approach and

describe my upbringing in Hallingdal. Or I could do the exact opposite: I could open with a few notable events that have taken place here on the island as recently as this afternoon – since those too must take their place in my tale – linking these back to our encounter in Arendal a month ago, then following the threads first to that upsetting dinner a year ago – one of the worst days of your life, Agnes – and then all the way back to Erik Lundin's funeral in the early 2000s. That kind of retrospective orientation could finally pan out into a depiction of some of my childhood experiences, which might allow for a little understanding, not to mention forgiveness, once my confession is concluded.

What is the easiest way to make sense of our lives? Is it when we sum up from the beginning, or is it when we start from the present day, which of course is freshest in our minds, and from that point reminisce our way back to where it all began? The flaw in this second method is that there is no absolute causality in people's lives.

It's not possible to prove why one has become the way one has. Many have tried to do just that, but they haven't got much further than underlining their humanity.

*

I've been over by the window again. The three sailing boats haven't moved an inch in the still air. I know it's a bizarre idea, but they make me think of the three of *us*: of you and me – and Pelle, he has to be included too.

It's embarrassing, but an old Sunday-school song starts to hum itself in the very back of my head: *My boat is so little, the sea is so wide . . .*

And I come to a decision: I will open my narrative in the middle of the voyage. I will begin at the point I met your cousin at Erik Lundin's funeral. From that point I will follow threads that lead directly to our first encounter almost ten years later. The burden I bear from Hallingdal – that will take second place.

My beloved Erik, our dear father and stepfather,
our much-loved grandfather and great-grandfather
Erik Lundin
Born 14 March 1913
Fell asleep for the last time today
Oslo 28 August 2001

Ingeborg
Jon-Petter   Lise
Marianne   Sverre
Liv-Berit   Truls
Sigrid, Ylva, Fredrik, Tuva, Joakim and Mia
Great-grandchildren and other family

The funeral will take place at West Aker Church
Wednesday 5 September, 14:00

All those paying their last respects are welcome to
join the memorial service at the church hall.

Erik

There were many of us paying our last respects to Erik Lundin that afternoon in early September 2001. Among us was your cousin Truls, and that's why I have decided to begin my tale here. Ten years later I would meet him again, together with Liv-Berit and their two daughters. It was then I met you for the first time.

West Aker Church was packed to the rafters, and we walked in small clusters following the coffin down to the place where he was to be buried. The sun played in the leaves of the trees, but it shone in our eyes too, and for some it was a welcome excuse to take out sunglasses. In my head, the choir's song was still ringing; majestic trumpet solos and exhilarating organ chords.

After the scattering of the earth, we trudged back up to the church and the church hall. It was mild for the time of year, perhaps twenty degrees. But the sun went behind a cloud, and we felt the odd gust of cool air come up from the fjord and the lowlands.

At such a well-attended funeral, wandering alone under the trees without approaching any of the bereaved goes quite unnoticed. The inner circle are taken up with one another and their nearest and dearest. Why would anyone notice the odd figure with no connection to the rest of the mourners?

I had, however, encountered some of those in the funeral procession before, and I nodded to one of them – a former student – now; we'd never had a good relationship, so I didn't need to concern myself with him. I had also noticed the tall, dark man who I'd met on a handful of occasions, but he didn't count. He was an extra, and I didn't need to pay any attention to him. It occurred to me that I'd once dreamt of him. He'd been swinging a scythe around.

There was a good deal of waving and hugging, as well as more introductions and greetings, in the spacious forecourt in front of the church. Some of the oldest guests were led over to cars parked on the tarmac, which now moved, one by one, slowly down a slope that was already thronged with people in black finery.

I myself was set on staying and taking part in the memorial service. I was well aware that this social challenge might turn out to test my mettle, but pulling out didn't strike me as an option.

In the church, I'd sat almost right at the front, near the aisle, on the right-hand side of course. Because of this, I had a good view of the priest, who began the ceremony by coming down and greeting the Lundin family, all four generations: first the widow, Ingeborg Lundin, then the three children in their forties and fifties, all accompanied by their spouses. The grandchildren and great-grandchildren also sat there.

I tried to guess which of the daughters was Marianne and which was Liv-Berit. I knew only that Marianne was the eldest, but quickly realised there was a significant age gap between the two sisters, so it was easy to figure out. Liv-Berit could have been in her early forties, while her sister, Marianne, was perhaps about my own age, around fifty. Jon-Petter, the oldest, was sitting very close to Lise, and it wasn't hard to guess that she must be the daughter-in-law, since Jon-Petter, Marianne and Liv-Berit were all blonde, and quite astonishingly alike, but Lise's hair was decidedly dark. I made the connection between Marianne and

Sverre, who had been sitting hand in hand until the priest greeted them. A little later, I noticed that a man who must have been Truls passed Liv-Berit a hanky.

Then came the young people. It took me longer to identify them, but before we'd left the church, I had a certain degree of oversight here too. I'd found pictures of Ylva and Joakim online. If it had been now, I'm sure I would have found pictures of the whole clan on Facebook and Instagram. But the notice in the paper had at least given me useful pointers as to their order by age. So it was no insurmountable task to place Sigrid, Fredrik, Tuva and Mia as well. That must be Sigrid, the oldest grandchild, perhaps in her late twenties, with a three- or four-year-old boy in her arms – they were sitting with a man who must be the lad's father. And the girl of about fifteen must be Mia, as the next-youngest was Joakim. Tuva, apparently a couple of years older than Joakim, was a young lady whom there was little chance of mistaking for a teenager.

That was as far as the priest's hand-shaking went. But who of the young people was a sibling, and who was a cousin? The death notice hadn't been much help on that front, so I let that puzzle lie for the time being. Neither did I concern myself with speculating over the parents of each of the grandchildren. Much would presumably become clear during the memorial service.

On the death notice, which I had in my inside pocket, the list of children and grandchildren was rounded off with 'great-grandchildren and other family'. So I had no way of knowing how many of the young people had their own children, and therefore how many great-grandchildren the old professor had stayed around long enough to see. Because of a quirk of the Norwegian language, it could be just one, or it could be several. In many languages, it would have been abundantly clear, but in Norwegian, when we use the indefinite form, it's very rare that we differentiate between neutral singular and neutral plural when the word has only one syllable, such as in the words 'hus' (house) and 'barn' (child). Moreover, I had no way of knowing which of the siblings, brothers- and sisters-in-law or nephews and nieces, both on the Norwegian and Swedish side, were in the church, since they were all covered by the grouping 'other family'. Still, it struck me just how much one can glean from a death notice, and the priest's eulogy gave me an opportunity to fill in more of the gaps. As I had guessed, it was Sigrid who was accompanied by a son of almost four. He was called Morten. But Sigrid and Thomas also had a one-year-old daughter, Miriam, who was the very youngest of the clan.

The priest painted a beautiful picture of the Swedish scholar who came to Oslo in the autumn of 1946 to complete his doctoral studies in Old Norse mythology and the Eddic poems in the context of Magnus Olsen's half-century of studies. When he was a PhD candidate he met Ingeborg and started a family. He later became a university lecturer and reader, and for many years was a professor of Old Norse philology. It was this side of Erik's life I represented. If questioned, I would inform the family that I had sat in his lecture theatre, but that we'd maintained informal contact over many years and, in time, became what I would call close friends.

As we filed into the church hall, the tall, dark-haired man cast an inadvertent look at me, but I immediately saw a different route and took a step to the side.

Most people were already seated around tables when I came up from the cloakroom, and in the background someone was rushing around, trying to find seats for the last arrivals. I remember I ended up standing slightly helplessly in the middle of the room, and now it was Tuva who got up and on behalf of the family came towards me and asked

whether I had anywhere to sit. I can't remember
how I replied, or whether I got moved around, but
in the end I was shown to an empty chair at the
same table as the young people. There sat Tuva and
Mia, occupying the head and foot of the table. Ylva
was sitting diagonally opposite me, flanked by Fredrik and Joakim, who turned out to be her cousins,
both a few years younger than her. Fredrik was the
older of them, and I soon picked up the fact that
he was studying law and that Joakim had started
his third year at Fagerborg High School. I got the
impression they were Sigrid's brothers, the sons of
Jon-Petter and Lise. To my right sat Liv-Berit and
your cousin Truls. I soon realised that they were the
parents of Tuva and Mia, and you, of course, have
known them since they were little. I noted at once
that your cousin had an old scar right across the
right side of his forehead. It was so striking that I
soon fell to wondering what might have happened to
him. That story is one that you would tell me more
than ten years later.

Let me now interject that I understand you've just
been introduced to a lot of people – undoubtedly
too many to keep track of at once. But you may be
relieved to hear you'll meet every one of them again.
Because after Erik Lundin's funeral, in the years

that followed, I met all the old professor's children, children-in-law and grandchildren in new settings, not as many at once as at this memorial service, but in smaller portions. For that reason, you can view this first chapter of my tale as an introduction to the Lundin family. How or why I met each of them again, I'll let lie for the time being. I don't need to explain everything at once. Indeed, that would be impossible.

Nor is this cast of characters so immeasurably extensive. And who knows: perhaps, through Truls, you know these names from before? But just to summarise briefly: Erik Lundin had three children, *Jon-Petter* in his mid-fifties; *Marianne*, who was a couple of years younger; and *Liv-Berit*, who was in her forties. Jon-Petter and Lise had a daughter, Sigrid, and two sons, Fredrik and Joakim, and it's Sigrid in particular I will come to mention a few more times. Marianne and Sverre only had one daughter, Ylva, she was perhaps in her mid-twenties, and all these last three will, in time, come to play a central role in my story. There's nothing more to say, because Liv-Berit's husband is your cousin and, as you confided in me many years after this, you have been close ever since you were little. His wife has, in recent years, been like a friend to you, and you've known the two daughters, Tuva and Mia, since they came into the world. At their grandfather's funeral that September day, Tuva was around twenty and Mia maybe fifteen, but you'll know that better than me.

I looked out across the gathering and estimated that there must be over a hundred people. I had never thought, and neither of course had it been my intention, that I would be sitting so close to the bereaved. I had seen for myself a more withdrawn role, at a table further down the room together with a few other lone grievers – colleagues and acquaintances of Erik Lundin – and perhaps a niece or nephew with or without spouse. I disliked the situation I found myself in. I was cold, and my stomach felt unsettled.

Even though all those around the table were dressed in black, there was little about the Lundin family that was reminiscent of the Pietists of Victorian times. The smart, close-fitting dresses and chic suits cut in the best fabric were just the start. The young ladies had certainly not skimped on mascara, lipstick or nail polish that afternoon; in their ears and round their wrists, gold and precious stones glinted, and Ylva – I remember I noted it the very first time we met – had a sapphire-blue pendant at her throat. It looked almost like a third eye, for the jewel had exactly the same colour, and almost the same form, as her other two eyes. Another thing contributing to my bewilderment was the many scents around the table – a motley blend of different perfumes, eau de cologne and aftershave. I am perhaps particularly aware of such sensory impressions as I live alone. In the bathroom and the kitchen at home on Gaupefaret there are no smells other than my own.

At the next table, the rest of the immediate family had sat down. Sigrid, Thomas and little Morten were seated together with the young mother's parents, Jon-Petter and Lise, and for a long time it was Grandpa who held the child. At one end of the table sat Ingeborg, a beautiful old lady with silver-grey hair. Then came Marianne and Sverre, who were the parents of Ylva, the family's only child.

I felt a sting of déjà vu when I caught sight of Marianne and Sverre, this time at close quarters. Had I met them before? If so, it must have been a long time ago. I noticed that Sverre had a little red stone in his left earlobe – and there *was* something about that red stone that triggered my memory; I'd seen it before, and when I cast a glance over the table at Ylva, it was as though I inched closer to a memory of her mother in her younger years. I made note, meanwhile, of the fact that

Sverre had a distinct Sørland dialect, which came as no surprise. But perhaps I was just imagining that I knew them. As an adult, one has met many people.

At that table sat a few other people in their forties or fifties. They spoke Swedish, or, to be precise, Gotlandic, or Gutnish as people also say – this was clear from their characteristic diphthongs.

Sigrid stood up at one end of the large family table and tapped a teaspoon against a coffee cup. It was to little avail as the hall was full of the murmur and hum of voices. But Sigrid cleared her throat and tapped a wine glass, rather more decidedly this time, and began to speak loudly and clearly to the assembled guests.

'Dear family! Dear friends and colleagues of Erik Lundin, dear former students . . .'

Once again I felt a chill and my stomach was uneasy. I thought this could go very wrong. But Sigrid continued:

'My name is Sigrid and I am Erik's oldest grandchild, the daughter of Jon-Petter, who sits to my right here and is the oldest of Erik's offspring, currently with a representative of the very youngest generation on his lap. His name is Morten . . . *No, not now, Morten! You just sit there with Grandpa* . . . The family would like to thank everyone who has taken this last walk with Erik today, and we are grateful that so many have joined us for this memorial service. We had hoped many people would want to be here, but we could never have known we would see *so* many. But still, there's one who can't be here . . . Grandpa would have been overjoyed to see each and every one of you.'

A few sobs were heard from the guests, but Sigrid was not to be distracted:

'Soon, food will be put out on the tables, and we will eat together and try to get to know those sitting beside us a little better. After a time, you may wish to say something, but please give me a sign beforehand. As you will have guessed, I have been given the task of being Master of Ceremonies this afternoon. As part of this celebration of Erik's life, we will also be treated to a number of performances – what else would you expect? But first we will serve a selection of charcuterie with sour cream, egg salad, potato salad, flatbreads, beer and mineral water. We're not absolutely sure it's permitted here in this hall, but we've got a little dram too for those of you who can handle it and are old enough . . .'

Sigrid cast a glance at the table where I sat, and perhaps it was Mia she first set eyes on, the fifteen-year-old, but then she noticed me, the stranger. She went on:

'It's deeply sad that Grandpa has died, but I will tell you something funny: I promised Grandpa I would send you his good wishes, yes, to each and every one of you. He knew he was going to die soon, and wanted so dearly for one of his grandchildren to be "toastmaster", as he put it. The very last time I spoke to him properly, he glanced up at me and said: *I guess it will have to be you, then.* I nodded: I am the oldest, and it was already agreed among the family. He said: *Send my love. Don't forget to send my best wishes to all my friends and acquaintances one last time.*

'Grandpa had lived in Norway for forty-five years. This was the very first time I'd heard him speak Swedish. I nodded again, and perhaps I brushed away a tear. Then he added: *And you must sing! It has to be a celebration. A real party, Sigrid. A real Old Norse wake is what it must be! Can you promise me that?*

'And with these words, his own, we bid you welcome to Erik Lundin's memorial service. Stay as long as you have cause and desire. We have use of the hall until late in the evening.'

There was an impressive platter of cured meats on the table, and everyone except Mia poured a glass of beer. The beer was warm, but soon a few of the bottles of mineral water were replaced by new bottles of ice-cold beer, and a young man began to walk around the room serving aquavit. There were no aquavit glasses on the table, but the young man had a little bag of plastic shot glasses, and looked around to see whether anyone wanted a dram. In this way, the serving of aquavit took on – in typical Norwegian style – an air of being distributed on request, in addition to the official catering. At our table, it was only Ylva and I who accepted the offer.

Liv-Berit looked up at me, smiled warmly and said: 'Sigrid gave us an assignment. We're to try and get to know each other a little better . . .'

She introduced herself and her husband (your cousin Truls), her two daughters, her niece Ylva and nephews Fredrik and Joakim. For each of them, she gave a little more information than just their name and place in the family – it was for instance at this point that I found out that Fredrik was studying law and that Joakim was in his final year of high school. I was also informed that Tuva was studying singing at the Academy of Opera, and that Ylva had already completed her Masters in the history of religion. This last piece of information made my ears burn somewhat – perhaps in the same way a hypochondriac immediately starts to feel the blood pounding in his temples when he realises he's at the same table as a doctor – but I nodded, interested, and acted as though I had, up to that point, been completely unfamiliar both with the names around the table and everyone's close connection to the deceased. As one of the last arrivals, I'd been seated here only because there was an empty chair. I had no way of knowing I was seated among the professor's closest family.

Naturally, everyone was staring at me. No one but me had gazed around the table and looked at each person being introduced.

'And you?' Liv-Berit said finally, with a warm, welcoming smile.

'Jakop,' I said. Or I might have said Jakobsen. I only rarely use my full name: Jakop Jakobsen. How I've always hated that ridiculous combination!

Liv-Berit asked again: 'So how did you know Father?'

I explained that I'd been among Erik's students in the seventies, added a few words about brilliant lectures, and a few anecdotes from the academic life of that time. But they continued to look at me, and I was forced to go on: 'Even long after I had finished my degree in Norwegian, or Nordic Studies, we maintained contact and met fairly regularly to talk about the old Germanic religion: informal colloquia, upon which I naturally placed great value . . .'

Ylva interrupted me. She was a beautiful, expressive young woman with a delicate, almost fragile appearance. She said: '*Germanic* religion? We don't know all that much about that. We have Tacitus and the days of the week, but that's almost all . . .'

This had already taken a turn towards academic particularities that I hadn't anticipated. Beforehand, I had rather expected I would be the only source of information on this topic at the table. Where I had got that idea from, I wasn't sure. But it was too late to retrace my steps.

'Of course, your grandfather was of the old school,' I said. 'Or as the priest summed it up: he took after Magnus Olsen, roughly as Magnus Olsen had taken over from Sophus Bugge half a century earlier.'

Ylva nodded. I took this as a form of assent, and perhaps also as encouragement to continue.

Everyone at the table was now following closely.

I said: 'I tried to open Erik's eyes to Georges Dumézil's great breakthrough. In keeping with Dumézil's research, I attempted to draw Erik's attention to the Indo-European perspective – I mean the Indo-European pantheon as a reflection of the three classes or castes in society. Dumézil saw parallels between Odin and Ty – as the gods of the sovereignty function – equivalent to Varuna and Mitra of the Vedic religion; Tor with his hammer as the god of the war function, analogous to the Vedic thunder god Indra and his *vajra* or thunder bolt; and finally the Vanir: Njord, Frøy and Frøya, the gods of the productivity function, analogous to the Vedic twin-gods, the Nasatyas or Ashvins. Dumézil finds parallels like this all over the Indo-European region, in old Iranian religions, in Greek, Roman and Germanic areas . . .'

Ylva had taken on a pensive, almost sulky expression, one that put me in mind of Renée Zellweger in a film I'd recently seen at the Saga cinema. Just a few seconds before, she'd been grinning from ear to ear. She'd nodded in confirmation and with a glint in her eye at my placement of her grandfather in a disciplinary context. But now she countered:

'Dumézil has undeniably made some invigorating contributions to the field of the history of religion. But today it is perhaps he who is of the old school. He wasn't actually a historian of religion. He was a philologist, a linguist . . .'

I nodded.

'Like Erik Lundin and Magnus Olsen,' I said. 'Because, as you just touched upon, philology too can provide source material in the study of the history of religion. In cases where the written sources are lacking, as well as the archaeology, comparative linguistics can, in many instances, take us a step further. And for many years, your grandfather and I had mutual exchanges through our informal colloquia. Long after I myself became a teacher, we continued to meet, often over a lunch, and for a period of many years I visited him in his office at the university, where we engaged not least in Dumézil's readings of the Old Norse texts. We sometimes took a walk together around the Sognsvann lake and continued our conversation there. I myself ended up as a high-school teacher, and I am in no way embarrassed that I have not reached further up the academic ladder, but in my heart I hadn't completely given up hope of a career in research. It was at that time that your grandfather and I, rather for the fun of it, started to read a little Sanskrit. We read the Rigveda, and on a few occasions, we sat bent over a trilingual edition of the Bhagavad Gita. Norse languages and Vedic languages are, of course, two sides of the same coin, or in any case like two twigs on the same tree – on separate branches, admittedly, but still on the same tree.'

I thought that would do. Ylva's facial expression was like an open book, and she nodded, though perhaps only in anticipation. At that time, I wasn't aware that Lundin, in addition to being her grandfather, had also been her academic supervisor.

She said: 'You used the term "Germanic religion". Could you be a little more specific about what you and Grandpa talked about? He never mentioned anything to me about Dumézil. But we talked about Magnus Olsen, and we couldn't avoid talking about Anne Holtsmark's lectures on the Völuspá, for instance, or her many stimulating footnotes to P. A. Munch's sagas of gods and heroes, including a couple of references to the French guru you've just mentioned.'

Several of the people round the table had begun to lose interest. Fredrik and Joakim were already talking to their cousin Mia. They'd obviously decided that this former student, having been offered the only empty place at the family table, had begun to take up a disproportionate amount of space.

But I sat up, looked at Ylva and said: 'We were talking about Odin. I could picture a potential thesis on Odin with a Germanic and possibly also an Indo-European perspective. There's evidence that the figure of Odin – or Wodan/Wotan – may have been as widespread and as old in the Germanic world as the runes.'

'Great,' she said. 'Odin *is* an exciting figure, at least in the Norse context, by which I also mean the *historic* context, and I'm sure there's a lot more that can be written about him. Why did you give up?'

I said: 'Dumézil placed this particular deity in the same category as the Vedic god Varuna. He also pointed out the etymological similarity between Varuna and the Greek god Uranus.'

Ylva nodded: 'That's well known, but probably a fabrication . . .'

But I would not be discouraged. I said: 'And he connects Odin's *runes* to Varuna and Uranus.'

Ylva laughed: 'I know. I hope you'll excuse the Hindu metaphor, but I'm calling bullshit on that particular sacred cow.'

She refilled her beer glass, gazing open-mouthed at the others around the table, and laughed again, heartily, but condescendingly.

Liv-Berit must have seen that I felt bad. What must *she* have thought of this student showing up at the professor's funeral after almost thirty years? I don't know what she's said to you about it, but now she turned to me and said, with a humorous tone and a conciliatory look: 'Ylva has always had strong opinions. And she's never been able to avoid getting into trouble with teachers.'

Ylva acted as if she hadn't heard the retort. She just carried on laughing.

I disliked being in the role of middle-aged

schoolteacher put on the spot by a young academic. Matters weren't improved by the fact that I found her to be a worthy interlocutor – quite the opposite. But I didn't let the mask drop. In order to stop my gaze faltering – and to avoid looking my opponent in the eye – I glanced at the sapphire-blue pendant hanging at her throat. But this third eye was at least as piercing as the other two, and it made me feel even more humiliated. It struck me that it could have been Odin's eye, the one he sacrificed to Mimir's well.

Varuna and the rune god Odin! What an idiot! I'd never even believed that theory myself. It had been almost forty years since I was a student at Hallingdal School, where I borrowed a Danish translation of Dumézil's *Les dieux des Germains* from the Norwegian teacher. Even then it had struck me that the good Frenchman was a little too free with some of his etymologies.

An old adage occurred to me: 'If only time had been on your side!'

If only time had been on my side, I would still have been able to pass as a good linguist.

I was the only one who knew that I actually *am* a good linguist, and somewhat exceptional when it comes to Indo-European etymologies; the study of the origin of words had been a hobby for me ever since I was in my teens. Dumézil and the study of myths was something I'd only dwelt on for a short time during the 1970s. It should of course have occurred to me that the history of religion might have taken a new course in the intervening years. I felt like Ibsen's old Master Builder Solness, and Ylva, she was the bold young Miss Wangel.

I missed Skrindo. You've met him, of course, Agnes. Peder Ellingsen Skrindo would never have let himself be knocked off his perch by this young graduate with three eyes. Pelle has always had the gift of the gab and would most certainly have trumped both Ylva and me as far as Indo-European parallels like these were concerned. But he wasn't there, and thus had no way of coming to my aid.

Dearest Herr Skrindo was my best friend, not to mention my only one, but I never could have invited him along to places like this. He was much too wayward for that. He quite simply wouldn't have been able to behave himself. So I had no choice but to rely on myself, and if I got the chance, I'd probably get some small revenge.

Sigrid tapped her glass, and I noted how Tuva, who was sitting to my left at the end of the table, saw her chance to take out a little mirror and some bright red lipstick.

Sigrid looked out across the room before fixing her gaze on Ingeborg and saying: 'Grandma, you were a pillar of strength to Grandpa. Grandpa loved you. I think he saw you as the true embodiment of everything *Norway*, that other great love of his life. Those of us who were close to him know that he called you by two names. Ingeborg was just one of them, the other was the nickname Veslemøy – after Arne Garborg's *Haugtussa*, made so famous by Edvard Grieg. Sometimes he would stroke your hair – or just reach out to you wherever you might be in the room – and recite:

> *'Beneath her forehead, lovely but low,*
> *her eyes shine as though through mist;*
> *they seem to stare so as to go*
> *far into another world than this.*

'Tuva, you've agreed to sing some of *Haugtussa* for us. Please, do us the honour!'

Tuva walked up to a little podium at the front of the hall and sang three of the songs from Garborg's cycle of poems as set by Grieg. She began with 'Veslemøy', from which Sigrid had quoted, and followed up with the lively 'Blueberry Hill' and 'Little Goat's Dance'. It was compelling and beautiful.

After this artistic diversion, the talk at the table

turned to this and that. Fredrik and Joakim began to discuss politics with Liv-Berit and Truls. I got the impression it was blue against red. I myself began, like the teacher I am, to engage Tuva in a conversation about *Haugtussa* and the later visionary poem *I Helheim*, in which we meet Veslemøy again.

'In *Haugtussa*, Veslemøy has visionary powers, and sees spirits and *huldrefolk*, and in the sequel, she travels through *Helheim*, the land of the dead. I mentioned that the words *hulder* and *Hel*, the name both of the Norse land of the dead and the goddess who rules over it, could be traced back to the Indo-European root word for 'to conceal', from which came the Norse word *hylja*, related to the Norwegian *hylle* (to cover) or *innhylle* (to conceal), as well as the English *to hull*.'

Ylva had pricked up her ears, and it was not least for her that I spoke; perhaps I was in the midst of my planned revenge. But I continued to direct my words to Tuva, well aware that the three sapphire-blue eyes were staring at me across the table:

'*Huldra* comes up again as Mother *Hulda* or Frau *Holle* in European adventure and fairy tales, the same figure as in "The Spinning-Woman by the Spring". It's also related to other Norwegian words such as *heler*: that is, someone who hides or conceals stolen goods, or English words such as *helmet* and *holster*. But such words are found throughout the Germanic region . . . '

Ylva had waved over the aquavit man. We were both poured a brimming new shot glass. The first had already calmed my stomach and I felt it had acted as an injection of vitamins for my memory.

Tuva was all ears, but now Ylva wanted to be in on the action too. She wasn't unfriendly, just gently teasing:

'You're not about to tell us that *huldra* exists in Old Vedic religion too, are you?'

She laughed, and I laughed with her, but I still had my eyes on Tuva.

I said: 'That's not completely inconceivable. The Indo-European root is **kel*, which we find in the Latin word *celare* in the sense of hiding something or keeping someone in ignorance, from which comes English's *conceal*, related to *cell* and *cellar*. From the same Indo-European root follow Germanic words like Norse *hǫll*, Norwegian and English *hall*, and German *Halle*. The same root is found in *occult* or *occultism*, that is, something that is secret or hidden, and through the Greek verb *kalúptein* – to cover or hide – also in *apocalypse*, in the sense of disclosure or revelation.'

With this last detail I looked across to Ylva, since we were once more entering the field of the history of religion. She had again taken on something of that aggrieved Renée Zellweger look, though she dropped her grimace as soon as I looked at her. She said: 'But we don't find any mystical female figures that are etymologically related to *huldra* in the Greek or Indian contexts, do we?'

It was an irksome question, and I couldn't think of any good answer, so I was forced to reconsider. For a moment, I concentrated my mind on Pelle. He remembered all these things much better than me. He never needed a glass of anything to get that extra detail, but that – and it occurred to me only then – was perhaps because he is a teetotaller. At once it was as though he were there in the room and had just whispered something in my ear:

'Indeed we do!' I said. 'The Greek mountain nymph Calypso is actually an etymological relative of *huldra*. The word means to cover, conceal or hide, and goes in its first instance back to the same Indo-European root as *hulder*.'

Ylva lifted her shot glass and put it to her lips. She drained it in one gulp, and I was obliged to be chivalrous and do the same. It wasn't a case of any actual toast, but now we were even.

Ylva proclaimed playfully to the table: 'This man is either very learned – or he's an excellent bluffer.'

This was before the smartphone era. Today the

young graduate's reservations wouldn't have been so necessary. We don't talk the same way about questions of fact any more. If we disagree about something when we're on a family trip to our cabin in the mountains, we don't have to wait a whole week to find out the answer. We google. These days, factual disagreements need not last longer than a few seconds.

Sigrid tapped her glass again, and now it was Ylva who got out her mirror: 'Dear family and friends. Erik spent his whole life steeped in the Norse worldview, with the precarious power balance that once prevailed between gods and trolls, Aesir and giants. In celebration of this, we're going to have another performance, before we open things up to commemorations and informal contributions. Please, dear cousin Ylva. You have agreed to recite the whole of the monumental Eddic poem *Völuspá* for us, and we are all ears.'

Ylva walked up to the podium. She first gave a short introduction to the poem, the oral form of which she dated towards the end of the Viking Age, when the Christian influence had begun in earnest to make itself felt, leaving clear traces in the Norse religion. She informed the mostly uninitiated guests that Völuspá meant 'seeress's prophecy', and that it was at the request of Odin himself that the seeress's apocalypse was proclaimed. As she said 'apoca-lypse', she cast a sideways glance at me and smiled wryly.

As I sat and watched this dramatic performance of the beginning of the world, the complexity of intrigues, end times and a new world where fields will grow unsown, Ylva's voice and the seeress's became fused to form a higher entity.

I was transported. I was dumbstruck.

Hearing I ask from all the tribes,
greater and lesser, the offspring of Heimdall;
Father of the Slain, you wished me well to declare
living beings' ancient stories, those I remember
from furthest back . . .

Early in time Ymir made his settlement,
there was no sand nor sea nor cool waves;
earth was nowhere nor the sky above,
a void of yawning chaos, grass was there nowhere . . .

After resounding applause, Ylva was back at the table again. Fredrik and Joakim embraced her in turn, and I myself said: 'Fantastic!'

The dramatic young lady winked the aquavit server over, but now I declined. Ylva no longer needed anyone to defend her honour. This time too, she emptied her glass in one gulp, and I felt Liv-Berit nudge me in the side, a kind of familiar 'now you know who Ylva is'.

In the background I both saw and overheard Marianne, Ylva's mother, and her sister-in-law, Lise, chatting. With a loud voice and a strong Bergen accent, Lise exclaimed: 'She's magnificent! And that poem is just so gripping!'

'It's totally . . . psychedelic!' Marianne gasped.

At the exact moment she said psychedelic, she seemed to steal a glance at me, before she returned, quick as a flash, to the table she was sitting at.

Perhaps the most surprising thing that afternoon happened now. There were eight of us sitting around the table, but Ylva turned to me and asked: 'What do you think?'

'An absolutely fantastic performance,' I repeated.

'Thanks! But I mean the poem. Do you see that *Nordic* quality, something "Ur-Germanic", or first and foremost something "Indo-European" in *Völuspá* now?'

I think I looked over at Liv-Berit. Could I dare challenge her niece? She just rolled her eyes, and I interpreted that as a warning, but I said:

'I see a classic Indo-European cosmogony, a dualistic conception of reality of almost Iranian calibre, and an apocalypse that has naturally been coloured by the fact that it has been formed on Nordic soil. Then, of course, there may be a dash of Christian influence too – of a Christian eschatology – I think you're right in that. But the ancestral giant *Ymir*, the origin of the world, who is presented in the third verse of this mythological poem, is presumably of the same name as the deities *Yama* in the Vedic tradition and *Yima* in the Iranian. Isn't that fascinating? We may be talking about a few scattered remnants of ancient mythological ideas, which after all could derive from Indo-Europeans who lived five or six thousand years ago, probably on the steppes north of the Black and the Caspian Seas. The same applies to a host of persistent native words, for example the one we find in the name of my mentor and your grandfather: E*rik* is related to the Celtic word for king – **rix* – which in Latin is *rex* and in Sanskrit *raja*. Another example can be found in the Swedish name for Sweden: Sve*rige*. Everything comes from Indo-European **reg-*, meaning to move in a straight line, as in English's *right* and German *richtig*, or in loanwords such as *rector, reign* – or *correct!*'

I couldn't tell what Ylva was thinking, but she looked me deep in the eyes as she formulated a suitable response:

'You mean like in e*rec*tion? Or what?'

I didn't answer. I could have done, but I sensed she was making fun of me, so I only said: 'Pass!'

I thought she'd emptied her aquavit glass, but there was some left, and at this point she threw the last drops in my face. I jumped, but didn't have the strength to make a fuss. And with that, she simply got up and left the table.

Her male cousins laughed, they knew what Ylva was like, and I don't think they had any sympathy for me. But both Liv-Berit and Truls looked at me with worried expressions and shook their heads.

I noticed once again the distinct scar that ran across Truls' forehead and under his hairline. Liv-Berit had introduced him as a brain researcher, and for a moment I wondered whether that scar might have something to do with his chosen profession – a completely absurd idea, of course.

The time had come to say farewell.

Sigrid had once again tapped her glass and opened the floor for commemorations and eulogies. I thanked the others round the table, gave a plausible reason as to why I had to be on my way, and left the dinner.

In the entrance I bumped into Ylva again, and

now her face lit up. She stopped me on my way out, and asked with a sly smile: 'Would you sign a ten-year guarantee?'

I didn't understand: 'For what?'

'For body and soul.'

'I've never considered it . . .'

'You would be able to live without any kind of health troubles for ten years. But then it would all be over. Slash!'

'I really don't know . . . but perhaps I would accept such a contract. And you?'

Now she seemed agitated. Or was she just playing a role?

'What is it you're asking, Father Jakop?'

'Am I not asking exactly the same thing you just asked me?'

She shook her head sharply. Then she said:

'I'm only twenty-five years old.'

I walked quickly back to Kirkeveien and hailed a taxi home to Gaupefaret.

Letting myself into the apartment I had a dismal feeling. I wasn't sure whether I wanted to be there, not that afternoon. Everything felt so stuffy. It smelled stale.

I felt like I had escaped from the memorial service, and wasn't sure if I would be able to stay at home until it got late enough in the evening that it would be acceptable to go to bed.

I had at that time instructed myself not to turn in before eleven o'clock. More and more often, though, I ended up going to bed much earlier than that. Preferably with a book, but that wasn't the point.

'Would you sign a ten-year guarantee?'

And I had taken the bait.

I wasn't in my twenties any more. At that time, of course, I would never have signed a 'ten-year guarantee'. I might not have been born under the luckiest star in the heavens, but I've never been suicidal.

I had to go out again, it was as though the soles of my feet were itching, but first I did a little circuit of the apartment, going into the bathroom and looking in the mirror – almost fifty years old! – then going into the living room and opening a drawer in the wall unit to flick through a few old photos from Hallingdal.

In the end I found myself standing for a long time in front of the bookshelf, looking over all the books I'd used throughout my studies and the academic literature I'd bought more recently, such as Gro Steinsland and Preben Meulengracht Sørensen's brand new retranslation and annotated edition of *Völuspá* (which Ylva had read from at the memorial service) and a new etymological dictionary by Bjorvand and Lindeman: *Our Inherited Words*. This last volume stood alongside a facsimile of Falk and Torp's *Etymological Dictionary of the Norwegian and the Danish Languages*.

I went to get something from the wardrobe in the bedroom. Two of the compartments contained all the cigar boxes I'd collected over several decades. At one time I'd owned one box. By that point there were perhaps twenty of them, and as I write this now there are over thirty.

I thought about how much there is in the world that accumulates in drawers and cupboards. For me it was these cigar boxes. They were the only thing I collected.

I boiled some water and had a cup of Nescafé. It wasn't too difficult to shake off the two drams. I tried to shake off the wounds from my encounter with Ylva too, but that wasn't as easy.

In the end, the day came to a conciliatory conclusion. It ended with me getting Pelle to join me for a walk in the forest. He could have protested. He's not always up to such late expeditions, or in the mood for anything at all. But today he was quick to come along. That put me in better spirits straight away.

I confided in him that a young lady had insulted me. Then I got to the point:

'But this evening it's time to really stretch our legs, Pelle! There's a lot to talk about.'

'Suits me perfectly,' he replied. 'I've been sitting around all day.'

About an hour later we were on our way to Midt-stuen, and we walked on up through the forest to Frønsvollstråkka, from where we gradually made our way up a small track that took us to Fuglemyra.

We'd been here many times before. Now we sat on a knoll and looked out across the marsh and the few open pools gleaming softly in the evening sun.

'Wheat and barley were cultivated here in the early Iron Age,' I said. 'As indicated by pollen analysis.'

I said it with a degree of irony, as though I could actually *teach* Pelle anything about the prehistory of this terrain. But it was a rhetorical preamble, just to get the conversation going.

Pelle was clearly game, since he turned his sharp eyes on me and said:

'Under the marsh here, there may well be an old *tuft* or two, that the turf of forgetfulness has long since grown over. But once children ran on the meadow here, playing and singing. That's long since passed. Now it's only the black grouse that play here.'

I wasn't sure where he was headed, because his voice had taken on a strange, almost melancholy tone, a pathos. I tried to bring the conversation back to the path we usually stuck to.

'*Tuft* as in *toft*,' I said, 'from the Indo-European *demH-* meaning "to build", from which our Norwegian word *tømmer*, and the English *timber* come – that is, what one builds with, as in the German *Zimmer* for both *timber* and "room".'

Pelle nodded emphatically. He said: 'Precisely, yes, just as we find in the Norwegian *fruentimmer*, or in the German *Frauenzimmer*, both meaning "woman". Do you see where I'm going, boy?'

I looked at him. *Fruentimmer*? I'd never made that connection myself. But there it was, all right. It wasn't the first time I learned something from talking to Pelle. He cleared his throat twice before going on.

'From the root *demH-* for "to build" we also get a word for building or house, the Indo-European *domHos-*, as in the Latin *domus*.'

There he was, back again on a familiar track. I smiled:

'No bluffing now, Pelle? Tell me you're not bluffing?'

The comment was contrived, as we'd been through this series of etymologies many times before.

Pelle grabbed hold of my wrist so hard it almost hurt, stared intensely at me and said: 'Listen now! From *domus* we also get *dame*, from the Latin *domina* for "housewife", like the Italian *donna* for "woman" and the Spanish *doña* for "Mrs". That was where I was headed.'

I was astonished. I myself would never have connected the word *dame* with *Zimmer* or *timber*. But I realized immediately that the information must be correct. I gave in:

'Both *dame* and *fruentimmer*, then?'

'You said it. And Ma*dam* and *dam*sel . . .'

'And?'

I think he felt uncomfortable, as he sighed deeply:

'How are things with the ladies these days? It's been a long time, hasn't it? Though once, of course, you were actually a married man!'

I just shrugged. Was that something we needed to talk about now? It felt so unmusical. Weren't we boys on tour? Pelle went on:

'You're much too young to give up on finding someone to share your days with, Jakop. You shouldn't just be drifting about on your own.'

'No . . .'

I never liked it when Pelle got so personal. I don't

think either of us liked it, but perhaps Pelle felt a kind of comradely obligation to occasionally bring an existential question like this to bear. He had always been concerned with the weal and woe of my life.

'Perhaps you're no Don Juan,' he admitted now. 'But you could try and find yourself a friend. You wouldn't even need to live in the same flat. You wouldn't need to sleep in the same bed. Because this is not primarily about "to have and to hold". You could also travel together, to Stockholm or Lofoten, or to North Cape, Jakop, have you considered that?'

There's nothing more I need to tell you about that conversation. It could quickly become too personal: as the time passed we talked about everything. But now it's twelve years later, I've become a man of more than sixty and not a great deal has changed. Pelle has to this day continued to show consideration for me. He has never given up on me, not even in his recurring hope that I at some point will find someone to spend my life with. I find it touching. It is, moreover, selfless: the more time I spent with a lady friend, the less time Pelle and I would have together. I'm speaking from experience here. For the short time I was married, Pelle and I only saw one another now and then.

From Fuglemyra, we carried on up to Vettakollen, with its spectacular view out over Oslo, the fjord, and large parts of the Østland region, without a doubt the best lookout spot in the capital. It was eight o'clock, and we stood watching the sun sink behind the horizon in the west, still maintaining its northerly summertime slant.

There was no one but Pelle and me up here so late. We felt there was no rush to get back down to the lowlands, and we sat there on a log, talking about whatever occurred to us.

I pointed out the marine limit where the ice had melted 9,000 years previously. In this area it was 220 metres above today's sea level, and Vettakollen and Voksenåsen stuck out into the sea like low headlands divided by a little bay, where Skådalen is today. The sea stretched all the way up to the north end of Mjøsa, and Maridalen, Sørkedalen and Lommedalen tore into the land like the long limbs of fjords. Then the land slowly rose up after having been pressed down by the massive ice sheet over thousands of years. When the first humans began to cultivate the ground here, the shoreline was around sixty metres over today's level. But the land continued to rise, and that saga has still not reached its end.

And now we were here, Pelle and I.

If it had been broad daylight, there would have been people passing constantly, and we would not have been able to have such a tête-à-tête, or be so loose-tongued.

Neither of us has ever liked to chat away in earshot of others, especially passers-by. In this respect, we have maintained a state of inherent bashfulness almost throughout our acquaintance. The more personal a conversation becomes, or can be expected to become, the more it precludes an audience.

It's completely impossible to predict which way Pelle will steer a conversation. It's like he has no scruples. He still has a very childlike nature: once he has got going, nothing can stop him. As you yourself have experienced, Agnes.

But now we were sitting alone on a hill, high above the city's din, and we could talk undisturbed until a slightly waning moon rose over Groruddalen in the east. It was almost dark, an hour after the sun had set, but soon it grew lighter, and we began to pick our way down to the lowlands in the blueish moonlight. The long shadows from the trees made it even harder to find our way across the steep terrain.

I was in bed more or less on the dot of eleven, and was, all things considered, no longer so dissatisfied with this Wednesday.

And Ylva?

She had upset me.

But I would meet her again. Twice, I would meet her again.

The last time I saw her was here, on an island in the Baltic Sea. It was just a few hours ago.

Andrine

One spring day at the end of the eighties I had to pay a little visit, at short notice, to an old aunt in Åsgårdstrand. It was just a month or so after I'd separated from my wife and moved out to live on my own again.

We had managed, over the years my wife and I lived together, with one car, and the plan was that we might continue to share it until one of us got a new car. This was on a Tuesday, one of the days Reidun was using the car.

My days were Monday, Wednesday and Friday. Still, I hoped that my need to get to Åsgårdstrand would trump any possible objection she might have, and I was willing to swap for the following Wednesday. But Reidun had to go to the hairdresser and the dry-cleaners, as well as pop in to see a friend who lived a few streets away.

This was not the first time we'd got into a quarrel over the car. Unhappily, the week had an odd number of days, so one of the days – it ended up being Sundays – neither of us could claim first right to the car. In hindsight, I've wondered why we didn't just book in every other Sunday to each of us, or let one of us have the car until 3 p.m. every Sunday and the other from 3 p.m. onwards.

Perhaps the lack of a system governing the seventh day, the day of rest itself, could be attributed to the fact that both of us were waiting for the other to one day come and tell us that car number two had now been bought and that we could therefore keep the old Corolla.

It was these Sundays we argued about most. We had no children, and after I'd moved out, our only real point of conflict was the old Corolla – a last remnant of co-ownership with painful associations to the days when we both sat in the car. The rust-bucket was a paltry reminder of a life together, a marriage, now that that part of our existence had withered.

As I mentioned, I have had steady relationships – to outsiders we might have referred to ourselves as 'opera lovers', 'restaurant partners' or 'travel comrades' – but my only genuine live-in partner has been my wife. It lasted no more than a few years before Reidun first turned her back to me – I mean literally – in our double bed, and we finally moved into separate places. The only way to arrange it was for me to move out of the apartment that had once been mine.

The divorce had a lot to do with Pelle. Reidun couldn't bear the sight of Herr Skrindo. What's more, she said he had a horrible voice, a blatant insult, since she didn't hesitate to make him aware of her stance. But if she really couldn't stand to see me with Pelle, and wasn't even capable of tolerating the fact that we sat together in the living room and talked when she was out, it should have been up to her to move out. I said as much. But in the end, I was the one who ended up packing my things.

I had rather carefully asked whether I might take the car to Åsgårdstrand that afternoon, encountered massive resistance, and quickly backed down and ordered a taxi.

The taxi arrived – a red Mercedes – and I noted the sturdy vehicle with appreciation, thinking it would be a welcome addition for such a long and expensive car journey. I didn't give the striking colour of the car any thought until I'd opened the door and sat down in the back seat. That's when it struck me that the red colour suited the driver particularly well: Andrine Siggerud was a charming woman in her late thirties, perhaps a couple of years older than me, with brown eyes and long, wavy brown hair.

We hadn't driven far before we were deep in a rather merry conversation, which soon took a more existential turn. As we chatted, she glanced frequently at me in the mirror, and so I had a chance to follow her facial expressions. Her dialect bore clear traces of a childhood spent in the Sørland region, or to be precise, Mandal, as it turned out. A few years ago she had got divorced, and now she lived in Tonsenhagen, with her teenage daughter.

An almost intimate atmosphere can arise between two people driving together. A situation like that can give rise to a deep feeling of mutual understanding much faster than in any other circumstances. The intense togetherness a car journey engenders – on top of travelling through ever-changing landscapes – can stimulate conversations that otherwise never would have taken place.

With her driving and me getting a ride, we quickly realised we shared a finely woven net of common references, even if I with my academic qualifications and teaching experience, and she with her experience as a taxi driver, were a good distance apart in our daily occupations. It gave us more to talk about. And more to tell each other.

It struck me that a few months before I had been on car journeys with Reidun, and that we had also had intense conversations with one another while driving through the valleys. But that was before Pelle introduced himself.

The last few times we sat together in the old Toyota, neither of us said a word – perhaps we were both thinking about Pelle – and I believe it was during one of those journeys that it became clear to us that something had ended – or that everything had.

My visit to my aunt was only going to take an hour or so, she wouldn't have the energy for more than that. Andrine therefore decided to wait for me in Åsgårdstrand, to be able to put the trip back to Oslo on the taxi meter. She had a thick book with her, a novel with a yellow jacket and an unfamiliar author and title, possibly a translated book.

Before we set off for home, we ate a small lunch together in a friendly café in the idyllic village deep in the fjord, where Edvard Munch lived for a few summers and painted *The Girls on the Bridge*. We walked for a good while between the wooden houses that lined the narrow streets. A sweet and sour haze rose from the flowerbeds, the smell of April, one of us commented. Lastly, we wandered down to the lake and out onto one of the jetties where two swans were bobbing about in the harbour basin. 'Two souls,' – it just slipped out of me, or was it she who said it? One of us spoke those two words, and the other nodded.

When we walked back to the car again, it seemed natural for me to sit in the passenger seat beside Andrine. If I'd attempted to slide into the back seat as before, I think she would have felt offended. We had that day together, it was ours. It was already six o'clock, it would soon be May, and the afternoon was like a summer evening.

She started the car, and before putting the yellow book into the glove compartment, I started telling her about the relationship between some Indo-European inherited words. It was something Pelle and I had been discussing a few days before – Pelle and I being free to see each other again now I'd moved away from Reidun.

'*Gul*,' I said, pointing at the book, 'or in English, *yellow*.' I looked up at her: 'Do you know where these perfectly ordinary words come from?'

Andrine was concentrating hard on driving at that point, I think she was impatient to pass a tractor that was hogging the road. But I think she nodded. In any case, I said:

'The Germanic base form is *gula-*, which also forms the basis for the German word *gelb*, but also of course for Norwegian *gull*, English *gold* and German *Gold*.'

'Oh really?'

The charming driver shifted her gaze a second from the road she was driving along, and shot back at me:

'*Gul* and *gull*, I see. And yellow? I've never considered that.'

'But those kinds of similarities between words often go deeper than you think,' I said. 'And they can be many thousands of years old. We call ancient words like that "inherited words".'

'Inherited words?'

'Yes, because they're inherited from an original root or base form.'

'Loanwords, you mean?'

I shook my head: 'No, that's different. When words for the same thing, or more or less the same thing, resemble each other in two completely different languages, it can be because one of the languages long ago loaned that word from the other. That's what we call "loanwords". The Norwegian word "vin" is of course incredibly similar to the Italian word "vino", and that's because we loaned the word from an Italic language a long time ago. The fact that it's also called "wine" in English and "Wein" in German is because the English and German words are also imported from another language.'

She looked at me and smiled.

'Now I'm craving a glass of wine, you know,' she said.

She focused on the road again, but continued:

'And what about *gul* and *gull* – and *yellow*?'

I thought what an attentive student she was. I said:

'They're old inherited words, which we can trace thousands of years back through history. We can reconstruct the old Indo-European root **ghel-* "to shine", and that syllable is behind a number of living words across much of the Indo-European region, like the Latin *helvus* for "honey-coloured", English *golden*, as in *golden* hair or *golden* days, the old Dutch currency the *guilder*, and the Polish *złoty*.'

'And all these heritage words really mean the same thing?'

'Not necessarily,' I said. 'But the words I have mentioned can all be traced to the root **ghel-* "to shine". The same word also means "yellowy-green" in Greek, *khlorós*, which has given Norwegian the loanword *klor* and English the word *chlorine*, as well as the words *gall* and *cholera*, plus a whole host of words for yellow and green in the Slavic and Indo-Iranian languages.'

'Oof,' Andrine exclaimed. 'Well, I liked the golden version better.'

She turned to me and grinned.

But I was only just getting started. I explained that from the Indo-European root **ghel-*, came many other words from across the whole Germanic region, such as the English words *glow*, *glare*, *glaze*, *glance*, *glint*, *glimmer* and *garish*.

She cast a hasty glance at me again:

'All of them? *All* the words?'

And I nodded emphatically:

'When we *glare* at someone, when something *glows*, like a *glowworm*, or when something is *garish*, we're using words related to *yellow* or *chlorine*. Or when Germans drink mulled wine, they're drinking *Glühwein*, that is, a wine that glows with warmth, but in Scandinavia, of course, we drink *gløgg*, which we've taken from the Swedish *glödgad* or "glowing hot" drink. The interesting thing is that these relationships across languages can, in many cases, be traced back as far as six thousand years. So it's a question of paying attention.'

It was only now I put the yellow book in the glove box.

'How do you know this stuff?' she asked. 'Where do you pick it all up?'

I replied that I thought that was *glaringly* obvious: I loved languages.

One reason I'd reeled off this little string of etymologies just then was perhaps to test whether Andrine might share something of my fascination for language, for words and their origins. She said she was fond of reading, and that she was also fond of writing herself. That answer was good enough for me. If you're fond of reading and writing, then you're fond of language too.

She told me she'd long been toying with the idea of writing a book revolving around the stories she'd heard from the back seat of her taxi over the years. A taxi driver hears all manner of things, and sometimes that really means everything. In the course of her taxi-driving career, she'd experienced a need to act as a spiritual counsellor, a psychotherapist and a legal adviser.

On long trips, she said, she sometimes asked the passengers in the back seat to tell their life stories. This was often a way of making sure she didn't have to continue to steer the conversation herself, but it wasn't the only reason: Andrine genuinely enjoyed hearing people tell their tales.

She explained that taxi drivers, and in particular, perhaps, female taxi drivers, are sometimes exposed to long, exhausting, almost interrogatory interviews. 'You have to find a way to get the ball onto the other side of the court,' she explained. 'Tell me your story!' Andrine would say. And most people let themselves be drawn in. Everyone has a life story, life itself is an epic genre, and Andrine had experienced how little encouragement passengers needed in order to open up about their lives.

Andrine was fond of people, and one day she realised she'd heard so many stories they would fill a whole book. The book's title was already there. It would be called *Tales from the Back Seat*.

I don't want to call it a romance, but in the months after the trip to Åsgårdstrand we saw each other now and then. I took her card and rang a few times when I needed a taxi, like when I went up to Mylla, planning to cross the Nordmarka wilderness on skis, and one time out to Drøbak. One Sunday in September, we drove up to Sollihøgda to go for a walk together, and another Sunday, we drove all the way to Norefjell. She was the one who proposed these trips. On these journeys, of course, the taxi's meter wasn't running.

Only once did I invite Andrine out to a restaurant

in Oslo. There, on that one evening, I felt that we were perhaps on the way to becoming a couple. I took her hands in mine, and she let me hold them, but only for a short time before she pulled them slowly back towards her. A shadow fell across her face, and she looked me in the eye, fragile and nervous as quarry. But soon she patted me on the cheek, almost like a mother, or rather a walking partner, and told me she'd recently met a man named Rolf.

After that I didn't get in touch again.

I found her death notice in the paper many years later; it was New Year 2002. Andrine 'finally gave up her battle against cancer and went to sleep peacefully with her family at her side'. The service was to take place at Tonsen church on Tuesday 8 January at 1 p.m., and after the service, everyone was 'welcome to join the memorial service at Østreheim'. I didn't hesitate – I would attend the service.

It was just a few months since Erik Lundin's funeral in West Aker, and I started when I entered Tonsen church. There, on the very first bench to the left of the aisle, sat Ylva and her parents, Marianne and Sverre. The sight sent a shock through me and put me in mind of a scene from the film *Don't Look Now*, which was in cinemas at the beginning of the seventies: the one with Julie Christie and Donald Sutherland in Venice.

They hadn't seen me yet. I was late, and the priest, a young woman with blonde hair, was already there, greeting them. My immediate impulse was to leave the funeral entirely, but the next moment, the organist began to play, and I sank onto a bench right at the back of the church.

The airy church was almost half-full. I noticed that many of those present were wearing Oslo Taxi uniforms. As I'd walked into the church, I'd been given a programme. I sat looking down at a portrait of a good-looking brunette in her late forties. The photo was taken in front of a taxi, a red Mercedes.

The priest's eulogy started with Andrine's childhood in Mandal. She went on to tell of how Andrine had driven a taxi for almost thirty years, and that she'd never dreamt of any other career. When it began to become clear to the family and to Andrine herself that the disease would end in death, the doctor had offered her a sick note, but Andrine said there was no rush. After that, she drove with the incurable cancer for another three months before parking her car for good.

She had always emphasised the freedom that driving a taxi gave her. For the past fifteen years, she'd owned her own car, always a red Mercedes, and there was never any question of hiring a reserve driver – for instance, on public or private holidays, when she didn't drive herself.

But although she enjoyed her vocation, driving a taxi wasn't the only thing in Andrine's life. She had a lot of friends and acquaintances, she was family-oriented and socially engaged, not least when it came to the struggle for women's rights. The taxi could still be an outpost of civilisation when it came to respecting the integrity and dignity of women.

Andrine was also an avid reader and always had a book with her in the car. If she spent more than a couple of minutes on a taxi rank, she never just sat and stared out at the street life outside, nor was she particularly keen on listening to the radio or to music. No, Andrine read. It was probably less well known in taxi-driving circles that she also wrote her own stories. 'Even as a child she had a literary streak,' the priest told us. 'Many years ago she won a prize in a magazine, and, as her family know,' the priest went on, 'that one story wasn't the end of it. As the years passed, writing – in particular Andrine's poetry – became a valuable extra source of income.'

The priest went on to mention how Andrine's partner, Rolf, came into her life eleven years ago, just a few years after Petter and she had broken up. She mentioned Petter and Andrine's only child, their daughter Anlaug, and her husband, Aleksander. They had two small children, Kenneth and Maria. Maria, who was the younger of the grandchildren, was born only just in time to be held in her grandmother's arms before she died.

Inexorably, the moment I had been dreading approached: the postlude and the procession out of the church.

The coffin was borne down the aisle by three women and three men, all in Oslo Taxi uniforms. After the priest and the casket came Rolf, Anlaug and Aleksander, and then Petter with his new partner or wife, whose name had, understandably, not been mentioned in the priest's eulogy. After them came Sverre, Marianne and Ylva. I had long since deduced that Sverre must be the brother of Andrine.

I had a strong urge to hide, feeling that classic desire for 'the ground to swallow me', but in practice, I couldn't see any way out other than to stay standing there.

Ylva noticed me first. She rolled her eyes. Sverre and Marianne also gave me stern looks, but it was a formal situation, and the little procession of nearest and dearest had soon passed.

I had to get out of the church too. Outside, the coffin was put into a hearse, which soon drove away, and the grievers came together in clusters. It was overcast, almost completely windless, and just a few degrees below zero. On the tarmac, flagstones and the lawns around the church lay a thin coating of snow, unusually little for January.

What should I do now? Should I just sneak past the crowd and head for the Sinsen interchange without further ado?

But why should I? A woman who had once been a close acquaintance, if only for a limited period, had passed away. Why shouldn't I be present at her funeral? Only I could gauge how much she meant to me. Only I knew what sorrow and pain I was dealing with now, or how crushed I felt since the news had reached me through a notice in *Aftenposten*.

Why shouldn't I come to the memorial service when the death notice had clearly stated that 'after the funeral, everyone is welcome to join the memorial service at Østreheim'? I had been to the long-established inn only once before, back during my student days.

Ylva wasn't to be seen outside the church, nor was Anlaug, her cousin. Sverre and Marianne were standing there, and I nodded to them from a distance. After all, I wasn't one of the intimate circle.

But it struck me again that I must have met Sverre

and Marianne at some point earlier in my life. If I were to just stand there and observe them for two or three minutes, I might figure out from where we knew each other. But I couldn't, in all propriety, look at them a moment longer. I turned around, and a short while later I got into my car, which was parked on Traverveien a few hundred metres away.

I drove past the Årvoll Shopping Centre towards Stig and Østreheim. There's a steep path that runs down to Årvoll School, and on it I spotted Ylva and Anlaug, walking side by side, gesticulating energetically. I pulled up, rolled down the window, and asked if they wanted to hop in. But the cousins were happy to walk, understandably: perhaps this stroll was their only chance to talk in confidence. Anlaug had lost her mother, and Ylva an aunt on her father's side. Aleksander was probably following in the car, as, I assumed, Sverre and Marianne were too.

But Ylva stuck her head in through the window and said: 'Now, I'm curious to know how you knew Andrine.'

'Yes?'

She smelled of citrus and lavender.

'You're not going to tell me you were one of her passengers?'

I smiled: 'Yes, actually. When we met I was her passenger.'

Ylva's face had taken on an inscrutable expression.

'When you met . . .' she repeated.

'It was more than just an ordinary taxi ride,' I defended myself. 'But perhaps we'll speak at the memorial service?'

I couldn't let the car stand there in the road any longer. I waved to the two young women and drove on with a vague sense that it had been me they'd been talking about. Of course that could have been a figment of my imagination. I can sometimes accord myself a larger role than I really have.

I parked the car in front of the old firing range, just a stone's throw away from the Østreheim Inn and Social Hall, as the establishment was now known. It was a few months before the place was shut down, and a year or so before the almost one-hundred-year-old Swiss-style chalet was demolished, to a clamour of protests from the locals.

I stopped in front of the monument to Viggo Hansteen and Rolf Wickstrøm, who were executed here by the Gestapo on 10 September 1941 and buried at the firing range. Under the reliefs of the two resistance fighters were the words: IT WAS THE SACRIFICES OF THE LONELY THAT LIT UP THE SKY BEFORE DAYBREAK.

I pondered why the young war heroes were lonely,

and it struck me that perhaps I felt a little lonely myself – without drawing any other comparison.

People began to arrive from the church. I went into the hall exactly in the midst of the crowd, so I'd have some degree of choice over whom I ended up sitting with.

Somewhere between thirty and forty people came along to the memorial service. Of these, two or three were still dressed in Oslo Taxi uniforms. I ended up sitting at the same table as one of them. He was a man of my own age, who introduced himself as Rikard. He was a union official with the Norwegian Taxi Association. The priest was also at our table. Her name was Regina; she was new to the job and was probably in her early thirties.

I'd managed not to end up at the same table as any immediate family, but the two cousins soon sat at the neighbouring table.

Rolf welcomed us and briefly related the course Andrine's illness took once she'd got her tragic diagnosis six months previously. He went on to tell us about the radiotherapy and chemotherapy, about her fighting spirit and bravery, but also about her disdain for death and her consideration for those around her.

One of the taxi drivers – it wasn't Rikard – had started fiddling with a pack of cigarettes, and Rolf finished by explaining what food would be served, as well as informing us that smokers should make their way out onto the covered veranda – even though the room we were in bore the lingering smell of decades of cigarette smoke.

Five kinds of open sandwiches were served, along with macaroons, coffee and mineral water. Rikard asked how I knew Andrine. Was I part of the family, perhaps?

But I told my story of the trip to Åsgårdstrand, and of the months that followed. Rikard nodded in agreement: that was Andrine down to a tee. He recognised everything I said about long trips and what might be said or might take place on a taxi ride. He chuckled at Andrine's idea for *Tales from the Back Seat.* And he exclaimed: 'Why on earth didn't that book get written?'

I noted that Ylva, sitting at the next table, pricked up her ears. Rolf had been walking from table to table, greeting those guests he hadn't already met, me included. He stopped by our table and listened to what I was relating.

As I sketched a few pictures from the trip to Åsgårdstrand, and the grain of rapport Andrine and I had felt there, he became somewhat perplexed and commented that it was odd that she'd never mentioned anything about that trip to him.

Now Regina came to his aid. She came to *our* aid, I mean, since I was arguably in greater need of backup. The priest reminded him of the fact that this must have been before Rolf and Andrine had met each other. And to my relief I was able to take it from there. Only once had Andrine and I been out in town, I said. It was at the Theatre Café. She told me there that she'd met a man named Rolf, and that was the last time we saw one another.

At this point, Rolf planted a solid arm around my shoulders and gave me a comradely hug. But Ylva, who'd been listening to what I was saying all along, turned around in her chair and asked: 'Did you ask for a receipt on any of these taxi rides?'

She had that same sapphire-blue pendant at her throat. The previous time I'd seen her, I'd thought of it as a third eye. Now I had the feeling it was, in reality, a lens filming me.

Some people had gone out onto the veranda to smoke, and Rolf had taken one of the chairs at the table I was sitting at. We sat side by side for a long time, talking about Andrine. Just think, now she was gone!

It may be that my brain was multi-tasking, or perhaps Rolf was deaf in one ear, but as we exchanged our memories of Andrine, I was the only one who heard Ylva start bending her cousin's ear at the next table. She was talking heatedly about sexuality in myths and cults, describing Magnus Olsen's interpretation of *Skírnismál*, in which Freyr, the god of fertility, sends his servant Skírnir to the giantess Gerd to arrange an amorous meeting in the fields; ritual intercourse. It was as though she raised her voice and shot a glance in my direction every time she served up one of her juicy morsels. Tiny amulets bearing motifs depicting Freyr and Gerd were laid in the fields to ensure fertility and increase the harvest, and perhaps it wasn't unheard of for men and women to head out into the fields and have sex for the same reason. After a while, Ylva left behind the history of religion and began to talk about how the orgasm was the most significant sensory experience. Yes, she even went as far as suggesting that the orgasm could be the ultimate aim and objective of the universe. But was she being sarcastic? Or was she just overwrought?

She said: 'Just think about the fact that we're able to give each other such galactic sensory shocks, or ourselves for that matter. We don't even need one another!'

There was no longer any doubt: she was looking demonstratively at me as she spoke, as though she wanted to make it clear it was me she was addressing.

But why? Was it to test me? Or was she just being provocative?

I'd had enough. I bid farewell to Rolf and left the memorial service before most of the others. I was a peripheral guest in any case. I had no obligation to stay.

I had already put my coat on and was about to leave, when Ylva leaned over the back of her chair and reached out her right arm in an old-fashioned gesture, as though she wanted her hand kissed. But why? To humiliate me? Was it a way of making apparent the fact that I belonged to a completely different generation, that I was a remnant from another time? But I just nodded and said goodbye.

I waved over at Sverre and Marianne, and now it was unmistakeable: they'd recognised me! At least, I was *almost* sure they had. And with that they also probably had a clearer memory of how and when we'd met each other. It must have been a long time ago. But they chose not to confront me with it. I could clearly see Marianne flinch and look away. And I noticed once again the red gemstone in Sverre's ear.

A second later I'd left the building, and that was all that was needed for everything to fall into place: it was at Nisseberget! That was where I'd met Sverre and Marianne more than thirty years previously. We'd been living as hippies in Slottsparken. On my part it was no more than a few months – before I came to my senses, I must add. Marianne and Sverre kept it up much longer.

I walked to the car in front of the firing range and changed into hiking gear and winter boots. Minutes later I was scrambling up a gravel path towards Linderudkollen. In spite of the season, the path was only just covered with snow.

By the time I reached the little tarn and looked up at the brown ski lodge, it had begun to get dark. I'd been here once before, when I was a student, and I'd rounded off the day with a beer or two down at Østreheim.

It felt odd to be back after so many years. I was sure I recalled the brown lodge being red back then.

On the way back down I met – of course – Ylva and Anlaug, who, in spite of the dusk, were on their way up. They'd obviously had time to go home and change, or perhaps they'd had their hiking gear in the car, like I had. We were Norwegian, after all.

Both girls doubled over with laughter the moment they set eyes on me. The reaction wasn't intended nastily, but still I felt ridiculous. Ylva must have noticed, as she said in a somewhat teasing yet inclusive way:

'I've looked up your etymologies, Jakop. And they check out! So maybe your taxi story checks out too? In any case, no need to send me a receipt. Forget it!'

I think I might have given her a little bow, or at least a little nod. But at the same time I felt that I mustn't let events get out of hand. I felt vulnerable. Because I *was* lonely. So it came as a small consolation that the young scholar hadn't been capable of picking holes in my etymologies. She'd gone home that day in September and *looked up* the etymologies. She really had. And now she was telling me they checked out.

Anlaug started tugging Ylva's coat. They had so much to talk about, it would be getting dark soon, and they shouldn't spend more of the evening on me.

But I felt the need to make a point. I said, or more or less proclaimed:

'We rarely give it thought, but completely ordinary words, like cow and hound, way and wagon – or acre or axel, garden and land – have echoes across the whole of the Indo-European language region. Even short words like what and who, you and I, now and no – and all counting words from one to ten – not forgetting a host of prefixes like un-, as in unending, are among the five- or six-thousand-year-old inherited words from a Proto-Indo-European language, which has of course been lost, but which we can get a good way towards reconstructing by following a set of sound laws through the languages that have been preserved . . .'

'Is that true?' Anlaug interrupted. She turned to her cousin and said: 'Sooo interesting!'

But I caught the sarcasm in this response, and trying to make eye contact with Ylva, I concluded:

'It's also the case with some grammatical structures. Something as banal as our own possessive 's' has roots we can trace back thousands of years.'

I had to draw breath. In the gloom I was having trouble discerning Ylva's facial expressions, but now she said, possibly with respect, though also with a dose of irony, I'm sure:

'So you won't give up? Haven't I already declared you to be a fantastically learned person?'

I remembered the little dispute we'd had over Indo-European studies, and I suppose she interpreted it as rather odd to pick up the thread again. But I was trying to get at something, and I saw no shame in making a last attempt to keep the conversation going – a fleeting chat, a rare fragment of fellowship. I said:

'But I wonder: when so many languages, and so much culture, not least that connected to agriculture, animal husbandry and various crafts, has been passed down across thousands of years, why wouldn't it be possible for the same to be true of religious concepts?'

I didn't know how she'd react. I'd seen how unpredictable she could be, and I wouldn't have been altogether surprised if she'd given me a slap. What's more, her cousin had begun to pull at her coat again, markedly more determinedly this time.

But Ylva replied to my question. She said:

'Even if some words and expressions are inherited, and the odd deity name, that doesn't mean whole myths, or as you said, whole sets of religious concepts, have gone almost unchanged through thousands of years.'

The cousin insisted, openly now: 'Are you coming, Ylva?'

But I'd got Ylva's attention, because she went into detail:

'So, comparative linguistics can, with the help of sound laws, bring the old Indo-European language back, pull it into the light. It's fascinating. But there are none of these "sound laws" in the history of religion. I think the religious imagination of humans is something far more effervescent, plastic and mutable than the meaning of words and what you call grammatical structures. Perhaps these sustainable *mythical* structures just don't exist. Human nature is too inventive for that.'

I thought she'd given an intelligent response, and a qualified one. I said so too. But I added that the comparative study of Indo-European religions was a young field, more or less at the nappy stage, and that there was a risk of throwing the baby out with the bathwater.

They laughed, both girls laughed. But I wasn't able to figure out why, and perhaps that's an early sign of old age: no longer understanding why the young laugh.

They said they were heading deeper into the forest, hunting for giants and trolls, and I bid them good hunting.

After I'd got a few paces I stopped. I could hear Anlaug saying:

'What *is* it with that man?'

'It's shameless,' Ylva said. 'But I haven't got the energy to talk about it now . . .'

The rest of the conversation between the two cousins was beyond my earshot. It was lost in the night.

*

The clouds had parted, and long before I made it down to the firing range, I had a clear view of the universe surrounding me.

I thought of Ylva's bizarre assertion about the orgasm being the meaning of the universe. After casting a glance up at the Milky Way I felt convinced it must be an anthropocentric exaggeration. It occurred to me that the stars are sexless. And senseless for that matter. Not too many orgasms to be had there.

There is something above and beyond scx, I reasoned. The stars in the sky, for instance.

Saturday 18 May 2013, the eve of Whitsunday. Here in Visby it's been an unusually warm day for May. The sun has sunk beyond the water's mirrored surface, but the horizon in the north-west is still red. The sea, which was pale blue half an hour ago, has taken on a dark hue.

I look up at a waxing new moon, and I can make out its edge on the dark half too.

The Norwegian word *måne,* and its English equivalent *moon,* are of course connected to the word *month,* an ancient inherited word, which is still in use almost right across the Indo-European language area. The six-thousand-year-old gloss **mēnōs* for both *moon* and *month* is assumed to be linked to the root *mē- for 'measure', as in words like *meter*, *mail* and *meal*. Therefore the words *meter*, *mail* and *moon* are related.

The languages fit together. It's like a big family, or at least an extended one. I'm sometimes gripped by the thought that I belong to this massive family.

Funny to think of it now: it's almost exactly a month since you and I met in Arendal. It was a new moon then too.

I've opened both the windows in the room where I'm sitting, and more and more insects keep joining me; they'll be with me till the morning.

Outside, it's still twenty degrees.

Runar

I have to fast-forward many years before I meet any of Erik Lundin's descendants again. It's them I'm writing about. You may have noticed that there's a lot I'm leaving out. I'm only including in my tale those occasions when I met one or more of Erik's descendants, no more, no less – it's the red thread in this story, and soon you'll see that this thread leads to you.

The leap I'm about to make takes us right up to August 2008. I was in Bergen, where I'd spent a week before the start of the school term, among other things giving a talk at a folklore association out in Sandviken. The association asked what assumptions we can make about pre-Christian myths and cults based on Nordic place names, an area of research that owes much to the work of Magnus Olsen. I'd centred the talk on the gods Ullr and Týr.

Ullr occurs widely in place names in Norway and the central region of Sweden – as in Ullern,

Ullensvang, Ullevål and Ullevi – but is, in contrast, completely absent in both Denmark and Iceland. What's more, Ullr plays no major role in the mythology that has been passed down, and so obviously represents an older stratum in the development of religion than that reflected in the Poetic and the Prose Eddas. The name Ullr is derived from the Germanic *wulþuz*, meaning 'radiance' or 'glory', and it's probably a personification of the firmament we're talking about.

In contrast, Týr is not found in Norwegian or central-Swedish place names, but is widely found in Danish place names. This god plays a certain role in the mythical world drama as depicted in the work of Snorri Sturluson, but was certainly a much more central deity before the Viking Age and the mythological poems we find in the Poetic Edda. We're talking about a common Germanic deity, which in its origins is probably linked to the heavens and the firmament.

The name Týr is derived from the Germanic *tiwaz*, which can also mean 'god', in the plural form *tívar*, and we find this deity name in 'Tuesday', that is 'Týr's Day'. The word is related to the Proto-Indo-European word for 'god', *deiwos*; the Sanskrit *devas*; Latin *deus*; and therefore derived from the same root as the Vedic sky-god *Dyaus*; the Greek *Zeus*; and the Latin 'Father *Iov*' or *Iovpater* – that is *Jupiter*. In Latin, 'open-air' translates as *sub Iove*. Furthermore, the root is connected to the Indo-European word for 'day', as in the Latin *dies*, from which the loanword *diet* derives. The Proto-Indo-European god **Dyeus* was the god of day and daylight.

Much points to the worship in the Nordic region of either Ullr or Týr, but not both at the same time. Or is it conceivable that Ullr and Týr could have been two names for one and the same deity? Both are gods of the firmament, both can also be linked to a judicial function, and throughout the Nordic pantheon the same deities consistently appear under a range of names. Magnus Olsen states, in short, that 'Ullr and Týr are names for the same god'.

But it's also been suggested that the two gods could be linked to one another in a more intricate way. Týr could be the summer aspect of the Nordic sky god, related, as the word is, to the Indo-European word for 'day' and daylight. And Ullr could be the winter aspect of the Nordic sky god, with the name – **wulþuz*, meaning 'radiance' or 'glory' – possibly alluding to the shining of the winter stars. The Nordic winter nights – with their intense starlight, and in Norway and Sweden, the northern lights – were seen as something different, but just as divine, and just as otherworldly as daylight. In historic times, Ullr was also referred to as the 'ski god', an obviously wintery feature.

Reaching conclusions on this matter lies beyond the scope of this text, but these were the kind of issues I discussed.

One night, I dreamed I was giving the same talk to Erik Lundin as we took our few circuits around Sognsvann. And even though many years had passed since I'd last seen Ylva, or perhaps for precisely that reason, I will confess that in the days before the talk I found myself daydreaming that she unexpectedly turned up at the event in Sandviken and took a seat in the front row. (There had been a small notice in the local newspaper in Bergen.) I have a close attachment to this material, you might call it a romantic attachment, and I doubt the young genius would have had anything to pick holes in. Perhaps at the end of the talk she would have just put her hands together and led the applause!

But Peder Skrindo was there. He sat and listened to everything I said, and he also made his own contributions at various points. It's not often we appear together, but it does happen. When I clam up, or have forgotten to include a point or two, I have nothing against Pelle taking the initiative and putting me back on the right track, or, if the worst comes to the worst, putting me in my place.

You're familiar with my connection to Bergen, of course. I can't remember precisely what I said in the car on the way back from Arendal, but I told you some of it.

My father was from Bergen. I still have a cousin in the Hanseatic city. However, I've never met him, and so it's not for family reasons that I've made something of a tradition out of spending a week in Western Norway before the school year begins in mid-August.

Indeed, it's strange to see from the screen in front of me that I've used the word 'tradition'. Because I've been alone in this custom. This is worth highlighting, because when you start to develop an inner respect for the kind of habits that involve no one other than yourself, the power of the habit starts to come perilously close to what many would call a compulsive neurosis. But I don't see it that way. I have a great deal of respect for contracts I've entered into with myself. There's nothing more to be said on the matter.

In recent years I've been happy to give a talk during the week I've spent in Bergen, whether in the town itself or out in Fana, Os or Åsane. In folklore circles I've gradually made a name for myself in Western Norway, not just in Bergen, but also in Hardanger and Sogn. 'Inspiring speaker ... An inexhaustible stream of Indo-European links and lineages ... An entertaining voyage through our shared Nordic heritage ...' Or: 'The Jakobsen and Skrindo double-act took the audience by storm ...'

In Bergen I always stay at Hotel Norge. When I check in on the 8th of August – always the 8th of August, my birthday – the receptionist has been known to recognise me from the previous year and to say, for instance: 'Here at the hotel we've started setting our clocks by you, Jakobsen. Welcome back to Bergen!'

I do like things like that. It shows consideration. It makes me feel as though I belong to a community.

There aren't many guests that spend a whole week at the Hotel Norge.

As I sat on the plane over to Bergen that year, I came across a death notice in *Bergens Tidende*, the local Bergen paper. Runar Friele had died, and it had happened under the most tragic circumstances, because the notice stated simply that he'd 'died in his home at Kalfaret in June 2008'.

You must have heard about his death, Agnes. Truls must have told you something. You said you're in touch with him regularly.

Runar died in his home 'in June 2008'. This line

stood out, for its vagueness, I mean. According to the notice, the deceased was to be 'buried after a service at the Chapel of Hope in Møllendal, Thursday 14 August at 15:00', that is, many weeks after he had died.

Agnes, you *must* have heard about it!

The end of the notice announced that 'everyone who knew Runar is welcome to the memorial service at Hotel Terminus . . .'

Runar, I thought. What have they done to you?

I had to go to the service, I was absolutely set on that. But I probably wouldn't have done so if I hadn't already been in Bergen. In any case, my making the trip across the mountains would have been dependent on my happening to flick through *Bergens Tidende* that day – for example in a newsagent's kiosk on Stortingsgaten or on Karl Johan's Gate, otherwise the information about Runar's passing away wouldn't have reached me; I don't often buy *Bergens Tidende* when at home in Eastern Norway, *Aftenposten* and the other Oslo papers are generally enough.

My original plan had been to check out of the hotel that very Thursday, that is the 14th of August, and come home to Oslo in good time for the school governance meeting, and what we call the work-scheme days. But now I rebooked my tickets, booked an extra night at Hotel Norge and bought myself a dark suit.

As soon as I stepped into the Chapel of Hope that Thursday, I spotted Lise and Jon-Petter Lundin right up in the front row. What's more, I caught sight of Sigrid, who'd led the memorial service after her grandfather's funeral many years before. A shudder passed through me. I'd had no idea there was any family connection between them and Runar Friele.

Sigrid sat alongside Thomas, so they must still be together. Seven years ago, they'd had two children, Morten and Miriam, and soon I was to find out that the family had since increased in size. But here, in the chapel, there were no children.

A thought struck me: not a single one of the people gathered was under eighteen. I had studied the death notice carefully and already had a sense the funeral service would be under some kind of censorship. By which I mean an age limit.

Up on the third row of pews I recognised Fredrik, who was a law student at the beginning of the 2000s. Now he was building a career as a corporate lawyer, which I was given an extensive briefing on a few hours later. Also sitting there was his little brother, Joakim, who had been in the last year at the Fagerborg High School and who would soon be starting the residency that would conclude his medical studies. Both Fredrik and Joakim were sitting with their wives or partners.

I realised from the first instant that Lise must be Runar's sister, and it occurred to me that at her father-in-law's memorial service she'd talked loudly across the table with an unmistakeable Bergen dialect.

Later that day I was to find out that the others sitting at the front of the chapel were Lise and Runar's other siblings, something that was also clear from the death notice: Øivind, Bernt and Mildrid, all accompanied by spouses in their fifties. It occurred to me that a cluster of young people between twenty and thirty were possibly nephews and nieces of the deceased, probably with their girlfriends and boyfriends and so on.

I took a seat right at the back of the chapel, though there were empty pews in front of me. No one from the Lundin clan had noticed me.

The priest was an almost bald man in his forties, with a sing-song Sunnhordland dialect – after some analysis I decided he must be from Bømlo. He began his eulogy for the deceased more or less as follows (I'm relating freely from memory):

'We are gathered here today to say our final

farewells to Runar Friele – a brother, brother-in-law, uncle and great-uncle.

'Runar grew up as the youngest boy in a privileged home and was from childhood blessed with a large family. It's tempting to quote the British baroque poet John Donne here: "*No man is an island entire of itself: every man is a piece of the continent, a part of the main . . . any man's death diminishes me, because I am involved in mankind. And therefore never send to know for whom the bell tolls; it tolls for thee . . .*"

'But we know that as an adult Runar lived practically isolated from his own family, *in* his own family. What's more, he died alone and in extreme distress. As a priest standing by the coffin of this solitary man, it is my duty to remind you that Runar really did have a large number of siblings. But they did not welcome him. Quite the opposite, my dear people. Runar's siblings pushed him away.

'Before a funeral like this I always have a long, in-depth conversation with the bereaved. I need to form for myself an image of who the person was, what they did. But after I met with the family – with the exception of Lise, who lives in Oslo, and wasn't able to take part in the conversation – I went home almost empty-handed. I went home full of sadness. I went home with my head full of slander and resentment.

'It was impossible to avoid the fact that Runar's siblings had not been in the same room as their brother for almost twenty years.'

No one in the chapel was crying. But the shame was there for all to see and sense. I could almost smell it: the embarrassment became tangible and reached my nostrils as a nauseating stench. The priest continued:

'Runar was a skilled businessman, extremely skilled in fact. It put him in the position to buy out his siblings after both their parents had died, and take over the Kalfaret mansion, so steeped in tradition. He painted the house, brightening it and freshening it up. He redesigned and replanted the garden, putting his stamp on the estate both externally and internally, *his* stamp.

'It hasn't escaped my attention that the prevailing impression within the family has been that Runar got his hands on the old family estate much too cheaply, and that he went on to ruin it with his drastic changes. In his first years as the owner of the house, however, he tried to turn it into a meeting place for the whole family, at times like Christmas and New Year, and also for the long succession of fortieth and fiftieth birthdays. Because "no man is an island entire of itself: every man is a piece of the continent, a part of the main". But Runar's hospitality was in vain. Runar's *call for help* was in vain.

'Runar was a homosexual and lived those first few years at Kalfaret together with Knut, to whom he was extremely close. When Knut become ill and died of AIDS in November 1988, Runar's world shattered. Only occasionally during the years that followed did he have a relationship. Some of these friends, or acquaintances, lived with him for short periods, but he never truly cohabited with anyone else.

'For some of us, such fleeting ephemeral meetings or *trysts* are an important part of life. Because we have nothing else. Not everyone is blessed with a life-long marriage. Not everyone is blessed with children and grandchildren of their own.

'Runar never found anyone who could replace Knut. He never started his own family. So he became all the more eager in his renewed attempts to gather his siblings and siblings-in-law, along with their families, to Sunday dinners and Christmas gatherings. But when they – I mean you – continued to refuse to grace your brother and brother-in-law with a visit, Runar's invitations gradually fell silent.

'None of this should go unsaid, *can* go unsaid. But I must add that it is in consultation with the bereaved that I have given Runar's isolation such harsh treatment here. As one of you said: "This is something we have to hear, because it is the truth."'

The priest gazed out over the mourners, and now several people were crying openly, not least on the front pews. The priest let the feeling of unease take hold of the congregation before continuing in a milder tone:

'"The Oslo lot", that was the name Runar gave to Lise and Jon-Petter, Sigrid, Fredrik and Joakim, the Oslo lot always got in touch with Runar when they were in Bergen, even though years could pass between visits. Later, it was Sigrid and Thomas and their children who established a relationship with Uncle Runar. After my unsuccessful conversation with the rest of the family, I was forced in the end to get on the phone to Sigrid . . .

'As recently as May this year you were on an extended Whitsun holiday to Bergen and spent a week staying at the mansion out at Kalfaret, where Lise had grown up. You arrived to freshly made-up beds, fires roaring in the hearths. Vintage wines carefully selected from the cellar were served during the beautifully prepared dinners. Or as you said, Sigrid: it was as though you were being treated to everything the rest of the family had turned their noses up at. You were the last members of the family to see him. It's not known whether anyone saw Runar after that. No one has got in touch to say so.

'Over the course of these days in May, Runar was happily engaged in building a treehouse in the old pear tree with Morten and Miriam, and from that same pear tree he hung a swing, so that little Olivia would have something to do while the others sat up in the tree, sawing and hammering. Because Mum and Dad were at Grieg Hall, or they were at the theatre, at the cinema, out dining at Holbergstuen.

'There was no mention of Mum or Dad during those days just a few months ago.'

Once again the priest paused for effect, and I began to give thought to my relationship to the deceased . . .

I could tell the family how Runar and I, seven or eight years ago, had got to know each other at Hotel Norge, where Runar was a regular, and always sat at the same table with a view out over Festplassen and Lille Lungegårdsvann. There was no reason the family would have been familiar with Runar's dining habits.

I'd been sitting alone at my table, and he at his. We were two solitary men who got chatting with one another over something as banal as the weather – it hadn't rained in Bergen for many days, and after all a conversation has to start somewhere.

That first time we met, we took dessert and coffee at the same table, and before the evening was over, we'd got into our stride. We'd soon agreed that we were both outsiders with a skewed view of our surroundings, or for that matter, of existence in general. Even when it came to our families, we were both peripheral. Perhaps each of us could be characterised as 'an island entire of itself'.

Runar had no connection to Germanic philology, and I was equally blank when it came to his domain, that is, the business world. This meant that our sporadic encounters were not only pleasant, but mutually informative.

On one occasion I invited Runar to come and enter the complex world of comparative linguistics. He was a completely blank slate: he hadn't a clue what I meant by 'etymologies', 'inherited words' or 'sound law'. And he didn't know what I meant by 'Indo-European languages'. But if I said Indian languages, Iranian languages, Greek, Latin, Germanic or Slavic, he was at least partly with me. I explained that the Baltic language Lithuanian is the most archaic of the Indo-European languages still spoken. However, when it came to Celtic languages, I had to explain in more detail. People are often unaware that the Celts once dominated large parts of the European continent, before the Germanic tribes such as the Goths, the Franks, the Angles and the Saxons forced them into the northernmost and westernmost parts of the British Isles.

The first time we talked of these things – of my things – I gave him a few examples of inherited words that might be of interest to Runar as a businessman. I began with a few terms linked to the Norwegian word *fe*, meaning 'livestock', which, long before the first coins, actually served as a method of payment, and still does in many places. It wasn't hard to capture Runar's interest. He sat watching me with a playful smile. He was all ears.

The Norwegian word *fe*, from the Proto-Germanic **féhu-* goes back to the Indo-European **peku-*, meaning 'livestock', or 'sheep and goats' – corresponding to the Latin *pecus* for 'livestock', in Sanskrit known as *paśú*. In the Germanic region we also encounter the same root in **fahaz-*, which in Old Norse gives us *fær* and in Norwegian *får* for 'sheep'. This ancient inherited word has also provided many Indo-European languages with words for wealth, such as the Old Norse *fé* for 'property', 'ownership' and 'money', and from the same Germanic root, via the Gothic *faihu*, we get the English word *fee*. We see a similar development in Latin, where *pecus* for 'livestock' produces *pecunia* for property or fortune, from which we have the loanword *pecuniary*, from the Latin word *pecuniarius* for monetary transactions or anything concerning money.

I could also tell the family that Runar and I met once or twice a year, always on one of these evenings in August before the new school year came around. I had therefore been concerned when he hadn't got in touch this summer – he would always call me at some point in July – but I thought I'd just have to get in touch once I got to Bergen. We'd never exchanged email addresses or anything like that.

I wouldn't have said we were close friends, that would have been going too far, and I probably wouldn't have made the trip over the mountains to attend his funeral, but since I happened to be in Bergen, I couldn't resist saying a last farewell to my Hotel Norge dining companion of so many years. I knew Runar's family only through his stories. It wasn't without a look of sorrow that he had recited the names of his siblings, nephews and nieces. But his eyes lit up every time he mentioned Knut.

All in all we must have had around ten of these dinners together, with fine wines and always a glass of cognac with coffee. I tried a few times to beat him to it when it came to asking for the bill: I told him we should at least split it, or take turns paying; but Runar was of the opinion that teachers and lecturers were much too poorly paid. Still, he let me pay for one or two of those dinners, and I believe it was to ensure we could continue on equal terms as conversation partners. He could speak freely, even when he strongly disagreed with something I said. And he wanted me to be just as candid.

Through the years we got to know each other well, but we never socialised outside the Hotel Norge. We often concluded with a drink in the bar, but he never invited me back to the big house at Kalfaret.

The priest from Bømlo now presented an unembellished picture of what had happened in the old mansion a few months before. The main points, supplemented with what I later found out during a long chat with Sigrid as the memorial service was coming to an end, are these:

Runar had gone down into the cellar, apparently to fetch something from the freezer, and all the signs point to it being something as trifling as an ice cube for a glass of whisky, which was later found on the mantelpiece in one of the main rooms, although the contents of the glass had of course evaporated.

The freezer was located in a large cellar room, which had once housed bicycles, skis and prams. Now only the freezer remained. Runar had no children, and he neither cycled nor skied. What's more, his refined nature forbade him from letting old junk sit around just because he couldn't get round to removing it.

From the time he'd taken over the house, however, he'd lived with a cellar door that had an incorrectly mounted spring lock. The problem was that you needed a key to open the solid fire door from the inside, whereas it was easy to just turn the latch from the outside – no key required. It was impossible to be locked *out* of the cellar. It was only possible to be locked in.

Everyone in the family remembered there having been a key that always stayed in the lock on the inside of the cellar door. That was probably why the call to the locksmith to correct the fatal mistake was put off again and again. When the children lived at home, they always got an extra reminder to put something in front of the door any time someone went into the cellar, and to that end, a 2.5-kilo weight was left right by the heavy fire door. In the event anyone did absent-mindedly forget to push the weight between the door and the doorframe, you could just use the key on the inside, which was *never* to be removed.

But Runar went into the cellar that fateful evening or night sometime in the middle of June without pushing the weight into place in front of the door-frame. He might have forgotten to do it, or perhaps he had grown lazy and come to rely on the key to get out again on his way upstairs. The problem was that there was no key in the lock.

How and why the key came to be taken out of the lock is something no one has been able to explain, not Runar's siblings, not the police or the fire brigade. Perhaps Runar never gave the key – or the key's absence – so much as a thought before it was too late. He might have known it wasn't there, but in a second's thoughtlessness he forgot to push the weight across before finding himself locked in and all alone. We'll never know if the ice cube he was going to fetch that evening was the first.

With him in the cellar, Runar had a sturdy torch, most likely because the overhead light had gone. The overhead light had, in any case, gone before he was found a few weeks later and by that time the torch had also run out of battery. How long he had light from the torch, we can only speculate. But he left clear signs that he saved up the light. He was scared of being left in complete blackness without at least now and then being able to grant himself a few seconds' light in the darkness of his existence. When the battery was gone, it would be over. It would be pitch black.

But if Runar just needed an ice cube or two for a glass of whisky, why hadn't he taken his glass down with him into the cellar? That's easy to answer, and the answer is that he only had two hands. In one hand he was holding the heavy torch, and in the other he was holding his mobile phone. This last detail is interesting. Runar seems to have thought it likely that someone would ring him, so likely that he decided to take the phone with him, even for those few moments it took to fetch ice for his whisky glass. He wanted to avoid missing a call.

I mention the mobile phone in particular, because if only Runar had thought to take it with him into the cellar room, it would have been a small matter for him to ring for help. But just as he was about to turn the latch and open the door, he put the mobile down on the floor next to him, alongside the old weight. When the door closed after him, he was holding only the torch, and the mobile was irretrievably out of reach.

In the days that follow, he will sometimes hear the telephone ringing, once for a very long time. Of this too he has left clear evidence. There are also external witnesses. He called out, he shouted, to no avail of course, imprisoned as he was in a cellar room in a patrician mansion surrounded by a large garden, which, at the time, no one entered or exited apart from him. At least once there was a ring on the doorbell, which could be heard all the way from the cellar. We can confirm this, because a DHL courier attempted to deliver a package, which turned out to contain a couple of old films on VHS, both with Fred Astaire and Ginger Rogers in the leading roles.

There is one final prop in this thriller. Perhaps on his way down to the cellar, Runar picked up an Elizabeth Arden lipstick, which Sigrid might have left in the hall or put down on a dresser when she was visiting her uncle the month before. In any case, Runar had that lipstick with him in the cellar. It would come to play a central role. That it belonged to Sigrid is beyond all doubt.

From the moment the door closed on him – what a moment, Agnes! – until he drew his last breath down in the deep cellar, the police believe that around two weeks must have passed. It's not easy to confirm exactly, because even when it was all over, there were additional weeks before the sturdy steel door was forced open and Runar's body could be subject to autopsy, as well as a Christian burial.

Two weeks he lived in the cold cocoon. That so much time could pass was due to the deep freezer itself. For a couple of weeks, that was Runar's source of food and drink. Alongside the bread and meat, it was full of frozen redcurrant cordial, blackcurrant cordial and pear cider. From the day he had taken over the house, Runar had been a keen gardener. In the end it was probably the liquid that ran out first, because afterwards the freezer still contained bread and meat, but all the vegetables, juice and conserves were gone.

These special living conditions did of course lead to certain natural consequences, but I won't go into detail, except to intimate that Runar's polished nature was tested in the extreme during those last few days. The cellar had four corners, and the freezer occupied only one of these.

You must have heard something, Agnes, and maybe more than me. Or perhaps Lise also felt so ashamed of this disgraceful family tragedy that she chose to keep it to herself? I'm not in a position to rule it out. But in any case, after what happened when the two of us met some years later – you were in deep mourning, and I compromised your reputation – there will certainly have been a good deal of chatter among the family.

So you must have known something. It's hard to believe we didn't talk about it when the opportunity was granted us on that long car journey we took together just a few weeks ago. We talked about most other things.

I'll never forget the story you told me about your cousin falling down the well. It's rather touching to think how you and Truls grew up together.

He became a brain scientist, and you, Agnes, you became a psychotherapist. Brain and psyche: so fundamentally similar, and yet still so different.

It's not hard for me to grasp that you must have been jealous when Truls suddenly got together with Liv-Berit and began to take *her* out to the old summer house you'd both been so closely tied to since you were little, a paradise you'd conquered together and shared since the dawn of time. Yes, I can imagine it must have been disruptive and awful. So in the end you did the only thing you could. You made Liv-Berit a close friend!

But back to our car journey. You sat listening intently in the passenger seat even as I got deep into Indo-European philology, that marvel, as I put it – that strange forest full of adventure and verbal creations, with its mesmerising register of related inherited words as varied as the branches of zoology's manifold catalogue of cats, Compositae, sparrows or rodents.

Runar spent the last hours of his life daubing his thoughts and cries for help on the whitewashed walls with Sigrid's red lipstick. However, the scribbled notes found in the gloomy cellar were incoherent and in places hard to decipher. Letter by letter, word for word, and sentence for sentence, much of the material had to be interpreted, and in some cases even guessed at. The fact that the script was illegible here and there could be a sign that some of it was daubed in complete darkness. But the unclear letters – and therefore the difficulty of deciphering the message – might also be attributed to the writing implement itself, and in the end, of course, to the writer's gradual exhaustion.

The way it was told to me, I think it makes sense to compare Runar's report from the cellar room with the sparse remains of runic inscriptions from the third century onwards. We are dealing with occasional insights into thoughts and temperaments of Germanic tribes that lived many hundreds of years before history as we know it. An example is the famous Golden Horns of Gallehus from the fifth century: '*I, Lægest, son of Holt, made the horn . . .*' And we shouldn't forget the many rune sticks of the Middle Ages – the social media of the day – on which can you find everyday messages like: '*Ingebjørg made love to me when I was in Stavanger*'.

These brief runic inscriptions span a period of more than a thousand years. They provide only a small peephole into an ocean of time, and of space, since runic inscriptions are found across the whole of the Germanic region – which, because of migration, covers large parts of Europe.

What Runar daubed on the walls of the cellar with Sigrid's lipstick is just a fleeting glimpse of what passed through his mind during those last days before he died. There was nothing on the walls to indicate that Runar had any hope of being found before it was too late.

Before the funeral, Runar's siblings and their partners, along with some of the children, went to inspect the old mansion in Kalfaret. They felt they owed their brother a final visit, even though it was post mortem. It was an ordeal they couldn't avoid. Sooner or later, the house would have to be sold. Runar hadn't written a will.

They went from room to room, mouths agape. Occasionally, a loud sigh could be heard, but everyone tried to control themselves.

The house they had grown up in was completely unrecognisable. The hall, where the old Art Nouveau furnishings had stood adorning the entrance to the drawing room, was remodelled as a simple home cinema. The kitchen had been modernised and expanded through the demolition of the old pantry, and in the library, the grand old mahogany bookcases with all the antique books and old maps and almanacs were gone, replaced by elegant glass cases full of modern photography books, art books, film journals and films on VHS and DVD. Almost all the reception rooms had undergone similar transformations. Only the dining room was intact, including the three Munch prints.

Now everything had been cleaned up in the cellar, the siblings gathered and went down there too. It wasn't something they were looking forward to. It was something they imposed on one another, a duty.

They'd had a status report from the police in advance, and they'd given the cleaning firm notice not to touch the walls. That was another thing they were in agreement on. Before everything was white-washed over, the siblings felt it was only right for them to go down to the macabre death chamber and read what Runar had written. Perhaps the messages had been intended for them.

It was the siblings' visit to their childhood home, and not least this detour down to the cellar, that Sigrid related to me vividly when we were alone. She mentioned things that were barely spoken of at the funeral itself.

Sigrid emphasised that Runar's contact with me must have been of great significance to him. He didn't have that many friends or acquaintances. The charming niece confided in me that Runar was essentially very shy, and that he wasn't in the habit of making contact with strangers. Something about my character must have unlocked something in him, leading him to open up to me so quickly when we met in the dining room at Hotel Norge. It's always nice to hear things like that. People so seldom speak kind words to each other.

High up on the walls, Runar had written THE WRITING ON THE WALL in capitals, and Øivind, Bernt, Lise and Mildrid thought that was probably the first thing he'd written, like a title or heading. At least all the letters were whole and written in a straight line, in contrast to much of the rest.

Runar must originally – perhaps just minutes after the door slammed shut on him – have had a clear plan to leave a last farewell. Perhaps he'd even imagined his siblings one day standing gathered before these walls. Lise thought her brother had taken great pains to give the family a chance to get this insight into his last hours and days.

The cellar room had four walls, and each of the four heirs stood in front of a wall, reading – partly in their heads, partly in a low murmur to themselves, but after a while they began to read aloud to one another.

I'll now attempt to relate something from that corpus, based on what Sigrid told me. In order to make the sentences flow to some degree, I have been forced to employ a certain amount of poetic licence.

The fragments fall into three discrete categories. One group focuses on the room and the house Runar is in, a second group could perhaps best be described as aphorisms or philosophical crumbs, and the third points in the direction we could term 'confessional literature'.

Runar wrote:

Bad, bad . . . the telephone is ringing . . . the mobile's ringing again . . . someone's ringing the doorbell, hasn't happened for months, must be a salesman . . . I'm calling out, screaming . . . didn't hear me . . . the phone's ringing again, a long time . . . the light is getting weaker . . . saving it up as best I can . . . scared to lose the light . . . I've slept . . . such a stench in here . . . hours since I last had light . . . don't know what time of day, could be the middle of the night, or it could be the middle of the day . . . slept again . . . dreamed I swam into the innermost shaft and saw the answers to all life's mysteries . . . swam with the ease of a dolphin into the holiest of holies, but I've forgotten everything . . . the mobile's ringing, think it's Sigrid . . . dearest Sigrid . . . when I don't pick up, I hope you'll report me missing . . . I sleep and sleep . . . wake from one awesome adventure after another . . . the head's cooked, starting to cool now . . . don't give up hope ... only you can save me, Sigrid ... Morten, Miriam and Olivia – will I never hold you in my arms again?

On the white walls there was also a completely different kind of observation:

We were scared ... was I the only one who saw that we were trolls? ... The opposite of everything is nothing, and the opposite of nothing is everything. Take everything from me and give me everything back! ... Nothing can be said about everything ... The Milky Way is a street of theatre, like Broadway ... the globe is an illness, the famine emerged five million years ago ... There is a lot God can be criticised for. Perhaps his most brazen quality is that he doesn't exist. But OK, no one's perfect ... if there was no consciousness, there might have been something completely different here, *gmein* for instance, or *gloin*, generation follows generation ... and the others come into post, brand new birds on branches, the changing of the guards: tweet tweet!

And then:

Oh, how I've loved this life, this city, these mountains; all the pretty boys strutting about up on The

Meadow . . . Knut! Where are you now? . . . I just met a similar guy in town, divine . . .

Each time Runar heard the phone ringing in the corridor outside, he noted it on one of the walls. After he was found, the police examined the phone, the battery of which was by that point completely dead, and they were soon able to release the log to the bereaved.

All the calls were from Sigrid; it was of course her he'd been waiting for a call from when he went down into the cellar, and she was the one who raised the alarm in the end. She was worried that something might have happened to him. He might have fallen ill or been in no fit state to be on his own.

Sigrid insisted that someone had to get into the house and check on him. When none of her aunts or uncles in Bergen were willing to do that, she turned to the police. Still, it was a while before they took action. Mention was made of the fact that her uncle often went on long business trips. But in the end two police officers broke into the elegant mansion. They soon realised they would need assistance from the fire service.

The four heirs, both to the house and to the remainder of Runar's fortune, stood for a long time reading the red lettering on the cellar walls. They switched places, and switched again, so that each in turn had a chance to familiarise themselves with everything their brother had written.

The next day the walls were whitewashed.

Grethe Cecilie

On 22 December 2011, I'm at a funeral again. It takes place in the more than one-hundred-year-old chapel in West Gravlund, and it's at the memorial service after this funeral that I meet you, Agnes. We've never met one another before, but even at the chapel I can see you must be Grethe Cecilie's sister. You have the same sparkling eyes.

Here too I met some of Erik Lundin's descendants. Namely, Erik's daughter Liv-Berit and your cousin Truls, with their daughters Tuva and Mia. At that point I didn't know how closely you were connected to them.

It was Tuva who had sung so beautifully from *Haugtussa* at her grandfather's funeral ten years previously. Mia, who at that point was a lanky girl of fifteen, was today a fashionable woman of twenty-five. She had, if possible, grown up to be even more beautiful and brilliant than the sister who was five years her senior. Of all things, she now worked as an estate agent. If I'd had to guess, I probably would have settled on something completely different. The apple had fallen far from the tree of Yggdrasil, so to speak. But I'm sure she facilitated the sale of many apartments.

But why am I telling you this? You've known Tuva and Mia since they were little.

I hadn't met anyone from that branch of the Lundin family during the ten years that had passed. Even though Oslo is a small city, and Norway a small country, it still seemed mysterious that I should once again meet members of the same family at a funeral. This was the fourth time.

The pieces had all fallen into place, as now I had met each of Erik's children and their families at separate funerals, first Marianne, Sverre and Ylva at Andrine's funeral, then Jon-Petter and Lise with their children at Runar's funeral, and now Liv-Berit and Truls with their two daughters.

Were there some hidden ties between me and the Lundin family?

I think it's fitting to ask that question. Later I'll show that this red thread in my story, the epic element of my tale, has a completely natural explanation. At this point, however, I feel there's still something that prevents such an insight, but I promise to come back to it.

*

The death notice said 'My irreplaceable daughter, our beloved sister, sister-in-law, aunt and great-aunt, Grethe Cecilie Berg Olsen, born 8 February 1959, was taken from us suddenly on 13 December 2011 in Oslo . . .'

This dramatic statement was signed by Grethe Cecilie's mother, Nina, her brothers, Jan-Olav and Ulf, with their wives, Norunn and Ingrid, and finally you, Agnes, the youngest of the siblings, before the usual 'and other family'.

I didn't know any of you, but I was familiar with the tragic circumstances of Grethe Cecilie's death a few days before I saw the announcement in the paper, both via the descriptions in the media and through a colleague at the teaching board.

Grethe Cecilie was a teacher of maths and physics in another part of the town. She also had a PhD in astrophysics.

I remember walking from the car park at the end of Frogner Park that afternoon, just two days before Christmas. It had been a busy, almost exhausting autumn, both in the classroom and on the teaching board. I get on with some of the students – we have an almost collegial relationship with a mutual respect for each other's role – but these few tend to get lost in the grey mass of students who are easily bored and who therefore bore me too. How can Indo-European sound laws stand up against a hefty dose of testosterone?

The weather was wintery, heavily overcast, a few degrees below zero, and almost completely calm. On the way to the chapel, over the grass and the graves, and on the leafless oak trees in the avenue, lay a thin layer of fresh snow that had fallen during the morning. On several of the graves, candles had already been lit, even though it was still a couple of days until Christmas. Many people had obviously already left the city and gone off on their Christmas holidays.

I looked to my left and glanced at the stately grave of the gypsy queen Lola Karoli. I focused my thoughts on Grethe Cecilie and the tragic incident that had happened so suddenly during the Christmas rush . . .

She was about to cross Bogstadveien. It was at a pedestrian crossing, but perhaps she hadn't looked properly, perhaps she was hard to spot in the winter darkness, and that afternoon it was raining heavily with strong gusts of wind. In any case, she was run over by the Briskeby tram a block before it turns onto Holtegaten. Grethe Cecilie died almost immediately, and the tram driver was suspended straight away . . .

You know all this, of course, and I don't like to reopen old wounds, but you've asked me to do just that. You've asked me to tell you what that day was like for me – the whole day, you emphasised – and what I've told you here is what I was thinking about as I approached the people in front of the entrance to the old granite-and-soapstone chapel.

Even before I reached the large group I noticed and recognised Tuva, and I realised the young woman she was standing with must be her little sister, Mia, who as I've mentioned was no awkward teenager these days. The two young ladies, each wearing a smart hat, had turned up for their aunt's funeral. Yes, their aunt, I realised it at once: Grethe Cecilie was Truls' cousin. Even though Liv-Berit had kept her maiden name, I heard someone say across the table that Truls' name was Berg Olsen. At Erik Lundin's memorial service, he'd boasted a little that he was actually a distant relative of the legendary Old Norse scholar Magnus Olsen, who the priest, of course, had mentioned in his eulogy for Erik. I just hadn't made the connection when I read the death notice. A blunder, but sometimes there are a lot of names to keep track of.

Tuva and Mia soon made their way into the

chapel, and I don't think they noticed me before we met at the memorial service at Bakkekroen half an hour later. At which point Tuva started, and at the same moment it occurred to me that she must have got wind of my attendance at the funerals at both Tonsen church and in Bergen. I could read it in her alarmed expression.

When Tuva jumped I felt a little like a ghost – altogether not a pleasant feeling.

The history of literature and film is full of descriptions of the way people react when they see an apparition. They are horrified. But what about the apparitions themselves? After all phantoms have to put up with seeing their own descendants again, those who are still walking the earth.

Maybe even ghosts have an emotional life. As a literary device I think it's all too neglected. Or to take a similar example: there are plenty of films and tales of people traumatised by encounters with extraterrestrials. But what about the aliens themselves? How do they react when confronted with us? Shouldn't we make a little effort to ensure at least a modicum of empathy for their trauma?

We too are numinous. We too represent a *mysterium tremens et fascinans*, to borrow an expression from the German theologian Rudolf Otto. Anyone but us would be struck by our impenetrable mysteriousness. However, we can't see it. We are not astonished by what we are. Perhaps we are the greatest wonder in the universe, though we go about our business with no knowledge of it. Imagine if someone came along and discovered us!

When Tuva jumped, I also started. It's like playing hide-and-seek: both the seeker and the one being found sometimes find themselves shrieking in surprise.

As you will recall, in his eulogy the priest emphasised the striking fact that Grethe Cecilie, with her bright, cheerful disposition, died on St Lucy's Day, the festival of light. When he said that, the electric lights suddenly started flickering. Do you remember?

Outside it had already begun to get dark, it was the winter solstice, the darkest day in the year, and for a second the only light came from the candles. I believe many of us felt a special proximity to Grethe Cecilie at that moment, even though this sudden glitch in the electrics could scarcely be attributed to anything but coincidence. It still had an effect on the congregation, and it became even more painful to look at the white coffin that stood, almost weighed down with flowers, in front of the cold stained glass in the accent wall.

The priest made another parallel with the fact

that Grethe Cecilie had dedicated much of her life on earth to studying the distant lights of the heavens. Grethe Cecilie's interest in astrophysics was well known, as were her scholarly contributions. I'd studied her PhD thesis, and even for an amateur it was fascinating. The title itself set your thoughts in motion: *Is Consciousness a Cosmic Coincidence?*

Just from reading that title the core idea sank right into my bone marrow. Surely the question asked here must be the world's most timely question. However, on several occasions while reading, I felt astonished that the academy had accepted such a down-to-earth title for a scientific thesis.

You'll believe me when I say I understood almost nothing of the mathematics in Grethe Cecilie's work. But thanks to the clear arguments, I managed to keep up with much of the atomic physics. Yes, Agnes! I'm thinking of the breakneck journey – or ascent – from a quark-gluon plasma in the microsecond after the Big Bang, via atomic nuclei and whole electrons with their electron shells, to stars and planets, living cells, nerve cells and synapses. And then consciousness – a self-inclusive recognition of the universe itself! We're talking about a cosmic explosion – as far as we know, from zilch – which thirteen to fourteen billion years later conjures forth a consciousness of itself. This *is* thought-provoking!

Grethe Cecilie saw herself and her whole existence from a cosmic perspective. In our language, we already have words like 'cosmopolitan', but in your sister's case, this categorisation could be filled with a hugely expanded meaning, and the old-fashioned word could easily be replaced by 'earthly', or 'planetary'.

'Who am I?' mankind asks. When Grethe Cecilie asked that simple question, it was the universe asking itself: 'Where do I come from? Where am I going?'

Because through human intellect, the universe grabs hold of its own wonder and tries to wrest from itself its own secret.

You must be familiar with these thoughts from the foreword to Grethe Cecilie's thesis. Although siblings are not always so quick to get involved in each other's work: the sibling relationship can have a tendency to operate on its own terms, quite all-encompassing even in relation to points of view that might otherwise be thought of as having a universal scope.

While still in the chapel I caught sight of the tall, dark man who had also been at Erik Lundin's funeral.

I don't think he noticed me until we were gathered at Bakkekroen. But even there the turnout was so large I managed to avoid him. The thought of having to look him in the eye – after which the only proper thing to do would be to acknowledge him somehow – felt so appalling that I was careful to seek out the opposite end of the venue to him as soon as we were inside the distinctive functionalist restaurant.

And so I came to be sitting at the same table as you, Agnes. The tables were long, and grouped tightly together, and in the end, Tuva and Mia also plonked themselves down at our table. I have a feeling Tuva cast a look over her shoulder before she sat down, as though desperate to find a way to avoid ending up on the same table as me, but soon everyone had been seated, and the young singer no longer had any choice.

I don't think Mia would have recognised me from that time more than ten years before. To her I was probably a complete stranger, not to mention the fact that I was a middle-aged man, and therefore totally outside her sphere of interest.

Everyone around the table knew each other already. I was the only exception. I was the one with the most peripheral relationship to Grethe Cecilie.

Obligingly, perhaps to create a sense of normality or break the ice round the table before the informal talk took over, Tuva looked at me and said: 'I believe we've met before. Weren't you one of my grandfather's students?'

I nodded.

'Germanic gods and learned walks around Sognsvann?'

I nodded again, a little encouraged by the young lady's good memory. At the same time it must have occurred to Mia who I was: we'd been sitting at the same table back then too, Tuva, Mia and I, and both their parents, Liv-Berit and Truls, too. She might also have heard about me since then. To her I must have cut a grotesque figure.

It struck me that Tuva hadn't asked me these two questions for her own sake, nor for any kind of reassurance, but rather in order to discreetly make her little sister aware of who I was.

All this being as it was, it wasn't long before I was called on to give an idea of how I knew Grethe Cecilie. All eyes were on me. You know this of course, because you yourself were behind one of those questioning gazes. But the instruction you've given me is to relate everything as I experienced it, and now I'm sitting here in Gotland, writing.

I said a few introductory words about Grethe Cecilie's deep love of nature, a side of her that had made me think of Henrik Wergeland. She loved being in the mountains, and had a particular affinity for Sognefjorden and Western Norway. She might exclaim that the more untouched the nature around her, the more touched she felt. And you undeniably have to go pretty high into the mountains to find nature that is even partly untouched by human hand.

You nodded, almost energetically, and it gave me the courage to continue. I think I said something like:

'Though Grethe Cecilie had been so fascinated by the world we live in from the age of around seven, that didn't mean she was blind to the diversity of life she was surrounded by on her own planet. After all, what are the stars in the heavens compared to the complexity of a summer bird or a salamander? Even as a young child, she often asked how life on earth could have come into being. The deepest origins of astronomy were the fertile ground she tended to. How did all this come to pass?'

You nodded again, grateful, I think, for the tribute I was sharing with all those sitting around the table. You smiled.

I said: 'Grethe Cecilie often laughed over human ideas about supernatural beings, and she often said she never felt religious. I, however, saw a kind of nature mysticism in her. She might hold a violet between two fingers and say that no two violets were quite alike. She had an eye both for uniqueness in nature and for the unity of all things. Everything in the world, both in the natural world of our own planet, and out in the universe, is ultimately born out of the very same primordial force or cause. The existence of a pretty glacier crowfoot flower, or a bullfinch on a branch, presupposes the whole universe, with all its titanic drama, just as much as a moon, an asteroid or a black hole. Even the smallest components of all life are dependent on that which occurred in the first fraction of a second after the Big Bang. The atoms we are composed of were cooked up in stars, which then exploded, sending them out into space . . .'

You nodded a third time, you were enthused. But I doubt, for example, that Mia, the estate agent, had any notion of what I was talking about, or why I was expressing myself as formally as I was.

I had already introduced myself as a teacher, and you asked if I had perhaps been a colleague of Grethe Cecilie at the school where she had worked for years. How had we come to meet each other? Tuva wasn't the only one wondering that.

I explained how I had met Grethe Cecilie many years ago at Østerbø Tourist Lodge right up in Aurlandsdalen in the west country, where we'd both come as single travellers, on the same bus in fact, but quite separately from each other . . .

At this point you looked a little thoughtful, but only a little. I didn't quite get it. Was it wrong to describe us as single? And if I had accidentally said something amiss, was it really such a bad thing?

I said that we'd met one another over a glass of wine before next morning setting off on foot together on the long journey down through the spectacular valley to Vassbygdi, where we'd rung for a taxi and gone on together to Fretheim Hotel in Flåm.

Mia wrinkled her nose and looked up at her sister, who was wearing a sullen, almost disdainful expression. It was as though she were about to interrupt at any point. But without saying anything, you looked at Tuva with a stern glance, and it was as though you were signalling: 'No, Tuva, don't interrupt!' You moved your gaze across to Mia, once again as though you wanted to say: 'Not you either, Mia.' You let the same signal go round the table.

You looked at me again and nodded.

I then described in minute detail the route Grethe Cecilie and I had hiked through Aurlandsdalen. I boasted of the profound conversations we'd become enmeshed in on the very wonder of existence, against the backdrop of all we now know about the universe we are living in. What was that thing we call dark matter or dark energy? And above all: What *was* the

Big Bang? But we didn't just direct our attentions out into space. I described how we botanised and classified mountain and meadow flowers along our path. I told of campfires, naked dips in the river, and our sore feet.

And so, apropos 'feet': we were *on foot*, which gave me a nice opportunity to focus on my own specialism. I had tried to infect Grethe Cecilie with my enthusiasm for etymology as I picked out a few rare examples of my capacious treasure trove of old Indo-European glosses. One example was the Indo-European words for *foot*. I explained that the Old Norse *fótr*, in common with Norwegian *fot* and German *Fuss*, are derived from the Germanic **fōt-*, which can in turn be traced back to the Indo-European **ped-*, a root we find derivatives of across the Indo-European language area, for example in the Sanskrit *pad-* for 'foot'; the Buddhist script *Dhammapada*, written in Pali, thus means 'steps' or 'verse-feet'; Latin *pes*, in genitive form *pedis*, which we in turn find in loanwords such as *pedal* and *pedicure*; or the Greek *poús*, which we encounter in the loanword *podium*, that is, in the platform or ledge where one 'stands' – at this point in my explanation I stole a glance at Tuva – if, for example, one is to recite old mythological poems or sing songs from *Haugtussa*.

Anyway. I described how Grethe Cecilie and I, late one afternoon, had checked into the Fretheim Hotel, each in our own room of course. Here we dined on four wonderful courses together, before heading out again for a night-time wander and renewed discourses in the hotel grounds.

It was here that you intervened. You looked at me with an indescribable attempt at empathy, and you said: 'But Grethe Cecilie was paraplegic. She was paraplegic from the age of six, also from a terrible traffic accident. That was why she was given her first telescope at the age of seven . . .'

'Well,' was all I said. 'Well.'

You continued: 'Before she'd learned to read, she had told us everything she'd seen in the sky. For hours she could sit in her wheelchair, finely adjusting the eyepiece, whether it was focused on the moons of Jupiter, the craters on our own moon or the Andromeda nebula several million light years from our own galaxy. She was paralysed from the waist down, but *that* was no handicap when she could move at the speed of light.'

I was speechless. At long last I'd been found out. It felt good. The sensation fell over me like a form of closure and solace, a moment's rest after the defeat: now the battle had been lost.

Before I got away, however, I had to take a few gulps from the poisoned chalice.

Mia sat gaping. She'd seen for herself. Now she was witness to something she'd previously only heard second-hand. Tuva still had the same contemptuous look. Her face was completely frozen, as disdainful and imperious as a Venetian carnival mask.

I looked out across the hall, now so much was over. I'd begun to think about my exit. I was exhausted. I've been more or less exhausted ever since Mother died. I felt about ready for a cold glass of something in town. I could take a seat at Vinterhaven in the Hotel Bristol, or in Dagligstuen at the Hotel Continental.

At the other end of the hall, the tall, dark man sat chatting easily to the people around him, but somehow he had got wind of what had taken place at the table I was sitting at – the venue was cramped. For a second I fell victim to his gaze, and I noticed a cold sneer glide across his face. He was triumphant.

But I half stood, turned towards you, and said: 'You'll have to excuse me. I must have come to the wrong funeral . . .'

How should I describe your expression at that point? Rather than being hard and stern, it was questioning and open. But you said only: 'To the wrong funeral?'

My mind was completely blank, so painfully drained that I said: 'I think perhaps my Grethe Cecilie is alive and kicking.'

The statement was absurd. How many people named Grethe Cecilie had written doctoral theses in astrophysics?

I had got up by now and was on my way out. But at the same moment, you grabbed hold of my arm and entreated me to stay. You urged me to stay for the rest of the memorial service. You realised I was having a hard time, but you asked me not to go, you implored.

I found your reaction paradoxical and mysterious. But as you said in the end: you thought I'd painted a thoroughly accurate picture of your sister. You thanked me for the portrait I'd sketched. Everything I had said had been so consistent and accurate through and through. There was just one thing that didn't add up, something both you and Grethe Cecilie herself thought was given all too much significance while she was alive, namely the fact that she couldn't walk. That was why it wasn't mentioned in the chapel, and there hadn't been anything about it in the papers either, at the family's explicit request. There's nothing inherently interesting in whether an unlucky pedestrian has been on their own two feet or in a wheelchair. Not even my colleague, who'd studied with Grethe Cecilie for many years, had made any comment about this fellow student of his being paraplegic. That information wasn't essential, either to Grethe Cecilie's character or to what happened on Bogstadveien.

But you also added that you wished your sister could have taken that exact trip by foot, and, as you said, Agnes, with a man like me – a proper walk with sore feet, sweaty t-shirts, campfires and river-swims – and with whom she would have been able to continue this dialogue about the wonders of exist-ence out in the grounds of the old hotel long into the night.

The only thing that didn't fit in my account was this annoying walking trip across rugged terrain. But as you underlined: now I'd given her that. I had given Grethe Cecilie that walking trip.

I was touched by your forgiving words. As I left the memorial service a little later, I believe I leaned over to you and gave you a hug. No, I know I did just that, because such behaviour is not typical for me, neither does it come easily. But essentially it wasn't *I* who embraced you. It was in the role of Grethe Cecilie's affable hiking partner that I surrendered myself and gave you that hug.

As I turned and headed out to get my coat by the exit, I heard you say to the others sitting at the table:

'I don't know how he managed it . . .'

And I still don't understand why you almost begged me to stay until the end of the memorial service.

On the little lawn in front of Bakkekroen, I discovered a fine bronze sculpture of a little girl on a marble plinth. I bent forward over a metal plaque and saw that the title of this sculpture by Tor Vaa was 'Seven Years Old'.

I stood there, falling in love with the youngster. I'd never come close to having a daughter. It suddenly seemed unfathomably exotic.

The girl was exactly the same age as Grethe Cecilie would have been when she got her first telescope. By then she was already in a wheelchair.

Pelle

I started going to funerals when I first came to Oslo at the beginning of the seventies.

I was from Ål in Hallingdal in Eastern Norway, and knew no one in the capital, no one. Mother died the year before, and I hadn't been in touch with Father since I was five or six, but I remember him well. He had long dark hair and a large wart on his nose. And he laughed. Father laughed. He used to laugh at everything.

Father's name was Edvard Jakobsen and he came, as I mentioned, from Bergen. He was just passing through Ål. I can't recall him ever living in Ål for any length of time after I was born and gradually started toddling around the yard, hiding in the carpentry workshop or the barn. But something in the murky depths of time tells me he was only there now and then. Mother never expanded on such matters, nor did I ever ask. It meant nothing any more. In any case, a single mother is what she had been all year round since I was five or six years old. The pictures that existed of Father and me, some with fishing rods or waders down by the river, some from the yard at home on the farm, and a few others from Vats and up near Reineskarvet, could just as well have been evidence that Father never lived in Ål. You didn't run round taking pictures of the people you lived with every day, not back then. My theory is that Mother took these pictures to document the fact that I had once had a father, or for that matter, some kind of family background.

At the beginning of August the summer I started school, Mother took me up to Holsdagen, where a bride and bridegroom on a horse were either getting married for real, or were just taking the chance to experience how people celebrated a traditional Halling wedding in the olden days. We were among a large party of guests who followed the couple along the Hol fjord, almost like a 17 May National Day procession in the middle of summer. I don't recall much of this – I was only seven – but when we came to the local museum in Hol, I was given a few crowns by Mother and managed to win a hand-crafted hand puppet in the tombola. The puppet was Pelle, or Peder Ellingsen Skrindo, as he introduces himself in more formal settings.

You've met him of course, Agnes. I couldn't help but notice that you got a good impression of him that time even before we'd set off from Arendal. You fell for him, you said. A few kilometres later you said you were head over heels.

So it's not quite without including Pelle that I'm writing to you now. I'm writing from the both of us.

When I pulled Pelle onto my arm that first time, he reached up to my shoulder. On Mother he only came up to the elbow.

As you've seen, Herr Skrindo is a man in his prime, of indeterminate vocation, but dressed in a navy blue blazer with silver buttons, and white trousers. As a child I was convinced he must have been a sea captain, but these days I'm not so sure. I know nothing of Pelle's history. He's like an adopted child: I know nothing about Pelle from before he came to me. But from that point on we've been almost inseparable.

On the way home from Hol that first afternoon in August, Pelle started talking to me, and I took his cheerful utterances completely seriously, so I answered him open-heartedly. From that point we were off: a lifelong conversation had begun.

I've never doubted that it's Pelle speaking when we talk. He's just had to borrow my voice.

*

Herr Skrindo's entrance into my life is an important moment for me in more than one sense. For
example, I can be certain that I never saw Father
again after that day in Hol in 1959. If Father had
met Pelle, I wouldn't have forgotten it, and neither
would Father, probably, because if there's one thing
Pelle excels at, it's speaking his mind. He often says
things I would choose to withhold – things I neither
wish nor in any way dare to bring up.

Back in Arendal, you saw how shameless he can
be. Pelle asked you some questions, totally obvious
in themselves, but questions that I would never have
been able to bring myself to ask you. I thought he
was crossing the line – he didn't know you, he'd
never met you – but you immediately opened up to
him and didn't get annoyed. You just looked Pelle in
the eye and gave him honest answers to everything
he asked you.

When we turned onto the E18 motorway to Oslo,
I turned to you and apologised for Skrindo's disrespectful behaviour, but you pointed out that perhaps
I couldn't be held responsible for all of Pelle's verbal
capers. I said I quite agreed. I thought it was a sensible and insightful thing to say: I don't feel responsible
for all the things the fellow witters on about.

Something tells me that if Father had met Herr Skrindo and had had to deal with his unusual demands for truth and honesty all the time, he probably would have grabbed him and twisted his head off his shoulders, or more likely thrown him in the fire.

Father wasn't violent towards me. He never had any reason to be. The question of how tolerant a person he was will therefore remain unanswered. I never tested him. But it's difficult to imagine he would have abided Pelle.

Pelle has been my main source of support from the time I started school for almost my whole life. The time I was married was a short interlude. During those years he lived a wretched life in the wardrobe, and I really felt bad for him. So when he did come out, it was painful to witness how intensely my wife despised him.

When I talked to Pelle as a child, normally behind the barn or in the carpentry workshop, it was always out loud. I spoke with my own voice, and Pelle replied in a slightly deeper voice than mine: his own voice through and through, even though he depended on my vocal chords to articulate the words. Sometimes, when he kept going on and on, I got irritated with him. I was the one who got a sore throat, not him. Cloth puppets don't get sore throats.

It was never hard to hear which of us was speaking. Not only did we have different voices, we also have different temperaments, and to a degree, conflicting opinions on many things. It's been surprising how much we have disagreed, given how closely we've lived together.

These disagreements have even spilled out into things as basic as when to end a discussion, and when one of us has wanted a break. Particularly in the evenings, when I've been trying to wind down before bed, Pelle has had a tendency to be particularly giddy and talkative, and I've had to hush him. It's become acutely troublesome on occasion over the last few years when I have to go to work the next day; I'm supposed to be well rested for my classes. But not Pelle. He'll just be at home having a good time. It's only as an adult I've made a habit of just pulling Pelle off my arm when I can no longer bear to listen to him. I hadn't the heart when I was younger.

I can't deny that our roles have sometimes been reversed in that respect, and looking at it like that, perhaps I don't have any reason to complain. I've sometimes turned to Pelle, and he's closed up like a clam, either because he's been annoyed about something, or maybe to get revenge, or just because he's been in a world of his own and has had enough to think about. Often I've felt rejected when that has happened. I've tried forcing him to respond to me, I've had him on my left arm, and have shouted at him or shaken him, but to no avail.

As I got older, Pelle was no longer dependent on me for his voice when addressing me. That brought the sale of throat lozenges down. We began to communicate more and more via a kind of thought transfer, and soon we didn't even need to be in the same room to exchange a squeak or two. I developed a talent for hearing what Pelle said inside my head, and needed only to think back to him in order to reply. And so Pelle became able to read my thoughts, a feat I still wonder at and feel a great respect for. And here I really must clarify: I don't see anything 'supernatural' in this connection. That's why I chose to write 'feat'.

There've been no absolute rules here, and I've also been able to give my replies to Pelle's comments via whispers or with short calls using my speaking voice, even when we've not been in physical contact. As I've walked through Oslo, or sat on the train or the bus, this has sometimes drawn the attention of those around me. With this I've indeed noted a radical social change over the last few years, one that has been to my advantage. Since mobile phones started coming with little microphones you can attach to your jacket or shirtfront, my behaviour has become less noteworthy. Previously people might have thought I had Tourette's syndrome, but today I'm not the only one walking the city streets – or a forest path – barking out replies to everyone and his dog. It's not easy to tell the difference between me talking to Pelle or on a mobile to a spouse. In both cases it's a matter of wireless connection.

Now this doesn't mean we've stopped conversing with one another normally. As a rule, Pelle sits on my arm when we're chatting, and if he's not sitting there it's rare these days that he can be bothered to engage in a real exchange. If we're not in the same room, and he's not sitting on my arm, it's mostly just a matter of short comments and calls, or perhaps a request to get up on my arm.

I often take Pelle along with me when I'm travelling, and not only for his sake, but so that I will have someone to talk to. The days can be long, and I'm not a big fan of TV, but I'm fine sitting in a hotel room with Pelle on my arm. We're never stuck for subjects to talk about, and I still find myself genuinely curious as to Pelle's thoughts on this and that. In breakfast lounges, I often see married couples sat in silence, perhaps because they have nothing to talk about. I sometimes feel very sorry for them.

I've also ascribed Pelle a certain role when I give these talks in Western Norway. I no longer just stand there, gabbing away by myself. Now I'll be in dialogue with Pelle, for example on some minute detail of an old myth or a word inherited from Indo-European. I feel quite sure that this is part of the secret to my reputation as an intermediary and speaker. 'The Jakobsen and Skrindo double-act took the audience by storm . . .'

I've tried to take Pelle into the classroom with me too, for example as a pedagogical aid in the review of New Norwegian grammar, but that hasn't been as successful. For a few years I had to put up with some of the students starting to call me Pelle, if not to my face, then behind my back. It became a subject of conversation in the staff room once. A colleague asked me why the students were calling me Pelle. It was the same colleague who'd studied physics with your sister.

When I sold the farm in Ål and moved to Oslo, Father was living in another valley that ran in a south-easterly direction just like mine, and just a few years later he died. He left a partner, or at least a woman he lived with – I think her name was Solveig – but no other children. As the only heir, I therefore received a good inheritance, so good in fact that I've sometimes wondered how my father came to have all of that money.

We hadn't seen each other since I was little, but it would have been completely impossible for him to wriggle out of his fatherly responsibilities, even if he'd tried. Not only did I own these pictures of him, but until the day I turned eighteen, he'd sent me Christmas and birthday cards. And I've kept these cards until this day.

During my time as a student, I lived for a moderate rent in the student village at Kringsjå, but I've always had my own means to fall back on: it was good to know that I could leave the student life behind and buy my own apartment if I so desired.

I don't have any siblings, but in Ål I have a male and a female cousin. I could have written their names here, but there's really no point. Their father was Mother's brother and only sibling, but Uncle Embrik died in a tractor accident shortly after Mother had passed away.

A couple of cousins in Ål wasn't sufficient reason to maintain any connection to the region where I grew up. These rudimentary expressions of familial belonging have never been enough to entice me back for a visit – at Christmas or New Year, or for the haymaking or sheep-gathering for that matter. I've been invited to some of the big occasions, like weddings and so on. It's just never been a good time.

If I'd had children myself, they would have had four second cousins in Ål. I've sometimes been sent photos of representatives of this younger generation. A few of them have already started their own families. A couple of months ago I got an MMS with a picture of a newborn. I think it was a boy. There was nothing wrong with him.

I love travelling, and I've been particularly fond of trips in my own country; I've really been to all the points of the compass here, though I've also taken a couple of holidays abroad, to Sweden and Denmark for instance, and actually one time to Iceland and the Faroe Islands. But I never visit Ål and there's just one reason for that: it's where I grew up, where I spent my early years living either with a father and a mother, or just with a mother who at irregular intervals received visits from the child's father.

It could sometimes be a vulnerable situation, being a single mother in the fifties and sixties, and I imagine that it must have been harder the narrower and more sparsely populated the village was. The offspring of single mothers too had an irreparable stigma attached to them, and things weren't necessarily improved by the fact that my father occasionally came for a sleepover – it might have been better if he hadn't shown his face at all. At least he came to his senses before I started school.

But still, everyone in the class knew that Mother and I lived alone on the farm and that my father was a wanderer. What's more, I would hear comments about the fact that he had a wart on his nose, and I was treated to some imaginative theories in relation to this, about why this wart had grown on him. It wasn't just because he was from Bergen.

I could write much more about this. But I don't need to write about everything.

And just to clarify: I don't have a bad word to say, either about Ål itself or the people who live or lived there. If I'd grown up in Oslo or Bergen, for example in Årvoll or in Fyllingsdalen, I might well have considered moving to Ål and settling there. Today the village has a decent cultural life, there are still fish in the river, and after a short drive you can be in that part of the country that has, over the last couple of decades, come to be called Skarvheimen.

I took many solitary walks up there in the mountains in my youth, particularly after I got my moped. I was given it by Mother on my sixteenth birthday, though lately I've been wondering if it wasn't bought with money that ultimately came from Father, particularly after I was made aware of the substantial inheritance he left. But even before I turned sixteen, I often headed up into the mountains. I either took my bike along the winding milk route, or I pedalled the twenty-odd kilometres from Ål and up through steep, birch-clad hillsides. It was all worth it though, since I could just glide the whole way back down the mountain, right across Leveld and Votndalen.

I never hitchhiked, even if there was already a fair bit of traffic up to the mountain in those days, especially in the summer months when tourists went up and down through the valleys and side valleys to their summer cabins. There were fewer cars than today, but the odds of a driver stopping to pick up a hitcher were much higher. There was a sort of general communal spirit on the roads: only very few could afford to keep their own car, and there was no shame in hitchhiking. But for me it was still too nerve-wracking to stand at the side of the road with my thumb out. I couldn't be sure who would stop and pick me up.

Along with a packed lunch and other necessities, I always had Pelle with me in my knapsack, and I was constantly scared someone would upend my bag and do Herr Skrindo a mischief.

People in the village didn't just know about my father. They also knew about Pelle. Only once did anyone overhear a chat between Pelle and me. It was in Nysetlia on the way up to the mountain. Two of the girls in my class were in the heather between the birch trees, each with a bucket, picking blueberries. I was standing on the path holding my bike with one hand, with Pelle over my left arm. Pelle was having a bad day and was talking nineteen to the dozen, but I too spoke out loud, telling him what I thought of the words pouring out of him. It wasn't until a good while had passed that the girls made their presence known, and they sniggered and laughed. Their eye-witness account spread like a virus in Leveld and Ål.

I realised early on that it wasn't only because of Father that I got beaten up by my peers. It quickly became apparent to my young self that there must also be something about my personality that warranted the heartless treatment I was subjected to. Even today, at my advanced age, I have self-awareness enough to think of myself as a loner and an outsider.

In villages like Ål there was no collective amnesia at that time. A certain village forgetfulness first started to make itself known when television arrived, but TVs weren't common until the seventies. The old village cinema in Sundre Hall only served to fan the spread of rumours, the meeting house too. I myself almost never went to the cinema before coming to Oslo. And I never set foot in the meeting house. But I did sometimes go to church. There, I could be among other people, watch them and experience them, perhaps even exchange a word or two with them, but still be left in peace.

Both in literal and figurative terms, it was loftier in the church than in the meeting house. I felt so comfortable in ecclesiastical settings that it may have been decisive in my choosing Christianity Studies as my last subject after my subsidiary of Nordic Studies and a basic course in Philosophy.

It was primarily out of interest that I chose the third subject, but as it was, I simultaneously gained teaching skills in two high-school subjects: Norwegian and Religious Studies. The combination of Philosophy and Christianity Studies was a solid background for the latter subject, which, in addition to the world religions, also covers different world-views and ethics, including a dose of philosophy.

I have taken the train through Hallingdal on the way to Bergen many times, and I have on occasion known tears come to my eyes and felt my heart in my throat as the train stops at Ål station. When it sets off again, I've experienced a certain shame at looking out the window, overtaken by nostalgia. Even when the train has stopped at the station for a few minutes, I've never got out onto the platform for fear

I might break down in tears. It was also not entirely impossible that someone from my old school would have either got a job with the train operator, or been a passenger themselves.

On a couple of occasions I've also driven through Ål on the way to Aurland or Geilo. But the main road has long since been rerouted away from the village. From the train I can still see the farm I lived on. You can't from the new road.

Only once, it must have been a year or so after I moved to the capital, did I take the train through Ål just to see the farm where I grew up. I got off the train at Finse and breathed the fresh mountain air before getting on the next train back to Oslo. And I looked up at the farm again. Other people were living there now. I wondered if they had children.

It has also happened that I've rambled along the old paths on the mountain, without coming through any of the villages up there. In the summer there's a private toll road up from Hemsedal, out over to Ål in Hallingdal. So in those months it's completely possible to get up to the top of Reineskarvet without driving through Leveld or Vats.

I never fell out of love with the mountains in Hallingdal. I feel no bitterness towards them, only pining. But visiting that landscape hasn't been wholly devoid of risk. I could have chanced upon an old acquaintance at any time, as it's no longer the case that villagers don't know the value of a proper hike in the mountains: it's almost a hundred and fifty years since William Cecil Slingsby terrified the farmers in Western Norway by going out hiking, and – even worse – climbing in the mountains.

But in the event of such an encounter, for example with the man who *knew* why Father had a wart on his nose, I'd thought up a possible explanation. I could make a point of having come up from Hemsedal, saying that I'd been down in the other valley for a particular, almost singular, reason. I'd concocted a couple of detailed stories I was eventually capable of firing off at will.

One of these walks through my old mountain stomping grounds I did with the woman I was married to. She sat with the Norwegian Automobile Association's walking guide open on her lap and couldn't understand why we had to take the same steep, uneven and uncomfortable route back down to the lowlands when it was both shorter and more pleasant to drive through Leveld and Votndalen to Highway 7 through Hallingdal. But distance and pleasantness can sometimes be relative. It's what's known as idiosyncrasy. For me, the route through Hemsedal felt much shorter.

A few days before this, I'd told my wife more than she'd previously known about my upbringing in Ål, and therefore about my past as a victim of bullying. The fact that I'd grown up without a father was something she'd known since we first met, and had completely come to terms with. But she couldn't bear the thought of being married to someone who'd been bullied. It was as though some of the shame of it spilled out over her too.

The hike took place just days after Reidun's fingers had first encountered Pelle deep in the wardrobe, or more specifically, in one of the many drawers that only I used. She stood in the hallway waving him about as I came home from an EGM at the teaching board. I thought it was a good time to introduce him to her properly, so I pulled him over my left arm and began a polite chat with him. I let Herr Skrindo talk freely in his distinctive voice, which was no longer any deeper than mine. In fact, now it was even a touch higher, but that was just because *my* voice had broken; Pelle talked just as he always had done. He addressed Reidun directly too. But she would not be charmed. In all truth it came as no surprise, and it was probably for that reason I'd kept him hidden in the wardrobe.

My wife was beautiful to look at, she had beautiful eyes at least, but she wasn't playful. She had no feeling for role-play, not in any arena. I had once tried to seduce her while wearing dark sunglasses, a white cap and multi-coloured Bermuda shorts. It got me nowhere. She wouldn't let me near her for several weeks after, for months I think. It went no better when we were going to bed one evening, and I'd put on her pink nightgown and laid down on her side of the bed. She was livid.

Still, if I were to pay my wife a compliment after all this time, it would be that she was orderly, and not at all false. We could drink wine and talk pleasantly, but Reidun would never get tipsy.

The hiking trip was an attempt by me to save our marriage, but it didn't work. I had a warped idea that Reidun might actually allow herself to be captivated by the terrain and the complex maze of meadow paths, and look with more forgiving eyes on the more humiliating aspects associated with the valley of my childhood. But she was immovable. The more I emphasised how much of a refuge these natural surroundings had been for me as a boy, the more she retreated. I felt under pressure to impress her, and started boasting about the 'wonderful things' I'd done in those mountains. But she was impervious. She saw nothing but the shadow of a pathetic bullied child in this landscape. She was, in contrast to Grethe Cecilie, no nature mystic. I pointed up at Lauvdalsbrea and explained how Peder Skrindo and I had sat up there deep in conversation on the mysteries of the universe. But she was deaf.

My wife showed no understanding for my objections to driving down through Leveld and Votndalen on the way home to the city. I was in no position to give in, I had no room for manoeuvre. It was completely impossible for me to drive down to Hallingdal, I protested, and I got my way.

As we approached Sokna, she announced from the passenger seat that she had to pee, and I stopped the car and let her out by Rustad Café. Those were the only words that were spoken during the long trip. I sat behind the wheel, waiting for her return. I don't know that I even turned off the engine.

An hour later we were home again. I knew Pelle was in the cupboard. But I lay awake until Reidun fell asleep, because I was scared she might attack him.

After secondary school I started at Hallingdal High School in Gol, twenty-odd kilometres along the valley. It was refreshing to meet young people who weren't Ål folk, but word travels – something I know all about, it's been that way for thousands of years, of course – and soon, nearly everyone at the high school knew who I was.

I might be standing in the schoolyard, talking to a girl from Nes, and suddenly she'd be holding me to account for the wart on Father's nose. I hadn't seen the man for more than ten years. And still this wart of his kept catching up with me! Another time, in conversation with a girl I found incredibly pretty, I was confronted with the fact that I played with puppets. This was many years after those two girls from my class had been out picking blueberries in Nysetlia.

Even though I already had my own moped before my first year in high school – something that for a short period of time managed to impress my peers so much it reduced the level of harassment consider-ably – I still took the school bus to and from school. The Ål–Gol–Ål journey was too long for a moped, and too expensive. But I took my driving test a mere week after turning eighteen, and bought a used car with the savings I'd earned at Bergo's grocery store over the summer months. So in my last year of high school I had use of my own car: I parked the old Ford in the teachers' car park in front of the school building, and it received due notice. I don't think I suffered any ill effects from this. I remained a loner for the rest of my schooldays, but from then on I was at least a loner with my own car. On a couple of occasions I was called in as a chauffeur on the weekends when the others were planning to drink, and I got to experience a few times what it felt like to be one of the gang.

Still, what saved me in Hallingdal High School was an inspiring Norwegian teacher. His name was Harald Indreeide and he was from Sunnmøre. It's no exaggeration to say that he made me the man I am today. He awakened my interest in languages and linguistics, and in particular in Old Norse culture, with the sagas and the wonders of the old mythology as the jewel in the crown. Though here we commit a grave injustice towards the Icelanders. Old Norse literature is not 'Old Norwegian'. It's Icelandic.

In the textbooks, 'Indo-European languages' were only discussed summarily as the background for Germanic and Proto-Nordic. But my curiosity was awoken. I was hungry for more. When I became aware that the possibility also existed of an equivalent Indo-European connection to Old Norse mythology, I was on the trail of the point at which I now find myself. Coincidentally – I repeat, coincidentally – Mr Indreeide had read his Georges Dumézil. He was, as he expressly stated, grateful to have a student like me, and he began to lend me books. Even before I came to Oslo, I had staked out my path. I was already a philologist.

The Norwegian teacher at Hallingdal High School cannot take all the credit for my disciplinary development, though. I also had considerable support from Peder Skrindo. He helped me daily to practise what I'd learned, primarily from the Norwegian teacher's lectures, and fascinatingly, he had an even better memory than me. It was something I never dared confess to my fellow students. Not even Harald Indreeide had any idea I was cheating, in a way, by teaming up with Pelle. Both in my final assessment and in the public examination I got the highest marks in Norwegian, that is, a 6. I should have written 'we'.

Once – it was just a few years later – Herr Skrindo suddenly burst out that he was a 'Skrindo-European'. He's always been a step ahead of me when it comes to such witticisms.

After the preparatory exams I started studying Norwegian, or rather Nordic Studies, which was the proper title. I was Norwegian, of course, and at that point it would have been absolutely unthinkable for me to study French or Italian, for example. The fact that Nordic Studies included a spell of Swedish and Norwegian was exotic enough back then. Not forgetting Old Norse. That was a little different to

Swedish and Danish, but no less spellbinding. We are talking, of course, about the very root of my own language, which is a branch of West Norse or North Germanic. But Germanic was in turn only one of many branches on the Indo-European language tree, on which the other branches were the Indo-Iranian languages, Italic languages, Celtic languages, Balto-Slavic languages, Greek, Armenian and Albanian, alongside the extinct groups, such as the Anatolian languages and the Tocharian.

Unique to Norwegian was that motley discipline we called 'målføre' back then – an area of study that was about me, in a way. I was a living example of 'målføre' or dialects, or to be precise 'dalføre' – valley dialects. It's the valleys, fjords and mountains that have created and kept alive the many distinct Norwegian dialects. People simply didn't drive over the mountain to another valley before the Oslo Electricity Board laid the new roads to build the hydroelectric plants that Norway's increasing living standards depended on until oil was discovered in the North Sea.

In the early seventies, it could still be seen as embarrassing in some contexts to speak dølemål, my regional variant. But that wasn't the case among students in the Nordic Institute, or for that matter in the Institute for Folklore Studies, which was one of the more lucrative arts subjects at the time. In these settings it was an honour to be able to speak a bona fide dialect, particularly when you could dazzle the others with archaic words and expressions featuring the racy dative case and titillating plural forms of verbs. Underneath all this lurked ancient declensions and conjugations. A dialect like mine contained living traces of prehistoric patterns from Indo-European times. In Hallingdal we still distinguished between the singular and plural second person in the present form.

Now I'm not going to get lost in philology. Allow me just to add that I was completely bi-dialectal that whole time. My Hallingdal dialect was – and is to this day – well and truly intact. At the same time I have also, from my very first days in Oslo, been completely competent in Bokmål, the modern standard language. Once upon a time I had a father who spoke his conservative, old-fashioned Riksmål. It's probably more significant that much of the literature I've read has been in Bokmål, and first and foremost, that I have a good ear for language.

The choice between two dialects at times had a value in itself. It has been a bonus not to have to declare where I'm from. In other situations though, it's been advantageous to speak Hallingdal dialect. In recent years, it's almost become a rule that I speak to Pelle in Bokmål and he replies in Halling. Or the reverse! Neither of us has any difficulty swapping roles in this way. We're both equally bi-dialectal.

I don't know, Agnes, if you've reflected on my use of language. If I were to guess, I'd assume you hadn't given it so much as a thought, because though I don't speak with a typical Eastern Norwegian accent, I've expressed myself in flawless Bokmål. But just you wait until the next time we see each other, I'll switch to 1960s-era Halling. What a lark it would be to see how you'd respond to that.

No, I shouldn't be too cocky. To tell the truth, I don't know whether we'll ever see each other again.

Those first months in Oslo, I lived a hippie life. I guess I've never mentioned that. It was in that context I met Marianne and Sverre, and also Jon-Jon, who, with the exception of Pelle, has probably been my only real friend in life, even though it was just for a few weeks, at most a month.

Enough of that! That's a whole other story, and it belongs in another time too. But in my isolation I sought some kind of community in Slottsparken. I wasn't the only one to have come to the capital alone. Some of us came together, camouflaged by one another. Essentially, I think many of us were more than averagely well-read, but I could be wrong here.

You should have seen us up there on Nisseberget, draped in our typical hippie robes! You never would have suspected I was a farmer-student from Ål.

I'll mention a little curiosity: in that subculture I called myself Pelle. And when I on one occasion introduced Jon-Jon to Herr Skrindo, Pelle announced his name was Jakop. That's just how it was, I can't really remember why, but I found that in that hippie theatre I was playing a *role*, and perhaps I felt at the same time that Jakop wasn't a very fitting name for a flower child. At university, on the other hand, I was Jakop Jakobsen, in keeping with my admission documents. I had two identities. While I was in the reading room or listening to lectures in the Sophus Bugge Building, Pelle sat waiting for me on the windowsill at home in Kringsjå.

This attraction to the flower children in the park was not completely arbitrary. The hippie movement was in many ways a philosophical one, with partly Indian roots. Even before coming to Oslo, I was inspired by Indian philosophy, particularly the school named *Advaita Vedanta*.

The Sanskrit word *advaita* means 'not-two' or 'not-dual'. That is to say, we're talking about a monistic or non-dualistic philosophy. The 'A' in *a-dvaita* is the ancient negation prefix, like the Greek *a-* (in *a*-gnostic), Norwegian *u-*, or English *un-* (as in *un*-done), and *dvaita*, the name of the dualistic philosophy in India, is etymologically related to the word *two*, from the Proto-Indo-European **dwo-*, in Gothic *twai*, German *zwei*, Norwegian *to* and Latin *duo*; the Indo-European link can also be seen in the Swedish *två*, and in words such as *twin, twice, two-fold, twine,* and *between*. Almost all Indo-European languages have retained this Proto-Indo-European number word, and *dvaita* is of course related to the Latin loanword *dualism*, both in its etymological and its philosophical meanings.

In fact – and it bothers me that I didn't manage to explain this to Ylva when I met her on the forest path after her aunt's funeral – it's not only the Indo-European words that are related. Many Indo-European *modes of thought* show signs of similar relationships, because thoughts follow words, and vice versa. Now, there is of course a certain degree of cultural contact between India and the countries around the Mediterranean. Ylva would have pointed that out. I will nevertheless mention that Indian philosophy has its dualism (dvaita), just as we find it in Western thinkers such as Plato and Descartes. The Pre-Socratic philosopher Heraclitus has a way of thinking reminiscent of Buddha's philosophy. The two also lived at around the same time, long before Buddhist missionaries came to the Mediterranean countries. And we must not forget that Indian philosophy has had a Spinoza of its own. His name was Shankara, and his influence flourished at the beginning of the ninth century. It was he who developed a philosophical system based on the Advaita – a non-dualistic (*a-dvaita*) or even pantheistic philosophy: there's no distinction between the divine and the material world. That such a distinction is felt to exist comes down to *maya*, an illusion. But everything that exists is a single indivisible unit. Everything is God.

When I made my entrance to Slottsparken, I'd read the *Upanishads* as well as the *Bhagavad Gita* – which, truth be told, is just a small parenthesis in the *Mahabharata*, that huge epic, which with its 100,000 double verses is the world's largest heroic epic. So I knew enough to stand on my own two feet in this community.

However, I had to be careful not to use academic turns of phrase. I just mentioned things off-hand, let the associations carry me, expounding on existential matters in the best hippie style. It made an impression. Neither did I mind reeling off a few words in Sanskrit. *Aham brahmāsi*, I might say: 'I am Brahman', or 'I am the universe', 'I am all that is'. Or I might point at some rosebush up on Nisseberget and as an expression of my cool attitude to life, utter the following explanation with its almost infinite insight: *tat tvam asi* – 'that is you!'

That rosebush, that is you! But of course I never mentioned that *tat* is actually etymologically related to *that*, *twam* with *you*, and *asi* with *to be*. It would have been like kicking a soap bubble. My credibility probably would have burst. And my time on Nisseberget would have been over before it had even begun.

After these first months in the capital I started going to funerals. Though perhaps I should choose my words more carefully. I never 'began' any such activity. I just remember Pelle and I sitting together, flicking through the evening paper, and our eyes falling on a death notice that immediately piqued my interest, not to mention longing or a strange sense of loss.

Behind all the flickering names, I detected the contours of a large family, who were to come together after the passing of their *pater familias*. The notice was bursting with a sense of belonging and togetherness, and there was that enticing phrase at the very end: everyone was welcome to join the memorial service after the funeral.

I got out the dark suit I'd brought with me from Ål: it was actually my confirmation suit. And I went to that very first funeral. You could say it was my debut. Though only now in hindsight is that expression accurate. It was the first time I attended a funeral like that, but I didn't think it would be anything other than a one-off, so perhaps I saw it as a social experiment.

I don't think my emotional life is any less intense that most people's; perhaps in some situations I'm actually *more* sensitive than most – tears come quickly at times – but I've never been particularly nervous. I already had experience of playing the role of the hippie; it seemed no more daredevil to turn up at a crowded funeral, since that too was a kind of theatre, though with a more sombre undertone than the colourful games of the flower children.

I didn't break a sweat as I walked into Nordstrand church, which was full of people, unsurprisingly, given all the names in the funeral announcement. I had also grown up accustomed to the big farmers' funerals in Hallingdal.

There were several reasons for my lack of nerves. Apart from the hippies, and perhaps a couple of students at the university campus, I didn't know a soul in this city, which meant there was no platform for shame. Shame can only exist if there is someone to see you feel it. So in a way, feeling shame is a luxury: only those living with a certain degree of social network are in a position to carry its weight. That doesn't mean I was shameless, because even shamelessness requires there to be someone you choose not to feel shame towards. Both shame and shamelessness demand a collective 'other', or at least a 'you'. I don't think I'm exaggerating when I confess that you, Agnes, are the person in whose presence I've felt most ashamed.

With the help of an extensive obituary, I had, in addition, done sufficient research to enable me to get me through brief conversations on how I'd met the deceased, if it became necessary. Something like that would have been absolutely surplus to requirements in Hallingdal. I mention this in passing. To attend a funeral there, you only needed to be from the same valley or side valley. And the more distant your relation to the deceased, the greater respect you were accorded for attending. Urban funerals seem like the absolute opposite in that sense.

Unpractised as I was, I made sure to stay in the background. I had prepared a short narrative about how I knew the deceased – it was not excessively elegant or inventive – but as I'd guessed, I didn't even have a use for it. At one point over coffee I was asked if I was part of the family. I was of course a very young man, more than sixty years younger than the deceased, but I just shook my head, and something in my expression must have meant that no more questions were asked.

A week later I went to another funeral, and the following week yet another, and I suppose these visits, with time, came to be a habit, or a lifestyle – many would surely call it a vice. But I've had no other family life.

I remember one time I sat with Pelle at my desk in Kringsjå. We were going through long lists of the forms taken by words for *father*, *mother*, *sister*, *brother*, *son*, and *daughter* in the various Indo-European languages, both dead and living. The fact is that each of these six words can be traced back to the Proto-Indo-European forms *$ph^{\text{?}}t\bar{e}r$, *$me^{\text{?}}ht\bar{e}r$, *$swes\bar{o}r$, *$b^hreh^2t\bar{e}r$, *$suHnus$ and *$d^hugh^2t\bar{e}r$. (The phonetic symbols indicate the word's pronunciation. We can guess to some degree how the Indo-European languages *sounded*.) The aforementioned familial bonds are also fundamental for most people, the pillars of life. But I had none of them. I'd never had a real father, and I no longer had a mother. I had never had a sister or a brother. I was hardly going to have a son or a daughter.

Agnes! You're the one who asked for an explanation as to my presence at Grethe Cecilie's funeral, and I dearly want you to at least try to understand what the root cause could have been: my familial relations were sparse. Even as a child I was branded an outsider, though it wasn't me who shied away from 'The Big Community', that ambiguous term that was so prevalent in Norway in the first decades after the Second World War.

The pictures of Father and me, the ones Mother had hung all over the house, couldn't undo the fact that Father had only rarely been to the valley to visit his own son and his child's mother. Further details of our story, of which the valley's sons and daughters had no more than a vague picture and very little context, were rounded out and embellished in minute detail by the adults. The oral traditions, and indeed a certain epic dimension, have for thousands of years thrived in the Norwegian valleys in particular. The winters and the winter nights are long, and people need things to talk about once the sun has set. Something as ordinary as a dinner with the family can become rich in epic elements. Into this maelstrom fell my mother and I.

Another more acute farmer's sin was this: that even though we lived well on the farm that had been in our family for generations, we weren't the ones who tilled the soil there, who had sheep on the hillside, cows and hens in the stalls, or who actually chopped down the wood in the farm's birch forest. I think I once heard that the circumstances in which we lived were the result of a district council order, and that Ål Savings Bank had come into the picture to ensure Mother's and my welfare. The debt – or the debt of gratitude – hung over me until I sold the farm and settled up. I didn't want to be indebted to anyone, not in Ål. I got exactly enough for the farm to pay off the debt. The contents of the house came on top of that. I sold them too.

We weren't like the others. We weren't part of the community. We were seen as parasites by many, and were shut out.

Since I came to Oslo and was able to start from scratch, I've felt an irresistible attraction to large, unified families, the desire to belong to that kind of extended community. I doubt I'm any fonder of people than the next man, but life has made me incredibly fond of families.

I like mothers and fathers, sons and daughters, brothers and sisters-in-law, cousins, nephews and nieces, aunts and uncles. I enjoy the warmth and togetherness in the density of these family networks. I am reassured by all the roles and relationships, and I've caught myself envying people who come from outside and suddenly – perhaps merely because of some arbitrary erotic impulse – get drawn into, tied to or even married into these unbreakable family bonds.

I have myself experienced being married and, with that at least, living a few years as one of a two. Once bitten, twice shy, you might say, so I won't get into idealising marriage or family life. Marital difficulties and sibling rivalry are very real. As is emotional cruelty. I know all that. But the woman I was married to for almost three years was from a small family too: she had no aunts or uncles, and she was an only child like me. Our marriage never became a family either. We were infertile. There wasn't even space for Pelle. In our coupledom, Reidun and I were as lonely as we would have been apart.

Being solitary can be empty enough for someone who has a tendency towards it. But I think even that might be preferable to being lonely with another person. If you live alone, at least you can do want you want. I imagine that freedom thrives better in large families than in claustrophobic marriages.

But enough of this!

It became a habit for me to go to funerals. I was crazy about family life because any kind of family connection other than the kind I stole was out of my reach.

*

I never attended any of these funerals as a voyeur, and I didn't enjoy my role as an outsider. On the contrary: I just wanted, as much as possible, and for as long as it lasted, to be part of the group.

When the church bells rang out for a funeral, they rang for me.

Every time, I've attended with genuine sympathy for the deceased – a living person whose time on this earth has come to an end – and with sincere consideration for the bereaved, who, if nothing else, I've known by name from the death notice.

Moreover, my thoughts have stayed with the family members I've met, and in most cases at least greeted. That's why, as an aid to thought and memory, I have been diligent in keeping all death notices, obituaries and orders of service for the funerals I've been to. These delicate documents, many of which are on newsprint, have been ordered chronologically in a little stack of cigar boxes. You might say they represent a portfolio of families and individuals I've met on the paths of life and death, or perhaps I could call it my *repertoire*. Maybe it sounds repellent to express it that way, but other people validate themselves on Facebook, and I don't do that. They also have their own family members whose funerals they can attend.

I myself prefer to think of the directory of names in these cigar boxes as a kind of list of life companions. Or as Pelle once said: 'This is your personal census. No one but you has this exact collection in their drawer.'

Peder Skrindo knew what he was talking about. He had spent a long time in a drawer himself, actually in the same wardrobe as the cigar boxes.

When my wife groped her way to Pelle, she'd already discovered these boxes, perhaps ten or twelve in number. She got most worked up about Pelle, especially after I'd pulled him onto my arm and he'd addressed her in a much franker manner than I ever would've dared to do myself. But then there were all these cigar boxes...

I didn't go to as many funerals during those years my wife and I were together. I tried to restrain myself, and now I had my own life too, I had Reidun. I still attended a few, though, and I sometimes wondered if my wife suspected I went to the funerals of people I had only the most superficial acquaintance with. Often when I came home I had to repeat what I'd said at the memorial service about my relationship to the deceased – of course these stories had already been put to the test: they were rock solid.

But I don't know if she believed me. Once she

asked me why I'd had so many friends early in life when I had no one but her now. Over the days that followed, she got more and more reproachful as we talked about it: why did we never have any visitors? Why were we never invited to dinner? Why did we spend all our time at home here in this apartment, getting on each other's nerves?

I've never premeditatedly pushed my way into a commemoration where clear signals have been given from the outset that the bereaved wanted to keep their sorrow to themselves, and therefore wished for as little fuss as possible to be made of their loss. When it has been stated that the service ends 'at the grave', 'in the chapel', or 'in the church', I've wisely stayed away. I've never attended any funerals where it has been made obvious in advance that there would be no memorial service to follow.

I've been drawn to open, light-hearted formulations, such as 'after the funeral, everyone is welcome to attend the memorial service' – whether this was to be held at a church hall, in a function room, or at one of the city's better restaurants.

Sometimes it's the priest who, on behalf of the family, concludes the ceremony by inviting all attendees to the memorial service. In such cases I've naturally taken this open invitation to include me.

Or should I assume the priest was lying, or spoke against their better judgement?

Not infrequently one of the bereaved, with the greatest of discretion, goes around filtering – that is to say selecting those who will, via a discreet whisper in the ear, be informed that they are welcome to join the memorial service to follow. I have taken such setbacks like a man, and simply nodded to someone near me as I've made my exit. I've played this kind of sheepish role ever since I was a child, of course. As I was already well dressed, there have been occasions when I've sat down at a restaurant or the bar of a nearby hotel. I've ordered a glass of wine and held a memorial by myself instead. The service in the church or chapel has usually been thought provoking enough. A commemorative service is often full of narrative elements, and I've always appreciated beautiful music and singing.

One time, due to my lack of common sense, I ended up in the bar of a little hotel where a closed memorial service of this kind was already under way. It happened that the bar and its high stools could be seen from the little dining room, and several people cast furtive glances over at me as I sat alone with my glass of white wine, or perhaps it was a glass of whisky. But I wasn't going to get up and head for the door because of that. This stingy family hadn't booked out the whole hotel. Or perhaps someone was envious of my wine or whisky: on the white damask tablecloths in the next room there were only soft drinks and alcohol-free beer. I ordered another glass, and made no effort to conceal myself.

Let me just add that I completely understand that certain families desire a memorial service that is closed to all but the innermost family circle. It's just that I would so love to be among the select few.

As I already hinted, I'm not alone. There was at least one other person doing the rounds of the funerals. It was the tall, dark-haired man who often turned up to the same functions I did. I wasn't the only stowaway aboard the church's ship.

I never knew what the other man thought about this thing he was part of. We never talked. We just knew of each other. At some point, many years ago, we started giving one another a quick nod, as it had become unavoidable. Still, our policy has been mutual avoidance of anything as intimate as eye contact.

I don't have a lot more to say about the tall, dark man – in some ways my colleague or competitor – other than that I hold him in the deepest contempt. Perhaps I should acknowledge that this anger is a form of self-hatred.

Of course it's not only this man I've met more than once. Over the years I've probably attended a couple of hundred funerals. In total we're talking about encounters with many thousands of people, perhaps twenty or thirty thousand. That's how extended my 'family' – or my 'clan', I should perhaps say – has become. So of course there are people I have met more than once along the way. A few I have chanced upon four or perhaps five times. But even then, a 'here again, eh?'-type comment would seem inappropriate. That applies just as much to the other person. Well, anyway, for my part it has been a matter of four or five *peripheral* acquaintances. I've never experienced the role of bereaved son or brother, nephew or close friend.

The fact that I, over the course of many years, happened to meet all of Erik Lundin's children and grandchildren again might seem intriguing on paper. But it's just because the material itself has been so extensive. The bigger the lottery, the more striking the main prize appears. Though you might have invested a whole fortune in tickets.

And apropos fortunes: I must add that a necessary prerequisite of my activities was the significant sum left by my father. It's meant that I've been able to work part-time all these years, and it's primarily the days on which I have no classes that I've been able to attend the funerals – my family replacement. I see a little paradox in that: if I'd had a real father, I would hardly have had a need for these funerals. But my inheritance from him has, at the same time, made it possible for me to alleviate my own lack of family life.

Before attending a funeral I have always striven to investigate the deceased and his or her family as thoroughly as possible. Up until a few years ago, this used to be a time-consuming process. Today it can be done with the greatest of ease, and if time is tight, simply by entering a few characters on the way to the church or the chapel: with the internet and social media, it's become almost too easy to live as I do. As the public realm has swollen in size, the private realm has shrunk accordingly. The Epicureans' motto of 'living unknown' has become more of a feat than it was in ancient times.

It's also been the case sometimes that I have chanced an improvisation, a 'blind encounter', that is, attending a funeral when I've known nothing at all beforehand about the person I'm going to say my final farewell to, other than what's been in the actual death notice. This has required a whole other form of attentiveness, spontaneity, and an almost chameleonic adaptability. This kind of practice is naturally bolder, and maybe also an inkling more audacious, than for example taking part in a funeral where the deceased has been a more or less public figure. There's not as much need for legitimacy when you are attending the funeral of a popular artist or politician.

I knew Erik Lundin well as a professor and lecturer at Oslo University in the seventies. It's true we never had any kind of personal relationship, but what I mean to say – and there's a kernel of truth in this, though ever such a small one – is that it was both right and proper that I should accompany him to the grave thirty years later as 'one of his students'.

Since Lundin had spent a few Tuesdays from 11:15 to 13:00 going through *Völuspá*, I was gripped by an inspiration and determination which at that time was rare for me. Overwhelmed at the thought that the world had been given a second chance after the great Ragnarok, I was left with a question pertaining to the very last line of verse in that monumental mythological poem.

So, before Lundin managed to leave the auditorium, I walked down from the far back of the large hall to ask the learned professor a question, as I knew he was to move on to *Grímnesmál* the following week. I had of course read carefully through the original text, both from the *Codex Regius* and *Hauksbók*, as well as a couple of modern versions.

In *Codex Regius*, the last verse was:

> *Þar kømr in dimmi*
> *dreki fliúgandi,*
> *naðr fránn, neðan*
> *frá niðafjǫllom.*
> *berr sér í fjǫðrom*
> *— flýgr vǫll yfir —*
> *Níðhǫggr nái —*
> *nú mun hón søkkvaz.*

Which in Benjamin Thorpe's English translation reads:

> *There comes the dark*
> *dragon flying*
> *the snake from below,*
> *from Nida-fells.*
> *Bearing on his wings*
> *flying over the plain,*
> *Nidhögg, a corpse.*
> *Now she will sink.*

My legs were shaking, I could feel my heart beating and my body sweating as it froze, and I remember I decided to address the professor in my broadest Hallingdal dialect in order to be treated with respect. I'd never spoken to him before.

I asked, as though spontaneously, whether the medieval source texts were completely unambiguous that it was the *volve*, the seeress, who was going to 'sink' and not the monster of chaos, Nidhögg. Because in my studies I had come across some speculation that pointed to the contrary.

The professor opened his eyes wide and agreed that was a relevant question. And then something unheard-of happened. He invited me over for a cup of coffee in the Wergeland Building, where he had his office. In the seventies, this kind of spontaneous invitation to an informal colloquium was extremely rare; indeed, it went beyond everything we were accustomed to, especially because a political schism had formed between the student body and the teaching staff. Professor Erik Lundin's invitation could therefore be seen as a minor sensation. And I, riff-raff from a mismanaged farm in Hallingdal, could barely control where I was putting my feet as I walked the short stretch down from the Sophus Bugge Building to the Wergeland Building.

There was something else. We disagreed, and it amused us both. The professor and I – at that time nothing more than a student on a subsidiary course

– were *in disagreement* about the exegesis of the apoca-
lyptic mythological poem.

At first, Lundin argued convincingly that it was
most likely to be the *volve*, who – her prophecy now
given – could withdraw and 'sink'. But, he pointed
out: it *could* also be argued that it was Nidhögg, who
in this very last scene after the clamour of the battle
– sure enough, a battle that had come to an end, in
which the good gods had won a final victory over
the forces of chaos – had to admit to being beaten by
the gods' power and 'sink' or pull back.

I disagreed with the professor about the plausibil-
ity of this latter interpretation. The pronoun 'hón'
or 'she' absolutely had to refer to the *volve*, since both
'dragon' and the name Nidhögg were masculine
words, requiring the pronoun 'hann' or 'he'.

Lundin, however, just as I had expected, was
able to explain that in the oldest source text *Codex
Regius*, the pronoun 'hón' wasn't written out in full.
On the old vellum was written only an 'h', and in
Sophus Bugge's edition this was extended to h*on* –
with a clear italicisation of the two letters that do not
appear in the manuscript. Formally, then, there was
nothing to prevent the reference being to Nidhögg.

I found this very entertaining. I asked if I could
borrow a pencil and a piece of paper.

'But in his scholarly edition of the Poetic Edda,

Sophus Bugge made a comment,' I asserted.

The professor gave me a questioning look, and I continued:

'He'd written a little abbreviation mark for himself after the 'h' on the vellum, and in the comment he writes "h*on written* h$^{\underline{o}}$, *which cannot be read as* hann".'

I'd written the comment out on the sheet of paper, which I handed to the professor. He sat staring at the letters for several seconds.

'But even Sophus Bugge could have been mistaken,' I said, mostly for politeness' sake.

I think Erik Lundin shook his head carefully. 'I'd completely forgotten that,' was all he said.

'And in *Hauksbók*,' I went on, 'the youngest source text, it unquestionably says "she". But even here Sophus Bugge has made a note, even though it is essentially superfluous. He writes: "'h'on' *with a dash above the* 'h', *not* 'han'".'

The professor nodded: 'Yes, where *Hauksbók* is concerned there's never been any doubt that the pronoun indicates the *volve* – who after completing her task could sink back into her *chthonic* or underground element.'

'And yet,' I concluded, 'in the case of both the two source texts, it has been important for the groundbreaking philologist to emphasise that it must be the *volve* who withdrew, *not* Nidhögg. So there must have been doubt about this before the Sophus Bugge edition of the Eddas in 1867.'

Lundin nodded graciously, and we looked at one another for a few seconds before he began to clear his desk, thereby marking the end of our audience.

We had never spoken previously, nor did we ever speak again. However, we did once meet among the few frail saplings that would over the next few decades grow to line the grand academic avenue that ran between the Sophus Bugge Building and the student services centre, Fredrikke. We nodded briefly to one another, thereby expressing mutual respect. It was that look I embellished a few decades later at the memorial service after Emeritus Professor Lundin's passing.

I've already said enough about my short marriage, and everything I've written on that matter I've told exactly as I remember it. It's true that one of the last things we quarrelled over after I'd moved out was the right to use an old Toyota Corolla, which we still owned between us. It's also true that I was at that time visiting an elderly aunt at an old people's home in Åsgårdstrand. I helped her with her tax returns. But I've never taken the taxi the whole way from Oslo to Åsgårdstrand.

I had neither met nor heard of Andrine Siggerud

before seeing her death notice in the paper. This then was one of my first unprepared attendances. My elaborate story at the memorial service at Østreheim came into existence as I listened to the priest's eulogy, assisted brilliantly by the beautiful photo of Andrine in front of her red Mercedes on the funeral's order of service. That was what I meant when I said I changed the order of my account: I described my alleged relationship to Andrine *before* referring to the priest's speech.

Bumping into Marianne, Sverre and Ylva there gave me a shock. But I didn't see it as an odd or striking coincidence. Given the number of burials I've attended, I've always expected these repeat encounters to occur. I'm surprised they haven't occurred more frequently. But this was the first time I'd come across any of the hippies I'd fraternised with in Slottsparken. I couldn't understand Marianne and Sverre's obvious need not to be remembered and recognised. Was it really that much of an awkward family secret that they'd been part of the hippie movement?

Everything I've written about Runar Friele's funeral, the priest's rebuke to the family and the subsequent memorial service at Hotel Terminus, I have tried to relate exactly as I experienced it. That includes all the insights Sigrid gave me into the family's visit to the old mansion after the death. But I never met the unlucky man himself, neither in the restaurant at Hotel Norge, nor at any other place. My only source material for the conversations between Runar and I over the dinner table was the good priest's eulogy in Møllendal.

I was, as described, on my way to my annual August stay in Bergen when I saw the strange death notice in *Bergens Tidende*. I stayed an extra night in the city, went into Dressman and bought myself a dark suit – an extra black suit would come in handy – and took a taxi out to the chapel at Møllendal.

This time too it was a case of going in blind. I was up to it. I'd given my lecture on Ullr and Tyr, with expert help from Herr Skrindo this time too, and was on top form. But that didn't mean I was any less emotionally engaged in the ceremony. I was deeply shaken just from reading the death notice.

Once again I met representatives from the Lundin family – the family who represent the red thread in this story.

And why is it this family in particular I am following, and not another? Because it was through them that the two of us met. And as you said, Agnes: those connections were the closest you had come to having your own family. Truls has always been like a brother to you, and Liv-Berit has come to be your closest friend. I was genuinely charmed by your stories of the summer house at Hvaler, I mean the ones you told in the car on the way home from Arendal.

You grabbed hold of me and almost entreated me not to leave the memorial service, even though I'd obviously lied my way to a closer relationship to Grethe Cecilie than I was able to defend. And I ask you again: why did you do that?

From that moment, you and your family became a part of the red thread of this tale.

At Grethe Cecilie's funeral, it was, as you know, not a case of going in blind. I'd conducted very thorough research. I'd spent a whole day at the university library, immersed in your sister's extremely original doctoral thesis.

To begin with, I was gripped by what I'd heard about the terrible traffic accident on Bogstadsveien. As I mentioned, I had a colleague on the teacher's board who'd studied with Grethe Cecilie and knew her very well. I had read with great interest everything on her website. It was all intensely stimulating. What's more, I found a number of photos of her, enough that I was able, several days later, to confirm how much you resembled her.

But no one, absolutely no one, especially not

Grethe Cecilie herself – on her website I mean – had given me any reason to suspect that she was paraplegic and in a wheelchair. As I have mentioned, even the priest didn't devote so much as a word to it at the funeral. We talked about that when we last met of course. As my colleague also mentioned, it was absolutely in keeping with Grethe Cecilie's approach to her own disability not to let it become something representative of her as an individual. It wasn't important, especially not when viewed in the context of her fascination with all the galaxies of the universe.

Still, my colleague might have warned me. But how could he know of my vice? How could it have occurred to him that I would get it into my head to turn up at Grethe Cecilie's funeral, and what's more, to the memorial service afterwards, only to come out with some elaborate story on our strenuous walking trip together down through the often steep and rugged terrain of Aurlandsdalen?

I was a little surprised that he didn't turn up to the funeral. Had I met him, I would have said something to the effect that I'd been so gripped by what I'd read and heard about the death that I'd felt a strong need to attend the memorial service. At worst, this would have been regarded as a little eccentric, and after all, that's how people see me.

If this colleague had turned up at the chapel, I wouldn't have attended the memorial service afterwards, I wouldn't have needed to introduce myself to anyone, and I wouldn't have given myself away. But then I wouldn't have met you, and I wouldn't have sat down and written this story.

There's no great art to imagining such counterfactual circumstances.

Andreas

We met again about half a year later, on 15 April 2013, to be specific. It was an odd coincidence. But I don't believe in divine providence, and there's nothing supernatural about short odds. That we should be at a funeral wasn't that surprising either. You had your own sombre reasons for being there, and so did I, though mine were of a different nature to yours.

After the wretched business of your sister's memorial service, I'd promised myself I'd never go to another stranger's funeral, at least not in Oslo, where I'd already begun to cross my own tracks.

More and more frequently, I had the sense of being stared at, or rather stared after, as I walked through the city. I might have been imagining it, but in the classroom too I sometimes had a feeling that some of the students had heard stories about me. I had, of course, met students, or former students, at funerals. With my many years of experience it wasn't paranoid to see warning lights flashing.

I was at a turning point. If I were to attend more funerals now, I had to get out of Oslo.

I was still reading death notices – that's something I'll never stop doing, even though I no longer maintain any kind of practice. I read the announcement of Andreas Dannevig's sudden passing, and after a little googling realised that this funeral in Arendal was one that I simply couldn't miss, though it might be my very last . . .

I parked the car in one of the side streets, said goodbye to Pelle and walked towards Trinity Church, set on the hill overlooking the town square and Tyholmen. I wasn't worried about being exposed here, so far from home. And yet – true to form – I'd prepared a watertight story on how the well-known marine researcher and I knew each other.

I was neither excited nor nervous, just expectant. I was eager to once again get to live a little family life. Moreover, it was distressing the way Andreas, completely without warning, at the age of just fifty-five, had had a heart attack out at sea, dying in his own little research vessel off Hisøya Island.

I was gripped by the death itself, and I harboured a genuine consideration for Andreas's family, his wife, Martine, and their four children: Barbro,

Aurora, Petter and Undine. I had with me a well-honed story about my acquaintance with Andreas, stimulated by articles and interviews I had found online, but of course with the addition of a few of my own anecdotes and references.

Had I chanced once again on a descendant of Erik Lundin, I would have had a watertight alibi. Even if Reidun had turned up, the woman who was once my wife, and who'd even found my cigar boxes, my story would have been totally incontrovertible. No one in the whole world could have questioned in the slightest my right to attend Andreas Dannevig's funeral.

Andreas had a lodge in Ål. It was on the birch-clad slopes by Hesthovda up from Vats. He had strong ties to this spot, and he was also fond of bringing his work with him and spending a few days alone without his family or colleagues around. He also had a connection to the whole wide mountain country, to which the birch slopes were the portal. He was a keen hiker, and in that we had something in common. We agreed that neither of us was much good at getting our thoughts moving without getting our bodies moving too. Walking in the mountains is a way of thinking. It is a form of understanding in itself.

The first time we met was at Reinestølen, one sunny day at the end of August. I think I remember the first sentences we exchanged being something about the old dairy farming ways on the mountains. But we got to know one another better, and as the years passed, we took a number of long, eventful trips together. A couple of times, we went up to Lauvdalsbrea, where we had a glittering 360-degree view over the whole of the Norwegian highlands, from Jotunheimen in the north, to Gaustatoppen in the south; and on a bitter autumn day – right after cloudberry season, while the autumn colours were still at their strongest – we hiked up to the top of Reineskarvet. We sat up there, I recall, and had a long conversation about our own generation's fatal combustion of fossil fuels, with the inexorable consequences of atmospheric warming, acidification of the world's oceans and widespread destruction of the Earth's habitats. I myself had, since the eighties, kept track of this development by reading the papers and so on, but up on Reineskarvet that day, more or less on the roof of the world, Andreas inducted me thoroughly in the scientific basis of it all. He explained how, 55 million years ago, the atmospheric CO_2 levels increased drastically, perhaps because the Indian sub-continent's drift northwards scraped the ocean floor, creating volcanic activity that released enormous quantities of carbon, with the result that temperatures increased drastically in a relatively short space of time, the land ice melted, and sea levels rose by a few dozen metres. And he added: 'Now humans are aping this global experiment, we're doing what the Indian subcontinent did with the carbonates on the ocean floor, just in a much shorter time period, and it will take around a hundred thousand years before the carbon balance is regained.'

I asked if he thought there was intelligent life on other planets in space. Andreas said:

'We can be pretty certain there's life. I'm less sure about intelligent life. We've not heard from anyone out there. And the reason we're not making contact with extra-terrestrial civilisations is perhaps due to what we're talking about, I mean the burning of carbon.'

I couldn't understand what he was talking about.

'How?' I asked.

Andreas gave me a thoughtful look. He said:

'Life can only exist where there is an atmosphere that can sustain it. A prerequisite for this is that large quantities of carbon must be locked into the ground of a rocky planet, in petrified sediments, but also in vegetation and in dead plant and animal remains; that is, in fossil layers. The paradox is that technologically advanced civilisations probably don't emerge before the extraction and combustion of these fossilised energy layers. This leads to radical changes in the planet's atmosphere, and before long the civilisation runs aground.'

We sat atop Reineskarvet. We sat atop a planet in the Milky Way. Perhaps we sat atop an ailing planet . . .

I would relate and expand all this, describing and fleshing it out, in my broadest Hallingdal dialect. That would be an extra plus. I was the farmer boy from the country turned hiking buddy and climate buddy to a marine researcher from Arendal. The fact I no longer lived in Ål was of little significance in this case; I still got into the car and drove up to the highlands I'd had such strong ties to since childhood. And should someone from my days in the village turn up at the funeral, against all reasonable odds, I had a nice little story on the back burner about how I'd got lodgings down in Hemsedal, which for many years had been my starting point for my mountain hikes in Ål.

But in the Trinity Church, you came up the aisle. As I said later, I think we set eyes on one another at exactly the same moment, and both jumped. Despite the circumstances you looked stunning, so glowing. In the black cape, with your dark hair over the collar, you were at once snug and elegant, gentle and indifferent. I was reminded of how much I'd thought of you over the year that had passed. What would it be like to meet you again?

You were at least as perturbed as me, and since I was already sitting on one of the pews, and it was a good spot, where were you going to sit? This was neither the time nor the place for me to gallantly wave my arm and invite you to sit at my side. I saw you hesitate, Agnes, but at the last moment you decided to walk past and sit a couple of rows closer to the altar.

And still: when we'd left the church and the black hearse had driven off, we came together, and joined the procession with many others down towards the Clarion Hotel Tyholmen. You told me you'd studied together with Andreas and that you'd stayed in contact ever since. I think you said something about a puppet theatre.

But you didn't ask how I knew Andreas. I interpreted that as a refined form of discretion. Or perhaps you just couldn't bear for me to get all lyrical again, that might well have been the case.

As we entered the hotel, you looked up at me and said: 'Perhaps we should sit at the same table?'

Why did you say that? I don't really know how I

reacted, but when we sat down, it was almost as though we represented the same family; for me a deeply unfamiliar feeling: being together with someone.

There were eight of us sitting around that table. I realised at once that the other seven of you knew one another, and I could guess at what relation each of you had to Andreas. Only I was an outsider, a role I was well accustomed to. No one but you had met me before.

The others looked at me with curiosity. Not sceptically, but in a friendly, inviting way. So came that unavoidable question: 'And how did you know Andreas?'

I had the answer ready, at my fingertips, as people say: Ål in Hallingdal, Vats, Reineskarvet, long walks in the mountains . . .

But I couldn't do it. Now you were sitting at my side, and you knew me. I couldn't tell any stories now. I didn't know how you would have reacted to yet another elaborate lie.

A few seconds passed, and I found myself unable to say anything. You saw this. Maybe you thought I was on the verge of running out.

I looked at you, and I thought: can I say that I didn't know Andreas? Can I say that I came to Arendal together with you?

The situation had become precarious. It was at breaking point.

But then you touched my shoulder. You looked round and said that I'd sadly never met Andreas, but that I'd come to Arendal as your companion.

It was as if the others round the table breathed sighs of relief, and I don't know whether it was because they'd now been able to place me, or because they felt pleased that you'd come to Arendal with an escort.

But you'd saved me. You've saved me twice.

We listened to the memorial speeches, made over an enormous PA system. Many of the speeches were read through tears. Andreas was torn away, completely without warning. There wasn't even time for him to be reported missing before a boat owner found his boat adrift. It was this boat owner, who was also in attendance at the memorial service, who found Andreas lying lifeless on the deck.

Around the table, too, there was naturally a lot of talk of the deceased. Many of those present were climate scientists, a couple of them colleagues of Andreas's from the Institute of Marine Research in Flødevigen outside Arendal. So there was also a fair bit of conversation about climate matters. For the first time in at least 800,000 years, more than

400 parts per million CO_2 had been measured in the atmosphere, a record that could be primarily attributed to humankind's combustion of carbon. It was asserted that it was no longer enough to stop the production of CO_2. Sooner or later, the gas would need to be sucked out of the atmosphere again, for instance by the extensive use of bio-fuels with carbon capture.

After the way you'd introduced me, it was not only natural but unavoidable that we should leave the memorial service together. As soon as we were outside the hotel, we were left alone, and it wasn't clear when or how we would go our separate ways.

We wandered about for an hour or so, talking of this and that. We went back and forth around Pollen, the small harbour inlet, and along the quays at Tyholmen. We were both bound for Oslo, and I had my own car with me, but you had a flight booked from Kjevik, departing in the early evening. We agreed I would drive you to the airport before turning round and heading northwards.

When we got to the car, I sat in the driver's seat, and you opened the passenger door alongside. There sat Pelle, as he usually did when I left him waiting for me. I picked him up, and for a moment I played with the thought of throwing him onto the back seat, something I could easily have done; it wouldn't have hurt him, after all, he's not alive . . .

But as you were getting into the car, I pulled Pelle over my left arm, and he immediately took the chance to address you. He made a kind of bow to you, bent deeply and introduced himself in his distinctive voice:

'Peder Skrindo here. But most people just call me Pelle.'

Your face shone. You looked at Pelle and said:

'And I'm Agnes. Agnes Berg Olsen.'

Pelle replied:

'Then perhaps you are related to the legendary Old Norse scholar Magnus Olsen?'

It was essentially an absurd question, given that Olsen is one of the most common names in the country. But you nodded.

'Yes, we actually are related, though many generations back.'

Pelle was trying to be funny, because he said:

'Well, that generates enough interest for me, milady. Did you know he grew up in the very town we now find ourselves in?'

Now you looked perplexed:

'No, I did not know that, I really didn't.'

'Or that his nephew, also from Arendal, became a professor of Old Norse philology at the University of Bergen? His name was Ludvig Holm-Olsen.'

You smiled, interested, and said:

'No, I did not know that either.'

'You can't be expected to know everything,' Herr Skrindo concluded.

You hadn't taken your eyes off him, but as you were thinking whether to say anything further, Pelle burst out:

'Are you married?'

You laughed. First you nodded. Then you just shook your head.

Pelle nodded backwards at me:

'Him neither.'

But you just went on looking Herr Skrindo in the eye without noticing me at all. A dark expression crossed your features.

'I have *been* married,' you said.

Pelle answered immediately, in a rather abrupt manner. Again he nodded at me. 'He's been married too actually. You'd never believe it. But now he's footloose and fancy free. How about you?'

Again you laughed. You were almost convulsed with laughter. You hadn't so much as glanced over at me, you only addressed Pelle, and you laughed, without stopping, you just carried on laughing.

Then I pulled Herr Skrindo off my arm and threw him over my shoulder into the back seat. I never knew where I stood with that guy. This time I thought he'd really crossed the line.

But when I started the engine and placed a hand on the automatic gear stick, you put your hand over mine at the same time. It lasted only a second, but you gave the back of my hand a definite squeeze. I put my foot down, and we were off.

Just before turning onto the E18, and taking a left to drive you to Kjevik, you asked if you might come with me all the way to Oslo. 'It doesn't feel right to travel in the opposite direction to the one I'm going in,' you said.

And so we spent many hours together on the way home to the capital. We talked about everything imaginable. You asked me to tell you more about Grethe Cecilie, and the walking trip we had taken together down through Aurlandsdalen. I looked over at you and asked if you really meant it: that I tell you *more* about Grethe Cecilie's walking trip in Aurlandsdalen? You smiled from ear to ear. It was as though you were a little child, and my tales had been plucked from a huge bag of sweets you could never eat your fill of. And I went on telling them.

We started talking about your cousin, Truls. Perhaps I started by asking how he'd got the distinctive scar on his forehead. But it was a long way to Oslo, and you went right back to the very beginning.

You said you were both born in November 1957, meaning you were exactly the same age. Your own brothers were many years older than you, and throughout your childhood Truls had acted as a foster-brother. Even as adults you'd remained close.

Truls met Liv-Berit as a young student, they had children early, and you'd seen a lot of their two daughters ever since they were little: you'd been like an aunt to them, you said, and of course you have no children of your own.

Today, Truls was a well-known neurologist and brain scientist, and you made no secret of the fact you were incredibly proud of him. In scientific circles, he'd already gained a global reputation, and he'd not long since organised an international conference in Oslo. The theme of the conference had been 'The Human Brain and Memory', which was Truls' own field of research.

'And how does he explain memory?' I asked.

You laughed. 'I've asked him that many times,' you said. 'And do you know what he says?'

I shook my head.

You said: 'He has *no idea*. Truls is among the world's most prominent brain scientists. But he doesn't know what memory is.'

Now it was my turn to laugh. I thought we were

having such a nice time together, Agnes.

'Every twelve-year-old knows what it is to think,' you added. 'And most boys know everything about the universe. But astronomers just wring their hands and admit they're clueless.'

Both of us laughed.

'And what about the scar on his forehead?' I brought up again. You had to tell the story then.

As children, you always spent holidays at your grandparents' place in the country, out at Hvaler, and even though Truls was a boy and you were a girl, you shared a bedroom until far into your teens. Your parents had started to propose other solutions after a while, but the two of you had protested.

Sometimes, you would lie there all night, talking until it grew light and the sun rose on a new day. In the summer holidays that might be as early as four o'clock. Or you might lie awake, listening to the nightingale. It sang so beautifully, with such a register and such power that sometimes you got the giggles.

One time when you were out in the orchard play-ing, something dramatic happened. You were only eight years old then, you were quite sure of that, because it was the first summer Grethe Cecilie was in a wheelchair. You and Truls were playing with the cover of the old well. The cover was just a thick wooden disc, and it was heavy, but it wasn't bolted to the concrete. You'd managed to shove the cover to one side so you could look down into the well. There was no water in it, but you could see several metres into the darkness.

'And speaking of memory . . .' you added now. You weren't able to remember what had actually happened, and you thought that perhaps some kind of repression was to blame, but the game ended with Truls falling headfirst into the well. You'd called for help, and four adults had come rushing over. They'd been quick to get the boy up out of the well, but again you stressed you could remember none of the details. It had just been engraved on your mind that your cousin had got a nasty cut on his head and had bled profusely. But he hadn't lost consciousness, and he didn't cry.

This was before the bridge and road connections came to the islands at Hvaler, so after having provisionally bandaged Truls, the adults had to quickly get a lift in a boat to Kråkerøy, where an ambulance stood waiting on the quayside ready to take the boy to the hospital in Fredrikstad. But you weren't allowed to go along, and the worst thing was having to stay on the island and wait. You felt like everyone was blaming you. It was as though there was no space for more accidents in the family now, after what had happened to Grethe Cecilie six months earlier.

Late that evening, Truls and his dad came back from town. There was a sturdy bandage wrapped around his head. They'd sewn seventeen stitches, and *that* was the reason for the scar.

Again, you had to emphasise that memory is a mysterious thing, and you weren't in a position to relate all the circumstances. But there was *one* thing you couldn't forget: Truls had come home with a bag of boiled sweets, and he'd refused to open them before he was back and could share them with you.

After you'd told me the whole story, you sat still for a few seconds, staring out at the road. But then you looked up at me again and exclaimed, almost embarrassed: 'I don't know why I'm telling you all this!'

But I did. It was me who'd asked you.

And everything was so good. It was nice to hear you tell the story! It was as though we'd known each other for years.

But – the question begs to be asked: why am *I* telling you this now? Why am I sitting in Gotland, going through everything again? You know what we talked about in the car.

Well, Agnes. You see, I enjoy going through it again. You described it all so vividly, so warmly and distinctly. It was so enlivening to listen to. I wasn't used to such *presence*.

It had been many years since I'd been on a long road trip with someone I could talk to. The trip with Andrine to Åsgårdstrand was all make-believe, of course – wishful thinking.

I've fooled myself in this way far too often.

At one point, you asked me to pull into a lay-by because you wanted to talk to Pelle. He behaved a little better this time, but even then the conversation took a turn that made me feel embarrassed on his behalf. I thought he asked far too many personal questions. You gave patient answers, and again you laughed, but you were also quick to ask Pelle a few choice questions in return, and in so doing, put the ball back on his side of the court. He chatted away merrily, going as far back as Holsdagen 1959, when Jakop, that is, I, had won him in the tombola. Before that he couldn't remember anything.

We approached Oslo, and I realised the long road trip was drawing to a close. One of us suggested we stop and eat dinner together at Marché at Holmestrand. It was over coffee that we agreed I could write to you. We didn't arrange to see each other again. We didn't even mention the possibility. But I could write. That's what you said. In the end you *asked* me to write. You wanted to try and understand what kind of person I was, and why I had turned up at Grethe Cecilie's funeral.

However, I have a crystal-clear memory of one more thing. Even if we didn't arrange to see each other again, there was something you said as we arrived in the capital. You said you would love to meet Pelle at some later date. And what's more: you made me promise. I had to promise you would have the chance to meet Pelle again.

I still haven't decided whether I'll send you my story. Before I do, I must tell you what has happened to me here on Gotland. Here, too, there was a little Lundin chapter.

Sven-Åke

Monday, 20 May 2013, Whitsun Bank Holiday. Here I sit, looking out over Almedalen and the Baltic Sea. The sea is flat and pale blue, the sun is setting over the water, and there is almost no wind.

I have both windows open. It's been the warmest Whitsun in living memory.

I've been sitting here in this room, writing, for four days already, interrupted only by a few brisk walks out into town to get something to eat, and a few glasses of wine in the evening. I always order by the glass, even if it never seems to add up to less than a bottle, but restraint is a virtue, and I like it when these glasses are put on the table, albeit in quick succession. My local here in Visby is called Bolaget, and the place got its name because the old building once housed the local Systembolaget, the state off-licence.

*

Aside from everything I've written about Halling-dal, my story extends across almost twelve years. Such a long time has passed since I met your cousin at Emeritus Professor Erik Lundin's funeral and had my little rumpus with Ylva about Indo-European matters. Only months later I met the young woman again. That was at the memorial service after Andrine's funeral, and then again, a few hours later, on a forest walk in Årvollskogen.

Since then I hadn't seen her. I write 'hadn't' because Ylva turned up suddenly when I was here in Gotland, and I'm getting to the point in my story where she will once again play a role. It was the afternoon of the 17th of May, my second day on the island.

I came to Gotland to isolate myself, literally. I'd managed to get through a great heap of marking, the last lot before the summer, and had a good long Whitsun break to spend sitting in my hotel room with my laptop, writing. To you, Agnes.

Now, I have to weave into my story something that happened to me just a week after we last saw each other. Late one morning, I had to run an errand in the Oppegård district. After completing my task, which was in a sense connected to my teaching duties, I walked past Kolbotn Church on my way to the railway station. I couldn't help noticing that something was happening in the old stone church: I caught sight of a hearse and realised it must be a funeral.

I went into the churchyard almost out of habit and snuck into the church. In front of the altar, there was a white coffin with a simple bouquet. A male priest was presiding, and three people were sitting beneath the pulpit to the left of the aisle. The two people from the undertakers sat in a pew right at the back of the church, just a few metres from where I was standing.

I had picked up an order of service from a white-painted wooden chair in the porch, and it was only now that I glanced at what I was holding. The front page was taken up by a picture of the deceased. It was the tall, dark man!

I lurched out in dismay, and set off at a run down towards Kolbotn station with just one thought in my head: it could have been me!

It was clear to me that an epoch had come to an end. Never again would I sneak around at funerals. And still: when I packed my case to come over to Gotland, I put in a black suit and a pair of freshly polished shoes, just to be on the safe side.

I also took Pelle along. He always joins me on long trips. I might get into a few pleasant conversations with him too.

While waiting for our luggage in the arrivals hall at the little airport in Visby, I caught sight of a copy of *Gotlands Allehanda* in a recycling bin. This would be four days ago now.

This paper was several days old, and when I later flicked through it at the hotel, I was made aware that the old theologian and priest Sven-Åke Gardell was to be buried the next morning at Bro Church, which turned out to be ten kilometres or so northeast of the old Hanseatic city, on the way to Fårö. The funeral was to be held on 17 May, the first full day of my little Whitsun holiday.

I read the death notice again, and soon began thinking about the man who'd passed away, and over the course of the evening I became convinced that I owed it to Sven-Åke to turn up to his funeral. It would be a fitting conclusion to a long and extensive career, especially since I had decided not to sneak around at funerals any more. I was abroad too, which made it an easy decision: when abroad, people often find they have no difficulty allowing themselves to do things they've stopped doing at home. I wasn't unique in that.

I sat in my hotel room googling Sven-Åke Gardell on my laptop. I had to be sure I had an indisputable explanation for showing up to the funeral the following day, and I concluded I had a whole series of extremely valid reasons: indeed, the more I thought about them, the more they became internalised; a part of myself and my own moral compass.

Gardell was one of the Swedish church's most high-profile liberal theologians, which made him very controversial, not just in Gotland but across Sweden. He had his own understanding of Jesus's position as God's son, a variant of Jesus being adopted as God's son on the strength of his deeds and not by birth. In all humility he thereby repudiated the Immaculate Conception as told in the Gospels according to Matthew and Luke, who on their part had perhaps no basis for their teachings other than an incorrectly translated verse from the prophet Isaiah (7:14). In accordance with the Hebrew original text, the prophet had foreseen that a 'young woman' (almá) would become pregnant, but in the *Septuagint*, the Greek translation from the Hebrew, around two centuries before Christ's birth, the word is inaccurately translated as 'virgin' (parthenos), and it is from this translation that both Matthew and Luke quote.

On one occasion, Gardell had gone so far as to assert that his Christian identity was no longer dependent on the dogma of Jesus's resurrection, in the literal sense, just as it was not dependent on the Ascension or the miracle of Pentecost. These uproarious words had been spoken in a renowned radio interview: 'If Christ is not risen, I am nevertheless one of Jesus Christ's priests.' Gardell was called upon to withdraw these words for many years, but he never did.

After a while, I had a detailed story of how, many years previously, the pastor and I had come to know each other well, not least through our theological debates, as well as through a strong personal affinity. The fact that I had studied Christianity meant I was well capable of speaking of the deeply considered sympathy I had developed for Gardell's theological opinions.

I was particularly impressed by his ability and courage with regards to confession and testimony. When it comes to their congregations, and the public in general, far too many theologians hold back from revealing their doubts about the church's dogma, let alone angels and demons, deadly sins and judgement day. I believe there are priests who have long since ceased to say their own private evening prayers, but who make their living by reeling off liturgical prayers during mass. There are religious leaders who recite the Apostle's Creed with their congregations without a trace of doubt, though they have not an ounce of personal belief, either in the first, second or third part of the creed.

I've always had a great tolerance for different visions of faith, something I took with me from my hippie days, perhaps. But I also have the greatest of respect for those who have lost all or part of their childhood beliefs, and who make no effort to conceal this, but instead go out into the public realm and give voice to these doubts. The opposite is what I call hypocrisy.

Nowhere else in the world are there more medieval churches, neither per square kilometre nor per capita, than here in Gotland, and Bro Church is said to be among the loveliest and most significant of them.

Built into the church's walls are pagan picture stones dating back to the fifth century. The most impressive of these has a large sun symbol, two rosettes, and at the bottom a ship full of oarsmen

– all widespread motifs found on Gotland's picture stones. Under the tower in the furthest reaches of the church is a huge font carved in sandstone from around 1200. It is touchingly beautiful, a little masterpiece, like a gigantic ceramic artwork. And the prettiest depiction I've ever seen of the Garden of Eden was one I found here on the backdrop up to the left of the altar. In all their grace, Adam and Eve are surrounded by predatory beasts and grazing animals in perfect unity, though the world's innocence is in the process of being torn down as Eve reaches out her hand and takes the forbidden fruit from the branch stretching from the tree of knowledge. Oh, Eve! Do you know what are doing?

I'd arrived just over an hour before the memorial service was set to begin. This gave me a chance to have a look around the church before other people arrived, and I had plenty of time to acquaint myself with the little churchyard that encircled the church, within the old boundary walls of limestone. I found the name Gardell on several of the gravestones. And now a grave had been prepared for the old priest.

Gardell is an old Gotland name, still widespread across the island. In the mid 1700s, the priest Lars

Berthold Hallgren took the name after the parish *Garde*, or *Garda*, meaning 'fenced-in area'. The names, as with the Norwegian surname *Gaarder*, are etymologically related to Norwegian's *gård* and *gjerde*; the German *Garten*; the French and Spanish *jardin*; the Italian *giardino*; and the English *garden*, or even *yard*, as in *courtyard*, and both terms can probably be traced back to one and the same Indo-European root, **gher-*, meaning 'to surround or fence in'. The root also forms the basis for the mythological *Midgard*, the very centre of the world, which forms humanity's playground; *Asgard*, the home of the gods; and Útgarðr, the stronghold in Jotunheim, which is the domain of the giants and trolls. Also, the Old Norse name for Constantinople or Byzantium was *Miklagarðr*, or 'the great city'. From the same Indo-European root **gher-* we also find *grhás* for house or place of residence; Latin *hortus* for garden, from which comes the name of the flowering garden shrub *hortensia*; Greek *khórtos* for pasture; the Irish *gort* for earth; the Church Slavic *grad* for castle or city, as in Leningrad, and Russian *gorod*, as in Nov*gorod* 'the new city', etc., etc.

Why is it that I'm so obsessed with these linguistic relationships? The answer is almost embarrassingly simple: other relationships are not mine to refer to.

I have no other extended family I can link myself to than the family of Indo-European languages.

Come now, don't say belonging and identity can't be connected to language: I grew up with the Halling dialect as my mother tongue, a branch of Norwegian, which is in turn a branch of the Scandinavian or Northern Germanic languages, which is once again a branch of the Germanic languages in line with the West Germanic languages such as English, German, Dutch, Frisian and Yiddish, alongside the East Germanic language Gothic, which has long been an extinct branch, though it was at one point a written language, leaving behind parts of a Bible from the mid-fourth century, the so-called Wulfila or Gothic Bible, which apart from a very few runic inscriptions is the oldest Germanic document. In its entirety, the Germanic branch of the Indo-European language family is one of several such major branches . . .

I have no living children or grandchildren, and I have no living siblings or parents, but I have living words in my mouth, and of these I can quite clearly see a multitude of relatives over the entire Indo-European language area, from Iceland to Sri Lanka, and what's more, they stretch over a historic time period of six thousand years!

The language I speak – and I'm not talking about

anything else now, I'm absolutely not talking about biological genes, which have nothing whatsoever to do with language – the language I speak, is derived from a small group of people, the Proto-Indo-Europeans, who lived five or six thousand years ago, possibly on the southern Russian steppe. This language of mine is my inheritance from them. A large proportion of the words I use are these Indo-European inherited words.

So I belong to a language family I feel strong ties to. It's here that my words have their grandparents, great-grandparents and great-great-grandparents, aunts and uncles, cousins, once-, twice- and three-times removed. I live with a certain overview of the various branches of this family tree across an era spanning several millennia. On the other hand, I'm completely blank when it comes to the Sino-Tibetan language family, though it's the world's second largest language family, or the Niger-Congo languages, which include around a thousand different languages in Africa, including all Bantu languages. Of the Afro-Asian languages, however, I've picked up a word or two, since this family covers languages like Hebrew, Arabic and Egyptian. I've already mentioned at least one word from this family, namely the Hebrew *almá* for 'young woman'. And I can name another here – the Aramaic *abba*, which means 'father' and which Jesus uses in the New Testament when he addresses God.

I don't have a bad word to say about these other language families. They're just not my family.

The old church lay alongside a country road in the midst of farmland. But soon, people began to arrive in droves, and I was reminded of the valley of my childhood, where people would come from afar for a wedding or a funeral. The reserved pews were soon packed. At the back of the church, a group of people were even standing between the old font and the aisle.

The priest professed his own and the church's faith in the resurrection of Christ, but he also emphasised that Jesus himself had never required that his disciples follow such doctrines. And was not the thief on the cross taken up into heaven without offering a confession? Who could then doubt that Sven-Åke Gardell was a servant of the church and a true Christian?

Right at the end, the priest said: 'The Church of Sweden must become a little more open-minded. We don't know exactly how Jesus expressed himself, and we can't really know how he saw himself and his role. But even today, at Sven-Åke Gardell's funeral, we must have a chance to say, as Paul did, that if

Christ is not risen, our message and our faith is meaningless. Sven-Åke is in God's hands now! Even if he was unable to believe in this miracle himself, we can believe for him. We can believe and hope that Sven-Åke will rise again!'

I was a little provoked by the priest's didactic, almost patronising words about a respected colleague's Christology. But I didn't show it. Perhaps I would get a chance to speak my thoughts later that day, I remember thinking. I felt as though I knew Sven-Åke so well it was my duty to defend his reputation, not to mention his spiritual testament.

At this point all those in attendance were invited to the memorial service after the burial. I didn't quite understand whether it was to take place at a public venue, or at one of the farms in the neighbourhood – all that was given was a name, and I didn't catch whether it was a place name or a family name, though of course these two categories often overlap. I'd never been to this area before.

When the postlude had faded out, the coffin was carried through the church and out to the grave that lay open only forty metres away. Under the baking sun, the priest read a few Bible verses, the coffin was lowered, the priest oversaw the casting of earth, and once again he said something about resurrection. A psalm was sung, and those attending, who had stood close together in the customary black-clad circle, began to drift off between the graves and out onto the narrow path. People hugged, and tears were shed, but I also noted a good-natured smile or two.

We left the churchyard through a white-washed gate-house, and it was only then, once we were outside the pale stone wall of the churchyard, that the attendees began to talk informally among themselves. We were a large gathering, I would estimate around a hundred and fifty people, and I was delighted to be among such full and varied company.

Not everyone was from Gotland. I realised that several people had come over from the mainland to say their last farewells to Sven-Åke Gardell. He may have been controversial, but the priest had been a central figure in the Church of Sweden, and naturally, he'd had his followers too.

Someone addressed me, and I answered in Norwegian. I needn't have done – I mean, I would have been fully capable of speaking the native language almost like a Swede, and eventually someone would have asked me which region I came from. Almost forty years previously, I'd taken a summer course in 'Swedish: Language and Literature' at the university in Lund. But a limit to the illusions had to be set somewhere, at a funeral at least, and particularly at the funeral of a man who was an icon of candour.

I had begun to dread spinning the whole tale of my encounter with Sven-Åke now, so close to his open grave. I thought about Arendal, and of our conversation at Marché. But as long as I was part of the party, I had to at least answer the questions I was asked. I said that I had met Sven-Åke many years ago at an Ecumenical conference in Stockholm, and that we had maintained some degree of contact over the years since. We were never close friends.

Mentally, I had begun to moderate myself. I explained that I had come to Gotland for a completely different reason than Sven-Åke's funeral, in fact, unaware of his passing, but that since I was on the island it had seemed like a pleasant duty to travel out to Bro this morning to take part in his funeral.

Part of my undoing was an encounter with a middle-aged couple who introduced themselves as Sven Bertil and Gunilla Lundin. I asked if they might by any chance be related to Erik Lundin, who had once been a respected philologist at the University of Oslo. They gaped, and I thought it was because I had hit the nail on the head. I must also have had in the back of my mind the couple who'd been speaking in broad Gotland dialect at the professor's funeral. Could it be them I was standing with now? That's why I began chatting away about my acquaintance with Erik Lundin, in addition to his children and all the grandchildren I'd come into contact with over the years. The two exchanged a look, before one of them reminded me that Lundin is one of the most common names in Sweden, more than fifteen thousand Swedes share that name, they said. And I felt embarrassed to have needed enlightening in this manner.

When at length I was invited to join the memorial service I declined politely. I must be getting back to Visby, I said, someone was waiting for me there.

It was strange to hear myself declining to take further part in such a warm and inclusive gathering. The language and dialects alone were a joy for the mind and the senses. But I was resolute: this game was to end once and for all.

Sometimes it can be a paradoxical experience to be witness to oneself and one's reactions. Occasionally it can be a thoroughly unpredictable one.

I'd begun to long for Pelle. He wasn't so far away. He was in the little knapsack I liked to take with me when I was in the mountains, along with a bottle of water and a book. I've never seen anything odd about wearing a dark suit and having a little backpack hanging from one shoulder, as long as it was also black.

I don't really recall how I came to be standing alone under the canopy of a large tree as the black-clad mourners broke up and disappeared, other than that it seemed to happen in slow motion. There were fewer and fewer people round me, I felt a lump in my throat, and soon I was all on my own outside the stone wall that surrounded the churchyard and the old medieval church. It was as though I'd been enchanted and at the last moment released from the sweet clutches of the spell.

I had no idea how to find my way back to Visby. I'd arrived in a taxi, but it was hardly likely I'd be able to procure another one here. I began to walk towards the town, and soon came upon a bus stop, without a shelter but with a beautiful, blue-painted bench for waiting passengers. A bus would be coming from Fårö in an hour. In that time I might be able to walk halfway back to Visby, but it was warm, and I opted to sit on the bench and wait.

I loosened the fastening on the little bag, drank a few slurps of water, and sat Pelle alongside me on the blue bench. But he wanted to get up on my arm straight away, he was as giddy as a top, and it was impossible to placate him, even though I would have appreciated the chance to catch my breath before we started talking. But Pelle could not be restrained, and barely had I pulled him onto my arm than he looked up at me and said:

'And now? What are we going to do now?'

'We're going to wait for the bus,' I said. 'For almost an hour.'

'Are we just going to sit here and gawp? For a whole hour?'

'We can pretend we're Odin's ravens,' I suggested. 'We can sit here and take a look around us. And we can tell each other what we see.'

He took his gaze from me, turned his head and looked out across the fields.

'Over there is a pathway. But did you know that the word *way* comes from the Old English *weg*, connected to the Old Norse *vegr*, which gives us the Norwegian *vei*, meaning road? All these are related to the word *wagon*, from the Germanic **wagna-*, from which we also find the Norwegian *vogn*, and the German *Wagen*, from the Indo-European root **wegh-*, meaning "to transport", as in the Latin *veho* for "to freight" or "to transport", which in turn gives us the loanword *vehicle*, and of course, the Latin *via*, meaning "road" or "road*way*". Or as in the present tense form *vahati* in Sanskrit, meaning "he transports", which in turn is also connected to Germanic words like the German *bewegen*, *beweglich* and *Bewegung*, meaning "to move", "movable", and "movement", as well as the English to *weigh*, and *weight*, from the Germanic root **wegan-* for to move, lift, weigh.'

Herr Skrindo looked up at me with an expression of concentration.

'Correct,' I said, and he relaxed.

I probably would have said roughly the same, though the loanword *vehicle* was a connection I certainly wouldn't have made myself. Sitting here with Pelle over my arm, I still couldn't remember ever having heard about or seen in print a reference to the connection with the loanword *vehicle*, but it seemed Pelle had, so I'd just have to make a note of it.

He interrupted me mid-thought.

'And you?' he said. 'What can you see?'

I looked in the same direction he had, across the fertile land, to a field that must have once been cultivated but was now full of weeds. I said:

'I can see an unploughed field. It's small, only

about an acre, but it might once have provided for a family. But if we take that word, *acre*, we can see its origins in the Germanic words for field, such as the Norwegian and Swedish word *åker*, tracing these back to the Proto-Germanic **akra-*, from the Indo-European root **agro-*, which also gives us *ajra* in Sanskrit, *ager* in Latin and *agros* in Greek, from which we get the loanword *agriculture*. Perhaps the original Indo-European meaning had to do with the land people "drove" the livestock on, since the Indo-European root **ag-* means "to drive" or "push", and also forms the basis for Old Norse *aka*, meaning "to drive", as with the Swedish åka "to drive" and Norwegian *ake*, to run or to skid, whether that happens on a sledge or on one's bottom. So Thor with his hammer was called *aka-Þór* because he drove across the heavens in his chariot or wagon. From the same Indo-European root we find a whole string of Latin loanwords such as *to act, agent, active* and *action*, and Greek loanwords such as *demagogue*, one who "drives" the people, *pedagogue*, one who "conducts" children, etc.'

I was no longer looking at the acre of land across the way. As a rule, I always looked at Pelle when I talked to him. It was the least I could do. I asked for a little affirmation.

'Right?'

Pelle nodded almost graciously:

'Sounds right, yes. The animals that pulled the plough were fastened to a *yoke*, the same word we use figuratively as a symbol of oppression or servitude. The Norwegian equivalent *åk* is derived from Old Norse *ok*, which in German becomes *Joch*, with all of them coming from the Proto-Germanic **juka-*, in turn derived from the Proto-Germanic **yugó-*, from the root **yeug-*, meaning "to connect", from which we also get the loanword *yoga* from Sanskrit, meaning "connection".'

It's possible I interrupted Pelle at this point. I said:

'The word for *yoke* – like the Norwegian *åk* – is found frequently across the Indo-European language area; it also occurs in Latin and Greek, in a string of Celtic and Balto-Slavic languages, in Tocharian and Hittite, telling us something about the culture the ancient Indo-Europeans lived in. They were hard-working farmers who had to struggle daily to survive.'

I felt Pelle jerking my wrist. This had happened before, and on a couple of similar occasions I'd ended up with tendonitis, or something I'd come to think of as Pelle-hand; luckily it wasn't the hand I write with.

He strained my muscles, saying:

'They had to *lift* – related to *loft* and aloft, as well

as the German and Scandinavian *Luft/luft*, meaning "air" – and *bear* weight, from the Germanic **beran-* meaning "to bear" as in both "to carry" and to "bear children", as in Germanic words *borne, burden, birth, bairn* and *birthday*. All these go back to the Proto-Indo-European root **bher-* meaning "to carry", as we find in the Indian word for India, *Bhārat*, from the legendary emperor *Bharata*, actually "the one who bears/carries". Think too of how the Latin word *ferre*, for "to bear/carry", from the same root, gives us a host of words such as *refer, differentiate, fertile*, etc, etc.'

Finally, he relaxed again . . .

As we sat talking, cars and motorcycles regularly passed us on the country road. Some probably thought it was strange to see a fully grown man sitting there, talking heatedly to a hand puppet. But I've often had to rise above this kind of attention, since I've not always had anyone else to talk to. And anyway, it wasn't as though we were sitting on a bench at home in one of Oslo's parks: we were deep in the countryside, on an island in the Baltic Sea. Many people are unafraid of swimming nude as long as they're far enough away from home: in the same way I felt no concern about sitting talking to Pelle on a country road in the middle of nowhere. OK, so I was exposing myself. But my students couldn't see me, and aside from them, I have no one to feel ashamed in front of.

'But they had *horses*,' I went on. 'Aside from that younger word we also have in Old Norse the Indo-European word *jór*, as in *Jórvík*, that is to say "Horse Bay", which was what the Vikings called the English town that came to be known as *York*, which in turn has given us *New York*. In Old Norse terms, we also find the same ancient name for horse in popular given names such as *Jostein*, "horse stone", perhaps a stone people would have stood upon to mount a horse, and *Jóarr* for a horseman and warrior. This comes from the Proto-Indo-European word **ekwos*, which we also find in the Latin *equus*, the Greek *hippos*, as in *hippodrome*, more easily recognisable in the Ionic dialect as *ikkos*, or for that matter in the Myceanean as *ikkwos*, and in Sanskrit *ásva-*. So the Indo-Europeans had horses . . .'

I felt my left forearm jerk, and Pelle interrupted:

'. . . and wagons.'

'What?'

'The Indo-Europeans had horses and wagons.'

'But we've already been over that. We talked about *way* and *wagon*.'

But Pelle wasn't giving in. My whole forearm was shaking. He said:

'A prerequisite for the invention of the horse and

wagon was that a pair of wheels had to be connected to an *axle*. It's the epitome of the egg of Columbus. And the Indo-Europeans must have known about this technology, because even *axle* is an Indo-European word that's found across large parts of the language area.'

He was right. The English word *axle*, and its Norwegian equivalent, *aksel*, from the Old Norse *ǫxull* meaning 'wheel axle', related to *ǫxl* and thus the Norwegian word *aksel*, for 'shoulder', go back to the Germanic **ahslō-*, the presumed Indo-European **aks-*, from which we find the Sanskrit *akṣa*, the Greek *aksōn* and the Latin *axis* for 'axle', the same word as the English *axis*, etc, etc.

We didn't get any further, because at this point the bus came along, hopefully on solid axles so that it wouldn't have any problem *accelerating*!

I pulled Pelle off my arm, folded him together neatly and put him back in the black bag.

As soon as he was off my hand, he lost the ability to protest. Sometimes I manage to tug him off fast as lightning, thereby stopping him from doing just that.

But I can sense when he's impatient to get up on my arm again. It takes the form of a peculiar kind of restlessness.

I found myself in this state frequently during the few years he was kept prisoner deep inside the wardrobe. I took him out into the light and held long conversations with him almost every time Reidun was out of the apartment. But this happened so rarely. And then he had to be safely back in place before she returned.

During the last months we lived together she would sometimes come home unannounced: I didn't like that, I thought it was odd, and over the course of a few weeks it seemed to happen more and more often.

I suspected her of having initiated a kind of espionage on Pelle and me. I believe she was taking note, on a daily basis, of Pelle's precise position in the wardrobe drawer – I mean, to the millimetre – in order to tell whether he'd been up, outside the drawer, in use, when she hadn't been home to observe us. I imagined Reidun had found out about Pelle's existence by going through the drawers in my wardrobe in search of something to get at me with, whatever that might be.

Her suspicions were confirmed when one day she suddenly stood there, waving him about when I got home from school. Perhaps she'd already figured out that Pelle and I lived in a kind of secret symbiosis. When I pulled him over my arm and let him talk freely, and she got confirmation of the accuracy of her suspicions, he had to get back in his drawer again. My wife would really have preferred it if I'd thrown Herr Skrindo in the bin.

Back at the hotel I changed my dark suit for something lighter, and walked up through the cobbled streets to Stora Torget and on up to Skafferiet, a café I'd passed on my evening stroll the previous day. I stepped into a lush garden full of rhododendrons, lilacs and oxeye daisies, as well as a couple of fruit trees that had not yet come into bloom.

It was warm – it might have been twenty-five degrees in the garden, but the trees and the white walls of the café provided a certain amount of shade from the sun. The sound of a little fountain between the trees also gave an impression of coolness.

A little blonde girl of five or six discovered the tiny fountain. She called to her grandfather, exclaiming: 'Look!'

I tried to put myself in the grandfather's shoes. It wasn't hard. When he put his hand on the little girl's head and stroked her hair, it was almost as though it was me doing it, and I could feel the girl's smooth hair on the palm of my hand long afterwards. It was a strange sensation, and surprising, as I've never stroked a little girl's hair in my life.

I'd been into the café and ordered a toasted sandwich with cheese and ham, a green salad and a glass of red wine, which was soon brought out to my table in the garden. The next day I was to learn that the young lady who'd brought me the food and wine was called Ida. Over the following days, I talked to her a little; perhaps she thought it amusing to speak to a Norwegian who, oddly enough, also spoke fluent Swedish. She told me she had a friend who lived and worked in Oslo, also in a café.

I sat there a while, people-watching, looking at all the plants in pots and tubs, at sparrows and thrushes pecking at crumbs on the garden path, at the tame jackdaws who threw themselves at the leftovers as the café's guests became sated with this idyll and took to the streets again.

It occurred to me that I wasn't missing the memorial service I'd declined to go to, not in the slightest.

And then Ylva Lundin comes rushing into the garden. She's carrying a mug of tea in one hand, and pulling a red suitcase along behind her. She's dressed in a black blouse and a black skirt. Both garments fit as though made for her, but it seems to me to be an odd outfit for this warm weather. Red and black form a beautiful contrast of course, and she could have dressed to match her suitcase as much as the reverse. The sunrays strike her throat, and even at this distance my eye is caught by the sapphire-blue pendant.

She catches sight of me and stops short. The astonishment at chancing upon each other here is perhaps equally split between us, though I am at a significant advantage as I am not standing with a mug of hot liquid in my hand. We haven't seen each other for more than ten years. But in the time that has passed I've met many of her family members, and I'm sure she's been given a few reports about me, the mystical, and perhaps dubious, Mr Incognito.

Her face lights up, I interpret it as delight at meeting me again, or delight of some kind, at least, and I offer her the empty chair at my table.

She sits down graciously and without affectation, almost as though this was an arranged meeting. She is now in her late thirties and her features have matured.

'Are you alone?' she asks.

I nod.

'And you?'

She wraps both hands around her mug of tea, bends over it, and she too nods.

It strikes me that for both of us there might be a double meaning in this half-verbal, half-mimetic dialogue.

On the roof of the café, two jackdaws sit, gazing down on us, or perhaps it's really the leftovers on my plate they're keeping an eye on. Ylva points up at them and says:

'They see it all.'

'You mean they see all the customers at the café?'

She shakes her head: 'It's Huginn and Muninn the ravens, and now they're looking down on you and me.'

I smile: 'And then they'll report back to Odin?'

She nods: 'And he's telling Grandfather – who's in Valhalla now. Soon he'll find out we met each other in Gotland. Grandfather loved Gotland. He had family here . . .'

I'd come to the island the previous day and was due to be in Visby until the end of the Whitsun holidays. Ylva had been here almost a week, and was heading back to Oslo that same afternoon. She was already on her way.

She'd just come up from Fornsalen, the cultural history museum in Visby, where she'd been studying a collection of Gotland's renowned picture stones with sun crosses, mythical motifs such as Odin and the eight-legged horse Sleipnir, or the heroes of Germanic sagas such as Sigurd Fåvnesbane. She'd spent the rest of the last few days sitting in Almedal

Library, reading up on Gotlandica, as she put it. She'd found books she didn't even know existed, and some of them had cast a new light on her own research, if just a glint.

Ylva had followed in her grandfather's footsteps. She was already a university lecturer in the history of religion, and was in the process of finishing her doctoral thesis on Odin in myths and cults. I asked if I was the one who had put her on to the idea, and at that point she gave me an inscrutable look. It was as though she hadn't thought about what I'd asked until this very moment. Several seconds passed, before she tilted her head to one side and said: 'Maybe?'

Early in the morning on that Friday, our very own national day, she'd hired an electric car and driven out to Fårö, where an older second cousin of hers had a summer house. On the way back, she'd passed by Bro Church, and now she began giving an account of the church I myself had just come from. She had a few interesting reflections on the fresco of the Garden of Eden, the same one I'd wondered at just a few hours previously. At that point, a white coffin had stood at the very front of the church. Why didn't Ylva say anything about it?

I started feeling dizzy. Was Ylva making fun of me?

There'd been many people at the funeral. Was it possible that Ylva too had been there, but that she had intentionally sought to avoid me and perhaps managed to get away in the electric car while I stood outside the church conversing with some of the funeral mourners? Or had she driven past me on the country road an hour later when I'd been on the blue bench talking to Pelle? But why hadn't she stopped and taken us with her? Was she scared of hand puppets, just like Reidun?

I'd even stood there talking to a middle-aged couple called Lundin. Was it conceivable that they had denied their relationship to the old professor? Perhaps because they had realised who it was they were talking to? It wasn't unthinkable that the rumours of my bragging had spread across the Keel to our brother nation in the east and found their way out onto an island in the Baltic Sea. They'd looked at one another so strangely when I asked if they were related to Erik Lundin.

So Ylva had been out to Fårö to visit an 'older second cousin' on her father's side. And perhaps his name was Sven Bertil?

Now she was sitting in front of me, more or less testing me with her tales of Bro Church, the Garden of Eden and the fall from grace. She was, in my opinion, rather too focused on the sexual aspect of the fall, though perhaps that was more to make me lose my cool, to get me into a state of imbalance. But I would not let myself be provoked. I mean, I acted as though I wasn't letting myself be provoked. I recalled a particularly outré outburst she'd casually let me overhear at Østreheim Inn and Social Hall.

I thought it would be most sensible not to hide anything; I had to go on the offensive. I expressed my dismay at her mentioning Bro Church a whole three times, since I too had been in the very same church earlier that day, at the funeral of Sven-Åke Gardell, the famous priest and theologian. Perhaps Ylva too was familiar with him? Perhaps in the course of her studies or academic work she'd come across the liberal priest who'd picked a fight with the church?

She said nothing. Her face remained perfectly calm. She just looked me in the eye, so intensely that I let my gaze fall to the sapphire-blue eye of Odin at her throat. She took note of that too.

I had no choice. I had to go on. I just had to lay it on. I was forced into telling the whole story of how Sven-Åke and I had met one another in Stockholm one time in the eighties. The die had been cast. It rolled there on the table between us.

*

I began to hold forth, and I think I gave her exactly what she wanted:

'During a period of my life when I had a certain degree of connection to the church, I had thought warmly of the Ecumenical idea. Christian faith and teachings: Christology, the doctrine of the Atonement, and eschatology alike, were in any case so overwhelming, and so irrational when seen through modern eyes, that it would have been almost uncanny if all religious communities had alighted on precisely the same interpretation of the Bible's message. Variety is the very quintessence of human existence: wasn't it therefore also natural that Christianity – after two thousand years – was characterised by a certain degree of diversity? But should that be a reason not to exchange thoughts and viewpoints, or to occasionally hold a joint service?'

After a few such introductory comments I paused for effect, once again making eye contact with Ylva to gauge her reaction to what I'd said so far, roughly in the way a fortune-teller might need small signals or affirmations from their client before proceeding with their predictions – or perhaps to avoid losing their compass and going completely off course. But Ylva was in no mood to collaborate: she gave no more than a minimal nod, and not as a confirmation of anything I'd said, but as a sign she wanted to hear more. She seemed neither sceptical nor dismissive. She was 'with me all the way', as they say.

'In 1986, twenty years after the big meeting of the church in Uppsala, an Ecumenical conference was held outside Stockholm,' I went on, 'and I had taken part, not as a delegate from any religious community, or a representative from any ecclesiastical group, but as a free observer, someone who had taught religion for many years in secondary schools, as simple as that. I'd taken this trip over to our neighbouring country to get a little top-up, in addition to the fact that I had, throughout my life, had what one might call a love affair with our brothers to the east. Because of this, the very arena for the conference became an added bonus. That was how I met Sven-Åke Gardell, the priest and intellectual from Gotland, and we hit it off so well, just from greeting one another and chatting briefly as we registered . . .'

She was bent forward over her mug of tea, holding it tight with both hands, and it couldn't be because her fingers were cold, because it must have been close to thirty degrees. But she looked up at me intensely, with a friendly expression, I thought, as though it pleased her to hear me telling my story.

She asked: 'Where was this conference, did you say?'

'In Stockholm,' I repeated.

Did I see a hint of a little grin? She said: 'But *where* in Stockholm? I'm familiar with the area.'

I acted as though I needed a moment before answering. 'I think I said *outside* of Stockholm,' I said. 'It was in Sigtuna, an old town between Stockholm and Uppsala, more specifically, at the north end of the Sigtuna fjord, an arm of Lake Mälaren.'

She smiled smoothly. But was she laughing? Maybe, maybe not. She said: 'It must have been at Sigtuna School, then?'

Wow, I thought. *That* familiar with the area. I said: 'And at the college too, actually. The conference was like a large festival, spread across the whole town, the streets themselves were part of it. As I'm sure you know, for the last hundred years, the old town has been a kind of centre for humanism and ecumenism in Sweden.'

She nodded again, and this time the signal seemed to mean a confirmation of my characterisation of Sigtuna, or at least a sign that I could go on telling her about how I'd come to know the liberal priest. I still had no idea whether she was connected to him, or if she really had been at his funeral, since she'd so quickly started expounding on the church he'd been buried at. She was dressed in black as well, of course.

She'd let go of the mug of tea, it was empty now, and she sat up straight.

'So how did you come to know the Gotland priest? You said you hit it off uncommonly well.'

I thought: 'Do you really want to hear all this? Do you have the time?'

The way she looked at me seemed to confirm she did, and from now on she was all ears.

'When the conference was over, Sven-Åke and I travelled together into Stockholm, and on the way into town it turned out that neither of us was due to travel onwards (that is, by air, to Oslo and Visby respectively) before late that evening. I told him I'd been considering a boat trip from Stadshusbron out to Drottningholm Palace. He thought that was such a good idea that he joined me. Soon we were sitting on a boat together, the old steamer SS *Drottningholm*, built at the beginning of the last century.

'On the way out we went down into the elegant restaurant, which was deep in the water, almost under the surface, and we consumed what I may as well call a liquid lunch. The trip took an hour, and we both managed a couple of glasses of white wine for starters, and a bottle of red wine as a main, before rounding off with coffee and cognac.

'I already knew that Sven-Åke had a chilly regard for the church's dogma, and that, at the same time, that was part of the power behind his ecumenical engagement. If only we could break down some of the church's dogmatic structures, it would be easier for the different communities to unite over what, in his opinion, was at the very core of Christianity: Jesus's teachings of charity and forgiveness, not forgetting his characteristically humane perspective on humankind's life and coexistence, partly in contrast to the Pharisees and the scribes, the "true believers" in his own historical context, and their rather doctrinaire concept of God.

'Even before we'd ordered the second glass of white wine, he bent over the table and said: "Listen! Throughout the ages people have had active spiritual lives. There's no place on earth, and no historical epoch either, in which the orientation of humans has not been steeped in a belief in an absolute swarm of supernatural beings, be that gods, angels and demons, or the spirits of their forebears, or a whole host of natural spirits. So perhaps the whole thing is nothing more than human mumbo-jumbo. I mean everything, all these concepts. Are you with me?"

'Did he even need to ask? I had no difficulty understanding where the priest was headed. There wasn't much left of what childhood faith I myself must have had. At that time, my connection to the church was more of a social nature than based on any engagement through faith. Then, as now, I like being around people, and I liked going to church coffee mornings, or to other church social events and discussions. Now I was sitting here with a central figure in the Church of Sweden, and I felt honoured.'

As I spoke, I was constantly looking at Ylva to check whether she was still following. She wasn't nodding any longer. She sat as though spellbound. There must have been something in my story that touched her deeply. Imagine, I thought. I enjoyed the fact that I was chatting away to a bona fide religious historian, who was moreover the granddaughter of the legendary Professor Lundin. But I was also aware of the possibility that she might be fascinated, first and foremost, by how I was able to sit there telling lie after lie.

Yet I went on with my account: 'I confided in the priest that I myself had lapsed in relation to all these kinds of supernatural visions of faith, but that I still reserved the right to call myself a Christian.

'And at that point my new friend lifted his glass of wine. "Listen, my good brother!" he exclaimed. "Maybe the question boils down to whether it's possible to live as a Christian without this thing you've just mentioned – swearing belief in revelation. Be that a belief in burning bushes and seas parting, or the resurrection of Jesus and his Ascension. And, well, we are both living proof of that. Perhaps there's not so many of us, though who knows? Who knows how many within the church just lack the courage, and perhaps the financial independence, to come out of the closet with their heresy."

'This was just a few years before Gardell gave his radio interview in which he uttered those famous words: "If Christ is not risen, I am nevertheless one of Jesus Christ's priests." I could have stopped him,' I said. 'I could have warned him. But I didn't.

'The old steamboat dropped anchor in front of Drottningholm Palace, and we wandered through the many gardens with plenty of time to explore a number of questions before boarding SS *Drottningholm* again a couple of hours later. By that point we were so worn out we probably could have slept up on the deck. But we saved the journey back to Stockholm with a bottle of Chablis, which we shared in brotherly fashion, almost like a sacrament, and the cold drink reinvigorated us.

'From Stadshusbron we travelled together out to Arlanda, and we didn't go our separate ways that

day until Sven-Åke headed for the domestic ter-
minal, and I headed for International Departures.'

'And they all lived happily ever after,' Ylva said with
a grin. The smile I understood, it was both warm
and genuine, but I couldn't be quite sure how to
interpret the comment.

She looked at the clock, excused herself, and
asked me to keep an eye on her red suitcase before
walking quickly across the cobbles and disappearing into the café. Almost immediately she returned,
much sooner than could be expected for a visit to
the toilet. I knew that for many women, the need for
a mirror could be as pressing as the need to visit the
toilet, and perhaps she had seen a mirror just inside
the café, but when she sat down, she was wearing
neither more lipstick, nor more mascara, and her
hair was just as it had been.

It was all a puzzle to me, but after a few minutes
Ida came out of the café with a bottle of Chablis,
fresh as dew, and two tall, stemmed glasses, which
she placed on the table between us. She opened the
bottle of wine and let me taste it, and I nodded my
affirmation. I was taken aback by this turn of events.
I remembered the glasses of aquavit at the grandfather's funeral.

Ylva lifted her glass and looked me in the eye.

'Cheers!' she said, and we toasted.

I thought that if she really did despise me, she wouldn't have needed to order this bottle of white wine and then come up with this cheerful toast.

Now, however, she had a couple of follow-up questions for me. One of them emerged out of her familiarity with the local area. Why hadn't we just stayed in Sigtuna and taken a boat trip on Lake Mälaren where we were already, before heading over to the airport, which is really only a stone's throw away from Sigtuna?

I had no difficulty talking myself out of that question. But, as though open-heartedly, she took on an expression of deep concern. As a scholar, it made her feel almost worried that she'd never heard anything about this ecumenical conference in Sigtuna, so magnificent that the whole town was involved. She confided in me that she was seriously worried she was beginning to lose her memory, because lately there had so often been things she'd forgotten. She said: 'I *must* have heard of this conference.' She threw her arms wide: 'But I've forgotten it!'

She was being ironic. I realised she hadn't for a second believed my story. She hadn't believed me at her grandfather's funeral, nor at her aunt's. I'd managed to convince everyone – apart from one person. And still – this was how I interpreted her look – still, this time she had enjoyed listening to me. Or perhaps she'd enjoyed it precisely because she didn't believe me. She took particular pleasure in hearing me tell tales, perhaps unsurprisingly: after all, wasn't she a scholar of myths?

Our ways would soon part, and I still didn't know whether she'd been at the funeral in Bro Church that day, or if she'd driven past Pelle and me on the way back from Fårö.

But neither of us was interested in shedding light on or clearing up such questions now. They weren't that important. It wasn't necessary to tie up the loose ends of what was historically correct and what was fiction.

So it was even more fun at that point to tell her the story of my visit to Erik Lundin's office during which the old professor and I, the young student, had sat over coffee, discussing the very last verse in *Völuspá*: *nú mun hón søkkvaz*.

Ylva laughed, not believing a word of what I was saying, and in doing so, she was lauding my talent for make-believe. She knew what a fool I was, and still she grinned at me and laughed. It was a real pleasure, because the story I had just told was as much fact as the rest was fiction.

I too grinned. I wasn't going to destroy the good atmosphere by trying to convince Ylva that I'd been telling the truth for once. In any case, it wasn't as though I had an ounce of credibility left.

Some way down the bottle of white wine, however, there was a question I wanted to see if I could get an answer to.

I started with a word or two about the memorial service at Østreheim. I mentioned the mythological poem *Skírnismál*, and touched on all the sex talk. But when she acted as though she had no idea what I was talking about, though in such a way that I would know she was only pretending – now she was laying the irony on thick – I did for once what Pelle would have done. I surprised her with a completely direct question.

'Have you had any powerful orgasms lately?' I asked. I looked her straight in the eye, and followed up with: 'I mean of cosmic dimensions?'

She sat for several seconds, looking at me. I think she was shocked at the audacity I had laid open so plainly, but she managed to retain her mask.

A shadow crossed her face. She said: 'What do you think? Why do you think I talked like that at my dear aunt Andrine's funeral?'

When I didn't reply, she said: 'You must know it was all for you . . .'

'Me?'

'Pah!' she practically breathed: 'At that funeral it was you who was most audacious. I tried to trump you, but it was completely impossible. Or did you keep hold of those taxi receipts?'

I laughed. Soon we were both laughing.

We drained the bottle before Ylva got ready to head off for her flight to Arlanda. As she stood up, she bent over me and gave me hug. It was good. She said: 'It was fun to meet you again, Jakop. And especially now you've been talking so nicely with Truls' cousin.'

She said it, Agnes. And the next moment, she sailed out of the idyllic garden, wheeling the red suitcase after her.

So she'd heard from someone in the family. She must have heard absolutely everything about the spectacular hiking trip through Aurlandsdalen.

It struck me that for all I knew, she'd also heard about Pelle.

I sat there gawping.

Ylva, I thought, or *she-wolf*, a fitting name through and through, hitting the nail on the head, from the Old Norse *ulfr*, from the Germanic **wulfa-*, which in German and English gives *Wolf / wolf*, from the Indo-European **wlk^wo-*, in Russian *volk*, in Sanskrit *vrka-s*, Greek *líkos* and Latin *lupus*.

Now I was running on empty, almost like Pelle. I wasn't capable of switching off: wheeling a *red* suitcase, from the Germanic **rauda-*, which in German gives us *Rot* and Norwegian *rød*, after the Indo-European **reudh-*, in Russian *rúdyi*, Sanskrit *rudhirá-*, Greek *eruthrós* and Latin *ruber*, as in the loanword *ruby*...

Of course! The stone in Sverre's ear had been a ruby! It was several decades since I'd first seen it.

Well wouldn't you know! I'd solved a little mystery. Things were beginning to fall into place.

Or were they falling apart?

Lofoten, July 2013

Jon-Jon

When I came home from Visby, there were just a few weeks left of the school year.

I'd resolved to use the first few days of the holiday to look through what I'd written. Only after that would I decide whether I dared send it to you. Then it would be up to you if you wanted to read it, and if you could perhaps bear the thought of meeting me again.

There are many things I can be criticised for, but among them is not a lack of self-awareness. I know I'm rather odd, an eccentric person, some might say monstrous. The fact that you didn't send me packing at Grethe Cecilie's funeral, or even let me leave, is beyond my ken. You also chose to come along for the whole ride home from Arendal, even though you wouldn't get so much as a krone back from your flight ticket, and you got home many hours later than you would have done by plane.

*

With Sven-Åke Gardell's funeral, my story had reached the end of the road. The whole time I've followed strictly my criteria for the small selection of funerals I've written about here: at each of them, one of Erik Lundin's descendants was present, perhaps with the exception of Andreas's funeral in Arendal, but then you were there. Whether Ylva actually was at Bro Church means nothing in this context. In any case I met her in the idyllic garden just afterwards, and it was there I made my memorial speech for Sven-Åke. What's more, after the funeral, I had spoken to the Lundin couple.

How loose this thread of my tale is, I may never find out.

I have made no mention of the other funerals I attended, not even my other escapades over to our brothers in the east, like my few trips this spring, to Sunne in Värmland and Fjällbacka in Bohuslän. What you've read here has been like a lottery in which only the winning tickets are visible.

My story is over. I thought it might be a fitting finale to my family chronicle to have a black-clad Ylva Lundin sail out of the garden at Skafferiet, wheeling a suitcase behind her. It would have made a good final scene in a film. I can almost see the credits rolling and hear the soulful soundtrack. One final image might have been of me, sitting there with the black jackdaws and an empty bottle of white wine, but that would be up to the director.

However, something happened then that gives my story a bit of a twist.

At the beginning of the school holidays I saw in a death notice that Jon-Jon, my friend when I was most lost, had just passed away. I sat bent over the kitchen table, and stiffened. It came as a bigger shock that he was alive – I mean, that he had lived so long – than that he was no longer living. Many of us had thought he'd passed many decades ago. The last sign of life was some time in the seventies.

Everything from that epoch immediately came back to me, clear as day. I thought of Marianne and Sverre, and not as the aging people they are today, but as pure young flower children.

We never used surnames at that time. Marianne was just Marianne, I had no idea she was the daughter of the renowned professor. Sverre was just Sverre from Southern Norway, and Johannes Skrova, who was now dead, had never been called anything but Jon-Jon. I myself went by the name of Pelle at that time, as I've already mentioned: when Jon-Jon met Pelle, and struck up a cheerful conversation with him, Pelle called himself Jakop, completely aware of the fact that I'd taken his name.

The notice stated that Johannes 'Jon-Jon' Skrova had passed peacefully in his sleep after a short illness, and the year of birth and other formulations confirmed that it was our own legendary Jon-Jon who was now dead.

I resolved to travel up to his funeral in Lofoten. I'd found the death notice in *Aftenposten*, so the family had obviously paid for an announcement in the capital's newspaper, perhaps with a thought to all his friends from the sixties and seventies, and I realised it was not impossible that Marianne and Sverre might also turn up. It would be the least they could do. Or was it likely that they might each see the notice without even mentioning it to one another?

Now there was something that occurred to me: if they came to Jon-Jon's funeral, it would surely be without Ylva. Naturally without Ylva. She'd never met Jon-Jon. She hadn't had anything to do with him. But why did this strike me now? The thought wasn't quite complete. It sometimes happens that our minds are struck by a partial impulse, that an idea doesn't quite gain purchase.

The possibility of meeting Marianne and Sverre again occupied my thoughts. If it hadn't already occurred to them that I was Pelle, and I couldn't be *completely* sure of that, it would immediately become apparent to them when we met in the presence of Jon-Jon's coffin. It was as Pelle, and only as Pelle, that I had introduced myself in that circle. Then they would realise that I didn't only go to funerals for fun. I saw an opportunity for a certain improvement in my reputation among the Lundin family. That too was an intriguing thought.

And so here I sit in a new hotel room, writing. I travelled with an early flight to Bodø, and onwards with the Coastal Express up to Svolvær, where I arrived at about nine last night.

I'll tell you about Jon-Jon's funeral, but first of all, a little digression. You've asked me to write as honestly as I can, and so I must be allowed a few such parentheses.

I don't really enjoy flying, and perhaps that's why I had a couple of glasses of white wine at Gardermoen before take-off. On the flight I was sat next to a woman in her thirties. Aside from a nod and a conventional 'Hi', as well as a few brief words relating to the arrangement of papers and cabin baggage as we were being seated, we didn't talk at all during the flight. I myself fell into a pleasant doze after the glasses of white wine I'd had, mostly with my eyes closed.

I sat to her left in the window seat, and once we had our seatbelts on, she happened to touch my forearm. We were both travelling in short sleeves: I was just wearing a black t-shirt, she a floral-print dress with several buttons undone down the front since it had been so hot on the ground. To speak plainly: the brief touch of skin on skin shot like a bolt of desire through my body. All the way to Bodø I sat hoping to feel another such unexpected touch. Probably on account of the two glasses of wine, I went as far in my excited state as wondering whether the young woman's contact could have been intentional, and wasn't merely due to an unconscious movement of the arm. Because she had been touching me for as long as three or four seconds, I was quite sure of that. She didn't jump as though she'd received an electric shock and pull her hand back straight away; after a short while, brief, but still a while, she just moved it slowly and carefully back, leaving me with a deep longing for more. Or course I didn't look up at her. I acted as though I was asleep.

I don't mean to say I interpreted her unexpected closeness as an erotic proposition, not at all, and neither was that something I fantasised about, far from it. No, I sat for over an hour, waiting for her to once again touch me, a middle-aged man, so that I could experience a sense of human warmth or thoughtfulness – for though there is much hate and evil in the world, there's also a lot of kindness. The young woman had spoken with an unmistakeable northern dialect, and I began to imagine that northerners might be more tactile in their dealings with others than the majority of Norwegians – we are as a nation, after all, known for being chilly and reserved. I'm probably easily affected by wine, at least that early in the day, and perhaps that was why I sat there, holding onto the warmth in the hope she would put her hand on my arm again, and now, this time, leave it there for a whole minute.

I don't know why I'm telling you this. But I think it belongs in my story. Now I come to think of it, I've never been lavished with bodily contact. I don't touch my students, nor they me, though I notice from those around me that some contact between teachers and students is not unusual.

The last phase of my short marriage to Reidun was without physical contact. We went on sleeping in the same bed, we didn't have any other, but we spread out each in their own direction on the wide double bed, and never even nudged each other, aside from an arm that might accidentally be slung across in one's sleep, and which had to be replaced carefully; carefully to avoid waking the other.

I've sat down in this hotel room in Svolvær in order to conclude my story. It just so happened that Marianne and Sverre *did* come to Lofoten. Had there been no Lundins present, this finale would have been irrelevant and wouldn't have been included in this manuscript.

It's Monday, 1st July 2013, and I have just come back from Jon-Jon's funeral at Vågan Church, also known as Lofoten Cathedral. The nickname is not without grounds, as the over one-hundred-year-old cruciform timber church, with over twelve hundred seats, is one of the country's largest churches. During the old cod-fishing days, the area would have been bustling from January to April, and the fishermen needed this huge cathedral where they could gather for services.

Even up here in the north, it's suffocatingly hot. My hotel room, actually a whole suite, includes a spacious veranda with a view of the mountains to the west and north. But it's far too warm to sit on the veranda, and too bright to see what I'm writing on the computer screen.

*

In the summer of 1967, the 'Summer of Love' itself, Jon-Jon was a central figure in the dawning hippie movement in the capital, despite his tender age – he was only seventeen. When I met him a few years later, he was already a mythical character on the scene, a cult figure. I came from Ål – about as far from Haight-Ashbury as you can imagine – had found some colourful rags to wear, and made my entrance to the Nisseberget hippie scene.

Here too I was an outcast of course, but no more than I had been at home in Hallingdal. There I wasn't really an outsider, I was a reject. In Slottsparken I felt included.

For the first time I experienced a positive sense of belonging. Jon-Jon knew nothing about my upbringing or lack of family, nor did he ever ask, but if he had known, he almost certainly would have seen it as a plus. There were many people in Slottsparken who didn't live at home with their mothers and fathers, many had broken with their families and moved away. I knew nothing about Jon-Jon's background either, apart from what I could hear from his northern dialect.

Even if the hippie movement was more inclusive in many ways, certain codes and nuances still prevailed. If you didn't know Jon-Jon, or you hadn't at least heard of him, it was a real handicap. So before long I found my way into one of his ritual 'sit-ins', which meant assuming the lotus position and sharing the little pipe that was passed round as a sacrament. This was undoubtedly part of what saved my reputation in the few months I was part of that scene.

Being at Slottsparken at the beginning of the seventies was in many ways like being a member of a large family. As in other clans, the sense of belonging was almost total, and at that point, it was exactly what I needed: an anchor. You just had to get used to listening to a lot of nonsense. There was no censorship or other form of monopoly on opinion at Slottsparken; thoughts and opinions sprawled in all directions. If it weren't for the fact we spent most of our time sitting outdoors, I'd say we found ourselves in a broad church. And it was much harder to have reservations about certain practices. You didn't refuse a chillum or a joint.

Later, when I began to study Norwegian and read about Peer Gynt in the hall of the Mountain King, I immediately thought back to Nisseberget. Even the name of that little mound – 'pixie mountain' – was an ironic parallel. The main difference was that the Mountain King's hall, formed as it was by the mountain trolls, was only a fantasy, and so psychedelic enough, while Nisseberget, with all its hippie-pixies, actually existed in the world.

Occasionally, in the years after I belonged to the hippie movement, I would look up at Nisseberget and think how I – just like Peer Gynt – had let myself be enchanted and actually become one of these pixies. After a while I began to think the hippies were simply narrow-minded. They just sat around on the grass. Then came the harder stuff.

Marianne Lundin was introduced to the scene as Jon-Jon's girlfriend. She was at his side right from the summer of 1967, she too only seventeen years old. In their flowing robes the pair came to represent Oslo's 'summer of love', and their pictures even appeared in the papers once or twice as they became icons of Norwegian hippiedom.

As I've explained, we were like a big family. Everyone was friends with everyone else, and you weren't supposed to have any 'best friends'. I at least never heard that term used, not in my time. But aside from Marianne, Jon-Jon had one, and only one, close friend, almost a protégé, and that was Sverre.

Both Sverre and Jon-Jon had run away from home, Sverre from the south, and Jon-Jon from Lofoten. They arrived in the capital the same day, meeting by chance at Østbanes station, and from day one they were exactly what we would now call best friends. This was just weeks before Marianne and Jon-Jon met for the first time and immediately got together. Where he and she met – I mean, whereabouts in the city – I was never told.

One day Jon-Jon had her with him in the park, perhaps just hours after picking her up on a street corner in the city, which wouldn't have been unusual for the time we're talking about. But his friendship with Sverre went on as before and the three of them hung out together. Sverre, Marianne and Jon-Jon were like the three leaves of a clover, almost like a holy trinity, and that was how I met them four years later, when I came from Ål in Hallingdal to register as a student at the University of Oslo.

Just a few months after I came on the scene, Marianne threw herself into Sverre's arms. It wasn't that unusual for a little love to be spread around, and there were no ideological barriers to that kind of behaviour; indeed, quite the opposite. But Marianne never went back to Jon-Jon. From then on he was a lone wolf, and the arch-hippie was no longer part of the movement. Jealousy, hatred and lovesickness were hard to reconcile with the flower children's light-heartedness. I had also lapsed. For Marianne and Sverre the reverie went deeper, and they lasted longer.

It was during those early days after the break-up with Marianne that I met Jon-Jon alone several times. He too had begun to attend the university, but I don't think he ever got a degree. He just hung around, going to seminars here and there, moving from faculty to faculty. One time he gave me a tattered copy of Gurdjieff's book *Meetings with Remarkable Men*. On another occasion it was J. D. Salinger's *The Catcher in the Rye*.

Only once did Jon-Jon come to visit me in my digs at Kringsjå. How we ended up there, or under what pretext I got him to come over, I am unable to recall. But that was where he met Pelle. I haven't forgotten that.

When we got to the digs, I felt a kind of gentle tingling in my left arm telling me that Pelle wanted to meet him. I fetched him from his spot by the window, pulled him over my hand with a practiced motion, and in typical Pelle fashion, he lost no time in getting started, though he was careful to introduce himself as Jakop, since I'd already taken the name Pelle in this context. He said:

'Jakop here. And you?'

It was as though Pelle ignited a spark in Jon-Jon. I've since pondered whether it was because Jon-Jon had also experienced some of the same loneliness as me. In any case, he was with us from the first moment. I think they talked for over an hour, just long enough for me to feel it was time to stop, but they showed no signs of doing so. I felt they might at least have involved me in the conversation, but neither Pelle nor Jon-Jon let me join in, they were completely absorbed in one another. I started to feel irritated with their familiarity. To tell the truth I thought they'd crossed the line a little.

For me it was a real coup to have Jon-Jon visit me at my digs. What's more we had a bottle of spirits to drink. Then along came Pelle, stealing the limelight. In a fraction of a second I'd pulled him off my arm, and from that moment he was as quiet as a mouse. Jon-Jon found that immensely amusing. At least he didn't ask me to put Pelle back on my arm again. We started on the liquor.

It's hard to be sure, but I think that might have been the last time I saw him.

The last time Marianne and Sverre saw Jon-Jon was at a much-discussed leap year masquerade in Oslo, on 29th February 1976. It was in a huge villa on Dr Holms vei at the top of Holmenkollåsen. To be precise, it was the last time *anyone* saw the legendary hippie guru – until thirty-seven years later, when I attend his funeral and find out he's lived ever since as a fisherman and handyman at a little fishing station in Lofoten.

I myself didn't go to that masquerade. I was quite simply not invited. But I still occasionally met someone from the scene, and I heard several detailed accounts of what had happened – as well as a certain blossoming of idle speculation and rumour.

Jon-Jon had arrived at the masquerade in a blue blazer with silver buttons, and white cotton trousers with sharp creases. I realised he'd come dressed as Pelle. When I heard many days later exactly how he had looked, I felt flattered, but simultaneously bitter about not being there myself. I imagined that when Jon-Jon had gone and dressed up as Pelle, he was probably thinking I'd be there too. We were both outside of the hippie scene now, but funnily enough, these parties up on the hill were much more open than the airy gatherings down in Slottsparken. The borderline between hippie parties and the trendy western Oslo parties was becoming blurred.

At that time, Sverre and Jon-Jon never went to the same parties. It was an unwritten rule in the scene that if one came, the other shouldn't or couldn't turn up. Sverre never let Marianne out of his sight, and so she never met her old boyfriend any more.

But Jon-Jon went uninvited to this masquerade. He forced his way in. He was on a mission, people said.

It was a particularly wild party, making use of the whole of the enormous house, including the bedrooms. The host was nineteen-year-old Julia, who had the house to herself because her mother and father were on holiday in Florida.

Jon-Jon had a peculiarly charismatic, almost magnetic, personality. You always knew where he was at a party. However, at one point on this occasion someone asked where he was – they were still unsure of whether he and Sverre would collide – and now it turned out no one had seen him for a few hours. So people started looking, and it was Sverre in the end who found his rival lying on the floor under a large mahogany desk in the spacious library. It wasn't easy to see whether he was OK, because his head and shoulders were camouflaged with Marianne's red chiffon scarf.

The alarm was raised. What had he taken? And where was Marianne?

Sverre took hold of Jon-Jon, but soon realised it was only his blazer and white trousers lying under the table, and the clothes were stuffed with rags, which later turned out to be clothes from the laundry in the cellar.

Not until later that night did Marianne appear at the party again. She wasn't the only one who'd fallen asleep in one of the bedrooms. When she finally came down to the living room, her eyelids were still almost glued together.

So what had happened? What had she taken? Her cheeks were burning and it was unlikely she'd only been sleeping.

The theories on what had happened to Jon-Jon during the masquerade in Holmenkollen were many. It wouldn't have been unusual for him to just vanish from a gathering. Still, this disappearing act had to be counted as a spectacular performance. After all, where had he gone? Had he left in just his underwear? Did he perhaps go out into the winter night to die? Would he be discovered in the Nordmarka forest when spring came and the snows melted? Or had he been dressed in a different outfit as he stuffed his costume full of rags and shoved it under the table? He'd come to the party completely empty-handed, but perhaps he'd found a costume in one of the wardrobes? Earlier that evening there'd been several people who'd briefly seen a guest dressed in a military uniform, or to be specific, as a private in the Norwegian Army. Then this stranger was suddenly gone, and there was no one who'd come forward to claim that costume.

And after that, in the days that followed, speculation swirled. What had happened to Jon-Jon? Had he left the country? Where was he living now? In Australia or Argentina? There was a wave of such rumours. No one could rule out the suggestion that he'd been knocked off. But who would have had a motive for something like that?

The police arrived at the house early in the morning, and no one would admit to having called the cops. It certainly hadn't been Julia. Because she wasn't legally old enough to drink, the police felt it necessary to let her parents know about the wild party that had been going all night. You certainly couldn't describe the elegant mansion as untouched.

All the next day the laundry was pored over by a forensics team. But they found no trace of Jon-Jon, and if, as the police eventually also concluded, this was a voluntary departure, it could hardly be a coincidence that Jon-Jon had chosen to make his exit in this way.

After that, no one had seen or heard from Jon-Jon, and with time people in town started to say that he was dead. And then this death notice appeared in *Aftenposten* thirty-seven years later. I almost choked on my coffee.

After the leap year masquerade, Jon-Jon had travelled home to Lofoten, where he'd eked out a living as a fisherman and jack-of-all-trades in the years ever since. He no longer had any business in the capital. And as I was told at the funeral: at home in Skrova he was never known by any name but his Christian name, Johannes.

Beneath it all lay a boundless heartbreak.

Marianne was expecting a child that year, that much I found out before giving up contact with my old hippie friends altogether. I had become a promising academic by that point. That the baby had been a girl wasn't something I heard about. But it struck me when I read the death notice: so, it was a girl Marianne was carrying at that point. Sometimes our lives circle back on themselves. Threads that have been long forgotten can be woven into the fabric of life again.

Marianne and Sverre had no more children after that.

I walked the five kilometres from Svolvær to the Lofoten Cathedral. I walked along the combined cycle and pedestrian path that followed the highway. I could have taken a taxi, but I needed to collect my thoughts on the short epoch of my life that Jon-Jon represented. It was warm, but not unpleasantly so at that time of the morning, and the weather was beautiful.

I was very anxious as to whether I would meet Marianne and Sverre. I hadn't seen them in Svolvær, neither the evening before nor that morning. But they might fly up from Oslo to Svolvær via Bodø just for the day. I tried to look into the passing cars, but they were driving too fast on the straight stretch of road for me to be able to see who was in them.

I came to the crest of a little hill, and caught sight of another lonely male figure in a dark suit, perhaps five hundred metres in front of me. A little later I cast a look back, and a second black-clad man was walking half a kilometre behind. That meant the man behind me had me in his sights the whole time, and if the man in front turned and looked back, he would see I was walking behind him.

I don't know why, but at the thought of being one of three men dressed in black, walking along

the highway between the sea and the high mountains on the way to Jon-Jon's funeral in the Lofoten
Cathedral, I was suddenly gripped by a deep
sorrow. I've felt a certain melancholy many times
before, but here and now – as part of a painterly
procession, an image that wouldn't have been out
of place in one of Magritte's canvases – I felt caught
by a despair so intense I was scared of breaking
down.

I thought: I know I'm leaving. I'm already on my
way. I'm going to leave this world. This time. This
whole universe.

If you live a civilised life, you look in the mirror
many times a day, and even if you were to see your
own face just once a week, or once a month, it would
be often enough that you wouldn't notice your face
changing. However, there have been times when
I've passed a mirror, and simply because it has been
a passing glance, it has struck me that I've become a
man of over sixty.

It occurred to me that the closer I am pulled to a
final departure, the more miraculous the world of
human beings begins to seem.

And, paradoxically enough, perhaps because I
was en route to the church, I experienced a hopeless
longing for religion, something to lean on.

I felt dispirited. I felt unredeemed.

*

I entered the Lofoten Cathedral as the bells were beginning to chime, just minutes before the service got under way. There were many people there, but because the church was so large, everyone was gathered under the pulpit to the left of the aisle. On the podium in front of the altar rail stood the white coffin, topped with yellow and blue flowers.

I noticed that Marianne and Sverre sat to the far right of one of the pews. It wasn't the first time I'd seen them hunched together at a funeral.

Poor Jon-Jon, I thought. Poor all of us.

I passed Marianne and Sverre, and when they caught sight of me, they both stood up to give me a hug, one after the other. 'Pelle,' was all they said, 'Pelle.' I felt sure they'd already recognised me at Erik Lundin's funeral, and that the memorial service after Andrine's funeral only served to confirm this. But there they'd bet everything on age and the passing of time preventing me from recognising them.

It was a simple funeral, and I soon realised that this had come at Jon-Jon's own request. It was a minimal ceremony in ecclesiastical terms too. I got the impression the priest had gone further than most bishops would have accepted in relation to the funeral liturgy, or lack thereof, that the church could allow.

I listened to the priest's eulogy and for a few seconds considered the Norwegian word for cod: *torsk*.

Cod fishing had been an important part of Jon-Jon's life, but he had perhaps never considered that the word *torsk* goes back to the old Indo-European root **ters-* meaning 'to dry'. Because *torsk*, from the Old Norse *þorskr*, has since time immemorial been synonymous with *torr-fisk* 'dry-fish', which, in addition, is related to Germanic words for thirst, like Norwegian's *tørst* and German's *Durst*, or for that matter the Sanskrit word for thirst, *trishna*, as in the Buddha's 'life thirst', the very root of *duḥkha*, suffering. Suffering is brought to an end by quenching the life thirst. A prerequisite for this is that a person is liberated from their lack of insight, for it is this that causes the life thirst. Not until this liberation does *nirvana* occur, the 'extinguishing' of this life thirst.

The Buddha in Benares and Jon-Jon in Lofoten. But they touched upon one another, both in Slottsparken, and at home in Skrova. I wished so keenly that they really could have met. They would have had so much to talk about.

*

If the service itself was simple, what followed was so impressive I still feel moved. The coffin was borne out of the church by six men dressed in black. Once outside, it was slid into a hearse, which soon began to drive slowly down the steep slope in front of the church with a huge funeral procession in tow. The black car crossed the highway and continued at a gentle pace into and through the vast graveyard, right up to the opposite end of the churchyard. After the hearse snaked a long procession of mourners, before the car stopped just a few metres from the grave that had been prepared for Jon-Jon. Again, I must say: painterly, but in black.

It was only natural that Marianne, Sverre and I should stay together. Now it was we three who were the clover leaf. As far as I could tell, we were the only hippies in attendance. Though it's not easy to tell that kind of thing once one has turned sixty. Sverre had the red ruby in his earlobe, that was the only relic that could be traced back to our colourful existence in the seventies.

After the burial, which also pushed the limits of what the bishop would have accepted, coming as it did without any promises of resurrection, the priest drew out a piece of paper and read a short message from Jon-Jon himself. No written text was distributed of course, so I am recording this last greeting from memory:

Thanks to everyone who has followed me back to nature. You have once again laid me in the strange treasure trove from which we were all brought forth. Outside that treasure trove I've been able to sample this world and something of its times. Now I have been gently returned.

There is a great degree of justice in what has happened. I have lived my life on credit. All the while I have known that my existence has been a loan that must be paid back at exactly face value.

But I am in good company, for we are all just as insolvent. Regardless of what we make of our lives, we can never buy ourselves out of this debt we carry with us like a shadow.

In light of this, I beg your forgiveness for the lack of invitation to a memorial service after this funeral. At times like this, there is a tendency for many ambiguous words to be spoken, and I am no longer here to contradict them.

As some among you may remember, I have in my life aired lofty visions of other worlds, on the lives after this one and on the transmigration of souls. I have found an antidote to such delusions here in Lofoten. I have come back to myself. I no longer believe in other worlds or lives after this one. So please spare me false words of any such hopes today. Let the furrows left by my plough grow in peace and with grace.

But smile! Don't worry! Peace on earth!
  And we'll say no more.
   The End

Many of us were crying openly. Marianne broke down completely, and in a flash I could see her as a young girl again. I noted that the muscles in Sverre's face were stiff and tense.

They had ordered a taxi in advance. Perhaps they'd known there would be no memorial service. And perhaps they were glad.

I sat in it with them on the way back to Svolvær, and we exchanged a few words about the old days. We didn't mention Jon-Jon at all, but I asked them to say hello to Ylva from me. I thought it completely natural, since it was just a few weeks since we'd met in Gotland.

They looked at me a little strangely when I asked. Sverre's face remained fixed.

Soon after that I arrived back in the hotel, where I have been sitting, writing these lines to you.

Now I return to my desk after a long break. I went into the town and made a couple of rounds along the quayside and through the narrow streets before sitting down in the hotel's restaurant and eating fresh shrimps with crusty bread, mayonnaise and lemon while looking out across the square with its motley street life. Here, the white gulls did the same sort of clearing-up job as the black jackdaws in Visby.

The southbound Coastal Express had moored in Svolvær from 6:30 until 8:30, and for a few hours the number of people on the streets had doubled. Now the ship had sailed further south towards Stamsund and Bodø, and a strange calm fell over Lofoten's capital, though it lasted only an hour before the northbound Coastal Express arrived at nine o'clock, and new hoards of tourists thronged the streets.

I sat there in the restaurant, enjoying the way the visitors took over the town. And then again, at ten o'clock, a glorious calm fell over Svolvær as the Coastal Express continued up towards Trollfjorden and Stormarknes. The stalls on the square were packed up, the shops closed. But in spite of the late hour, the sky was still light, the sun shining. The sun wouldn't set over Svolvær that night.

I've taken a seat out on the veranda. The sun is in the north-west, but it's still almost unbearably hot in the sunlight. I sit here with a cup of whisky, thinking through everything I remember from the seventies. I try to figure out what I might have forgotten. But my thoughts soon sweep over recent years too. I think about Grethe Cecilie and about you. And in my mind I see Truls falling headfirst into the well.

Old ever-young Jon-Jon lives no more. His first love and his best friend came to visit only after everything was over. I think about Ylva and the ravens, Huginn and Muninn, who see everything, and old Professor Lundin who sits now in eternal colloquia with Odin, discussing the life of human beings down on earth, and the precarious balance of power between gods and giants, and the powers of good and evil.

It's approaching midnight. Even though both Coastal Express ships have passed, there's still life in this Lofoten town, which is bathed in the ever-more golden light from the sun. It's warm, warm. There's a heatwave, just like on Gotland. And here there's the midnight sun too. Down on the square, people are skipping along in shorts and t-shirts. I see in them something strangely pompous and puppet-like. It's as though everything is objectified, like characters on a stage. It's as though something is about to happen.

I feel an irresistible desire to go back to the square, and all at once I'm there again, just one among many strutting figures.

I hear a ship's horn, turn to follow the sound, and see, to my surprise, that a new Coastal Express has docked, the MS *Polarbjørn*. I know there's no ship with that name – Polar Bear – and neither should a ship be docking at this time of the day, of course not; nowhere along the coast do more than two Coastal Express boats stop per day, one southbound and one northbound. But the ship that has docked has the Coastal Express logo on its horn, just like the other ships in the fleet.

The gangway is extended, but no one comes ashore from the ship this time. Instead, people in the town begin to board. Everyone on the streets joins this collective boarding, and while they tramp aboard ship, they gesticulate and conduct intense conversations. I spy the contours of Marianne and Sverre as they enter the ship, so they must have missed their flight. From the mass of talking puppets I hear words and fragments of sentences such as: 'no one can say what the Big Bang was', 'the moment of creation' and 'the age of the trilobites'. I also hear some interesting characteristics of the Proto-Indo-European language from five or six thousand years ago, and what's more, a bunch of good examples of inherited words that really *are* that old, and which can be found throughout the whole Indo-European area: *I, you, two, much, heart, warm, woman*. It's as if these scraps of inherited words transcend and become a unit, joining together to form an intense aggregate of opinion.

I'm afraid of being left in Svolvær, or of being left behind; soon I'm the only person still standing in the square. The town is empty, there's no one on the streets, at the restaurant tables or up on the verandas. I no longer have any choice, I too must board the ship, the MS *Polarbjörn*, though the name can't be noted in any shipping register, so it must be an apocryphal vessel.

I cast a look behind me and see that this small Lofoten town has been completely emptied of people, as through struck by a plague.

Aboard ship, people have formed groups out on the sun deck, in the café, the restaurant, the library, the bar and the large lounge up on the top deck. People around me are talking. They are talking about all possible subjects, a whole range relating to ontology, astrophysics and evolutionary biology. But people are also making small talk about everyday things; they are playing cards, solving crosswords and sudoku.

I continue to familiarise myself with the ship. Out on the promenade deck, two young women come walking towards me, arm in arm. They've both been my students, but not in the same year, so it's strange to see them together, thick as thieves. Both girls are wearing bright summer dresses, one yellow, the other blue. Together they seem like a bicoloured flower, to be more specific, a violet.

'Jakop!' one of them says as she catches sight of me, it's the one named Anne.

'Pelle!' the other says. Her name is Britt and she was a student the year I brought Pelle in as a pedagogical aid to liven up my New Norwegian grammar classes.

Both have sparkling blue eyes. It's as though they come from another reality and have brought with them an extrasensory gaze.

'What are you going to teach us today?' one of them asks with an infectious smile.

'Something *visionary*, please,' the other begs.

And I tell them how we can find examples of the Indo-European root *weid-* for 'to see' over much of the Indo-European region, as in the Greek word *idea* and *eidos* for 'appearance' or 'visible form', from which come the loanword *idea* and words such as *ideal* and *idealism*, and in Latin *videre* for 'to see', leading to *vision* or *visionary*.

Then I add: '*Quod erat demonstrandum!*'

The one who said she wanted something visionary puts her hand to her mouth and suppresses a yawn. But I won't be put off. I just go on with my lecture:

'When we "have seen" something, we might say we "are *wise*" to it. That word too stems from the Indo-European root **weid-*, meaning "to see", but now from the perfect form, as with the Sanskrit *veda*, which is the name of the holy scriptures; *vide* in Danish, *vite* in Norwegian, and *wissen* in German, all meaning "to know", the last of which gives us *Wissenschaft* or "science" and, in English, *wit* and *wisdom*, and accordingly, *wizard*.

I make a little bow and walk further on along the promenade deck. I'm in need of a cane. Out here on deck it would have been most fitting to have had a thin walking cane.

Behind me I hear one of the young women say: 'He's lost his mind.' And the other replies: 'Perhaps he's drowned in his own wisdom.'

The ship weighs anchor, backs out and sails south-west along the Lofoten Wall. South of the island of Moskenes, a westerly course is set, out across the open sea. We cross the whirlpools and eddies of the fabled Moskstraumen, and the ship rocks and writhes; bottles and coffee cups tinkle nervously, as on a car ferry, then it heads due west, out into the Norwegian Sea, which is now perfectly calm – never has a sea been calmer. We aren't moving towards the sunset, as there is no sun setting in the west: the sun hangs in the north, on the starboard side of the ship, continuing its 360 degree troll's dance through the time-addled summer's day.

I walk around the crowded ship and look about. The heated discussions are continuing, and I begin after a while to recognise some of the passengers. I noticed Marianne and Sverre as they boarded the ship. Now they're sitting in the panorama lounge, each holding a red cocktail, and Marianne has an oxeye daisy in her hair. We nod to one another, but I go on up to the sundeck.

I immediately lay eyes on Jon-Jon. He's wearing the old Afghan coat, just like back in Slottsparken, and is surrounded by a large group of young people dressed in billowing, colourful garments. He catches sight of me, puffing on a pipe filled with sweet hash, and waves at me cheerfully, as though we'd seen each other only yesterday rather than many, many years ago. The years have passed, but time and space are no longer absolute quantities, there are corridors criss-crossing not only space, but also time. I think of something Jon-Jon said on this very subject back in the seventies. He'd been reading Aldous Huxley's *The Doors of Perception* and Arthur Koestler's *The Roots of Coincidence*.

I don't see it as a contradiction that I was at Jon-Jon's funeral just a few hours previously. Some are living, some are dead, that's just how it is, but there's no sharp distinction between those living now and those who have toppled over the edge and are gone. Whole generations don't just fall away the way whole mountains can sometimes collapse into the sea creating huge tidal waves that wash away everything in their path, leaving no trace. We die one by one, alone, often at home, in our own bedrooms, on our own pillow, always with a web of memories behind us, stories of simple things, minor tales that are eventually lost, but for a time they survive, side by side and in among those left behind.

The essential difference is not between living and dead. There is another difference between people, which is much more important. Most people, alive or not, have one another, or have *had* one another – usually a little of each. They both *have* and *have had* family and friends. Yet I see myself once again as an outsider. Even aboard MS *Polarbjörn* I'm a stowaway. I'm not part of the social fabric of those now living and those who once lived. It was only as a result of an anomalous arm movement that the young woman on the flight happened to touch my arm.

While I still have the sweet scent of Jon-Jon's chillum in my nostrils, I think of you, Agnes. You were right. I have to stop leaning on others. Now I feel it myself; I can no longer bear the thought of being the uninvited guest in other people's lives.

I begin to walk from one end of the ship to the other, first at random, but then more systematically.

In the bar on the top deck stands Professor Erik Lundin, giving an informal lecture on Odin in myths and cults:

'. . . *Though the name of this god is also found beyond the Nordic region, the sources don't allow us to view our Odin as anything other than a genuinely Nordic deity . . . When something is original, it soon becomes a simplification of its unique qualities if one merely forces it into a schema, á la the French philologist Georges Dumézil . . .*'

In the library, Andrine Siggerud sits wearing her taxi uniform, reading to a group of listeners from the quirky book *Tales from the Back Seat*. The audience are grinning and laughing, they recognise themselves in many of the situations the author describes, and they're having a wonderful time.

I go down to the café on the fifth deck, where I find the Lundin cousins talking intimately. Ylva looks up at me and waves with two fingers, but she turns back to her cousin and picks up the thread of the conversation they're deeply engaged in. I hear her exclaim: '*The orgasm, yes, that's it!*'

But soon I've had enough of this cousinliness, and I poke my head into the little conference room, which is crammed full of people. People on the ship are not a grey mass: quite the opposite; each one glitters with personality and individuality to the point where it's almost painful on the eyes. It strikes me that nearly everyone I see is from the funerals I've visited. That might be the reason so many of them nod at me as I pass. But I also notice people I've only seen two-dimensional pictures of in a funeral's order of service.

At the front, on the podium, Runar Friele is giving a presentation using PowerPoint. It's an overview of American films and musicals from the fifties. Runar praises Doris Day, both as a singer and an actor. It's as though he knew her personally. He talks about the old star as though she were a close friend. 'Doris,' he says.

I feel restless from all the talking. I begin to walk around the ship again. There's something I've begun to look for. It strikes me that the ship I'm on is eternity itself. This is where I will find everything I'm searching for.

Every deck is thronged with people. I run into people I haven't seen since I lived in Ål in Hallingdal. In the bar on the eighth deck, Mother sits, knitting with a few other women, all from Hallingdal. She isn't the slightest bit surprised to see me. She just waves to me cheerfully, now we're on a boat trip together, far from Ål.

On the promenade deck, Father stands with a group of men, fishing with a rod over the railing. He doesn't notice me, and I don't approach him either. There are limits.

The thought strikes me that if the whole of humanity is on board this ship, or at least that section of humanity I've met, you must also be here somewhere. I try to think logically, because now I'm set on trying to find you. I think you probably wouldn't be in a large crowd. Perhaps you're up at the bow, watching the direction the ship is headed.

I know the promenade deck passes all the cabins and continues through a narrow opening in front of the two balcony suites up at the bow. I make for that point, and find you there. You're not surprised when I come to stand alongside you. I feel expected and welcome.

The sea is still perfectly calm, almost dead, and the sun maintains its grip on the summer's night, its privilege. The air is still warm, very warm.

You lay a hand on my bare forearm. But I feel nothing. You try to grasp harder. But I can't feel that either.

'Agnes,' I say, or perhaps I only think it.

You look up at me and smile. At the same time we both get the feeling the ship is no longer touching the water. It's now floating in mid-air. But still it travels due west.

'Agnes,' I say again. 'Do you think we'll be able to tear ourselves from this vessel of death and find a way back to life?'

Agnes

S ome time mid-morning I'm awoken by a banging on my hotel-room door.

Had I been dreaming? Or had I been sitting there
typing on my laptop until late at night before finally
crawling into bed?

I look over at an empty whisky bottle by one of
the narrow windows that stretch from floor to ceil-
ing, with tall, rugged mountains in the background.
I think I can sense, far back in my head, how empty
that bottle is.

I can also see Pelle, as cheerful as ever. The little
joker is leaning back against the window alongside
the whisky bottle, almost like a twin brother – to the
bottle, that is.

My body is telling me I've been out on the ocean
on my ghost ship. In the end I was standing with you
in the bow of the MS *Polarbjörn*. I turned to you and
asked whether there was any way of escaping this
dismal predicament we were in.

I hear the person banging on the door saying my name, and it's your voice I hear. Am I still aboard the apocryphal Coastal Express ship? If so, I must have been given the presidential cabin.

But I get out of bed, put on the hotel bathrobe, stagger across the floor and open the door to the corridor outside. You're standing there right in front of me, Agnes. In Svolvær, in Lofoten!

The last time I saw you was in the car on the way home from Arendal a few months previously, and we hadn't been in touch since. But I'd had you in my thoughts all the time, and in the café that time I did suggest I might write to you to explain how I'd turned up at your sister's funeral, rather than going into that troublesome subject in the car on the way back to Oslo. It was too much, I thought, to go through in the car – truth be told, explaining would mean talking about my whole life. It was too soon. I needed more distance, more time. And there was something else too: since I was driving the car, I couldn't let Pelle do the talking for me.

You see how astonished I am, and surely also how drunk I am. The very first thing you say is that you've come to talk to Pelle. In the midst of all the confusion, you also manage to explain that of course this meeting is no coincidence.

As soon as Marianne and Sverre had dropped me off in Svolvær and continued in the taxi to the airport, Marianne had rung the family and told them about their encounter with Pelle at the funeral of a mutual friend from their hippie days in the early seventies, and that Pelle, or Jakop, which was his real name, would be spending a few days in Svolvær, writing something, as he'd put it.

Truls hadn't hesitated to ring you. He knew that you also happened to be in Lofoten, assuming you weren't already on your way home to Oslo. But he got hold of you in Stamsund a few dozen kilometres south of Svolvær, just as you were about to board the southbound Coastal Express on the way home, and that, *that* is the only major coincidence in this tale. Though of course it's debatable how surprising it is to bump into friends and acquaintances in Lofoten while the midnight sun is at its highest point. I myself didn't have the imagination to see this encounter as anything other than a trick of fate.

As you said later that day, it was no secret among the family that you wanted to meet me again, something Ylva had also hinted in Visby only weeks previously. But why had *you* been in

Lofoten? In Stamsund? You still didn't want to tell me that.

In any case, here you were. You looked up at this drunken soul and were quick to emphasise that it was Pelle you'd come to see, not me.

I can't help admitting that this sentence hurt a little. But it didn't come completely without warning. You'd made me promise you'd get to meet Pelle again. And it wasn't me you'd fallen for in Arendal. It was Pelle, my best friend, and from that moment on, my rival too.

You headed over to him and picked him up without making a big deal of the empty bottle. You passed him to me and, believe me, I was quick to pull him over my hand and forearm. Pelle started talking straight away. It was like pouring beans from a sack.

I must add that due to my hangover I was having difficulty talking myself. That got me thinking about how the literal meaning of the Buddhist word for 'suffering', the Sanskrit *duhkha*, is 'a wheel or hub that turns badly' and that's exactly how I felt now. My axles were out of sync.

So it was liberating to let Pelle do the talking. I was lucky to be blessed with such a ready deputy. Pelle never has a hangover. He hadn't so much as touched a drop. Now he held forth with crystal clarity, and stunning sobriety. He said:

'Well met, Agnes!'

You immediately broke into a grin. You lit up.

'Well met indeed!' you replied.

Now Pelle got right to the point. Without any hesitation he took up the subject from Arendal, and this time he was unstoppable:

'When we met last time, you said you weren't married. Right? But how's your love life? Do you have a boyfriend or a partner?'

You shook your head, and I thought I detected a sad expression flitting across your features. But you didn't reply.

'But you have *been* married?'

You shook your head again. You said:

'Perhaps I am still married . . .'

My wrist quivered:

'You were never divorced? You just went your separate ways?'

But you shook your head a third time, and I thought I could see you were suffering. The questions that had been raining down on you were obviously not easy to answer.

'Agnes,' Pelle said then, and for once I approved of his intent: 'Tell me your story!'

*

We sat on the edge of the bed, you to my right, and I with Pelle over my left arm. You looked Pelle in the eye and began to speak.

You told us you'd been married to Marc for many years. Towards the end of the time you'd lived together, he'd worked as an archaeologist in the town of Sóller in Mallorca. You were working as a psychotherapist in Oslo, and during that time you travelled up and down to Mallorca during your holidays or on long weekends, or he would come up to Oslo.

On 11 May several years ago, Marc was pulled away from you in the crowds attending the festival *Es Firó de Sóller*, also known as *Moros i Cristians*, which commemorates the victory of the Christian Mallorcans over the pirates of North Africa, the Moros – that is the Moors, or Muslims, back in 1561. All the inhabitants of the town had taken to the streets, and children and adults alike were dressed in simple national costumes. Many of the men were blacked up, dressed in wide pantaloons and carrying swords and blunderbusses. They were the pirates. Cans of beer and big plastic glasses of sangria were being waved around, and from early morning on, the air was filled with the bang of firecrackers, as well as the heavy boom of bombs exploding. All day long, the local people took the tram between Sóller and the seaside village of Port de Sóller, or they walked back and forth along the tracks. The battle between the 'Moros' and the 'Cristians' was to take place in the little seaside village at midday.

I won't go into any more of that here. But: in all the chaos and the crowds, Marc was pulled away from you. You searched for him, walking for hour after hour, but you haven't seen him since.

Pelle remained calm, and allowed the story to sink in; he behaved in an exemplary manner, I must say. You'd talked for a long time, and he'd made no move to interrupt. It wasn't until this point in the story that he began to ask questions. He said:

'You must have had mobile phones? Didn't you try to call him?'

'Try?! You know, sometimes I still dial his number.'

I felt my wrist strain.

'Did you report him missing? Were there no police on duty that day? Wasn't there someone who could help you look for him?'

At this point you smiled exaltedly, Agnes, or perhaps it would be more accurate to write, theatrically. You said:

'Yes, the village was crawling with police, and I ran from officer to officer. They thought I was crazy.

I spoke relatively fluent Catalan, but they thought I was a crazy tourist.'

'Why?'

'There were huge crowds, and everyone was packed into a small space. Try to imagine someone losing contact with a companion on Karl Johan Gate on 17 May. Or on Petersplassen on Easter Sunday . . .'

'But afterwards? The party must have finished at some point.'

'And he didn't turn up. We lived in a little apartment up in the town, but he never came home. The rest of that evening and night he didn't come home. Each unbearable hour, every single minute, he didn't come home. Marc never came back.'

At one point I thought Pelle was being rather pitiless. It was completely unnecessary to go on as rapidly with his train of thought as he did. He said:

'Of course he could have used the big festival as an opportunity to run away from you. Perhaps these days he's living under an assumed name in Australia or Latin America. You said you'd been living separately for the past few years. Could there have been someone else? Could he have run away with her?'

Your mouth fell open. You just sat there, staring

at Herr Skrindo, but now I think that for the first time you were a little irritated by him. I certainly was.

On the whole, Pelle's a good guy. The problem is that he can be shamelessly direct. He says things others only think, and keep to themselves. To put it plainly, I've sometimes wondered if he has a touch of Asperger's syndrome.

When you didn't answer, he just went on with his inquisition:

'Was there never any police investigation?'

You nodded: 'But the police wouldn't touch it before many days had passed after *Es Firó*. Or as they put it: "It wouldn't be the first time the festival lasted several days for some people," and Marc wasn't the only one who hadn't headed straight home to his own bed.'

'The insolence!'

Insolence? *He* could talk!

But Pelle just went on: 'Pigs!'

I think he only said that to please the lady he was talking to. She continued:

'What's more, Marc had made a name for himself in the town. The police knew who he was. He was from Palma, but had worked on a number of important digs in the town. People have been living in Mallorca for many thousands of years: Phoenicians,

Romans, Vandals, Moors . . .'

It was as though a lightbulb lit up in Pelle's head. I felt my wrist jerk, so hard that it hurt for a long time afterwards. He said:

'Did he have any enemies?'

You laughed bitterly, Agnes. You sat there, looking down, looking twenty years younger than you are.

Pelle kept going:

'Could someone have kidnapped him?'

You looked straight at him again and answered loud and clear.

'Yes!' you said.

'But did anyone have a motive?'

You said: 'Working as the leader of archaeological digs can mean that people like Marc get into conflict with business interests and developers of various kinds. The discovery of an old hairpin can be enough to stop the construction of a hotel complex. Marc sometimes talked to me about this kind of thing. Someone could well have used the opportunity that day either to kidnap him or . . .'

You drew a deep breath, but then continued:

'Or to shoot him, with the sound well camouflaged by all the bangs and explosions that day. There was a whole battle going on down in Port de

Sóller, where we were before he disappeared. But no trace was ever found of him. The disappearance was never explained.'

'But they did investigate it?'

'Well yes, in the end it became a big police investigation. Then the case was closed. I suspect that in the end, the detectives came to the same conclusion as you did initially. I guess they thought Marc had vanished of his own free will. There have been examples of disappearing acts like that. But Marc and I lived together for many years, and were very close to one another.'

I felt a strange slackness in my left wrist and interpreted it as Pelle feeling a sincere empathy for you.

He said: 'What do you think now?'

You seemed to be weighing the question up: 'I have no way of knowing if Marc is alive or not. So I have no way of saying whether I *have been* married to him, or still am. But I've decided that I won't start a relationship with anyone else. Perhaps Marc is locked up somewhere. I can never be sure he won't return.'

You got up from the bed and walked over to the tall, narrow windows with their view of rugged peaks to the north and north-west. For some reason or other, you started kicking the empty whisky bottle, but only so much that it didn't tip. It was hard to tell whether you even realised what your left foot was touching, you certainly weren't looking down at it. Your thoughts were somewhere else altogether.

I hadn't pulled Pelle off my arm, but he was clearly moved by the situation and didn't say a word.

You sat down on the edge of the bed again. At that point, Pelle could no longer wait. He spoke up once more, and I thought he expressed himself coarsely, just to make that clear.

'Dear lady,' he said. 'I think it is best to say you may still be married. That is to say, I take you at your word.'

You had already begun to smile again. You looked at Pelle, measuring him with your gaze, and were surely wondering what he was about to say.

He went on: 'Now here is an honest man who also lives alone. His name is Jakop and he won't be asking for your hand any time soon. He's simply offering good companionship for the short time allotted to us on this earth. And should your archaeologist pop up again like a jack in the box, or like human beings rose up from the ashes of the titans, our lady here can be confident that he'll have tact enough to pack his things and never show his face again.'

I was on the verge of tearing Pelle off my arm, as I felt a strong aversion to the way he'd expressed himself. But at the same time I allowed myself to graze on his concern for my welfare, this time focusing on the stage of life I was at: I was no longer a young man.

You now did the only sensible thing you could have done in that situation – it's something I've been thinking about all day. You kicked the ball into our half. Effective tackling, if you ask me. You nodded at me before once again turning to Pelle:

'But he's been married too. What's the story there?'

How could you ask about it, Agnes, *so* directly? But of course it wasn't me you were asking. It was Pelle. And it became something altogether different. He'd been at least as direct towards you. What kind of mutual respect could there be between you unless you were as immediate and direct as he was?

Pelle looked up at you. I felt a quivering in my wrist, but I had no idea what he would answer. I was just relieved I didn't have to answer for myself. He said:

'Classic love triangle, my dear. Reidun was her name, and such a meddler as you never saw.'

'A meddler?'

'For the first couple of years of the marriage, I was kept mostly in a drawer along with all the cigar boxes . . .'

'Cigar boxes? No, now I'm not following you.'

My wrist twisted:

'Oh, never mind about them.'

'Well, go on?'

'I lived there with these boxes deep in a huge wardrobe, and very occasionally, when Reidun wasn't home, he would take me out and have a little chat with me. Those were some loooong years.'

You smiled, Agnes:

'I can imagine that. But you said the lady was "a meddler"?'

'"Such a meddler as you never saw", I said. It was his wardrobe, and the drawers were his personal drawers. A certain degree of private life is to be expected in a marriage, not to mention in a wardrobe. But the woman he was married to was such a meddler that one day she found both me and the cigar boxes. We were carefully concealed under a good layer of gentlemen's undergarments. That's why I say she was a meddler.'

'And how did she react to what she found?'

'She was incensed. When the gentleman currently sitting alongside you came back from work, he was met by Reidun in the doorway. She held me crumpled in her hand, had a bitter expression and thrust me forth with an accusing gesture. As though she was holding Jakop responsible for my very existence.'

'And what did he do?'

'Did he have any choice? He resolutely pulled me over his arm and put all his money on me being able to talk him out of the embarrassing situation we found ourselves in. It was no longer just the two of them living in the apartment. All of a sudden there were three of us.'

Your face was one big smile. It wasn't hard to see what a sucker you were for him. You said:

'But what happened? Did you manage to calm her down?'

'Not in the slightest, my dear lady! I talked as well as I could, but the woman was raging. I was extremely generous with my compliments, went on about her beautiful eyes, declared them to be like two beautiful jewels, that sometimes glittered like stars in the night sky, but it was no use. The thing she had the most disdain for was my voice. She said Jakop was putting it on for my sake, but it's not true, I've always had this very same voice. At that, the lady took a wrestling hold of me and tore me right off his arm. She said she wanted to throw me in the bin.'

This last detail really struck you, Agnes. At least, you raised your hand to your mouth and gave a little gasp.

Pelle nodded to me and said:

'But this noble man pleaded on my behalf. He said I'd been living with him since he was a child, and in the end he was allowed to put me back in the cupboard with a solemn promise not to take me out again.'

My arm was worn out. The rest of me felt pretty rough too. So I took Skrindo off and laid him carefully on the bed.

You said you'd been witness to a little puppet show. I think you called it exceptional. I couldn't make out what you meant.

You also pointed out that Reidun must have struggled with poor self-esteem since she'd been capable of losing her wits over a hand puppet.

I agreed on this last point. Reidun had some fine qualities. But she did have poor self-esteem. I guess you were also able to say that from a psychotherapeutic perspective.

And so you and I were left sitting there a while, with no one but ourselves and each other. But we were more awkward now that Pelle wasn't along for the ride any more.

I was incapable of saying anything at all. But I was thinking hard. It's strange how sometimes it's possible to be completely incapable of speaking, but still be mentally agile.

I thought about everything I had on my laptop, about the whole story I'd written for you, but also *about* you, Agnes. You still hadn't read any of it.

Wasn't it odd to think that we were sitting together on the edge of a bed in Lofoten? You and I! There was no other furniture in the room besides the big bed. It was only in the room alongside that there was a suite with a sofa that could be turned into an extra bed.

You were the one to break the silence at last. You stood up and announced that Pelle was 'absolutely priceless'. You reminded me it was him you had come to visit, and that you were still living, body and soul, in the hope Marc would return. It had been eight years since he disappeared.

You had once again positioned yourself by one of the narrow windows. With your back to me you spoke of why you were in Lofoten. When Truls rang you the previous evening, you were in Stamsund, where you'd been visiting the Nordland Visual Theatre. You thought it was fascinating that there was such a great centre for puppet theatre in a little fishing settlement in Lofoten.

It occurred to me that you had also mentioned something about puppet theatre when we met in Arendal. That was how you and the marine researcher had become acquainted during your time at university. The two of you had both been involved in setting up *Pinocchio* – the Student Union Puppet Theatre.

You said you thought you might have some plans for Pelle, and that of course you understood that this would also involve me. The whole thing was too complicated to go into now, you maintained. It was something you'd need to spend a little time figuring out. But it had to be decided that very day. That was why you'd stayed the night in Stamsund before taking a taxi up to Svolvær.

You turned to me again.

'And perhaps you should take a shower,' you said. I thought it was fair, given the whisky bottle.

But in the same breath you nodded over at the adjoining room and added: 'Can I stay here tonight? There's not a single hotel room free in this whole town.'

I'm unclear as to whether I gave an answer, or whether I just nodded. But I got in the shower, and you mentioned, as if in passing, that you were going down to the square to get a coffee and a pastry. You talked as though you were already staying here.

What you didn't say, but which I soon felt sure of, was that these potential 'plans' you had for Pelle would be dependent on how well the two of us got along that day. I had a feeling I was about to sit some kind of exam, and that it applied only to me, not to Pelle – he'd already passed.

I realised as I stood in the shower that I'd already begun to get exam nerves, and that the night's excesses, plus nerves, made a bit of an unfortunate combination.

Both at Hallingdal High School and at the University of Oslo I'd got good grades. It wasn't that surprising, because I was a dedicated student, or *prae céteris*, in Latin: 'before the others'. But I've not always passed the tests of the school of life.

We agreed to go for a walk while we talked. Since, as one of us said, it's often easier to have a proper conversation while you're walking than when you're sitting face to face. I added that this kind of consideration had never made any difference to Pelle. It was as though he was out for a stroll as soon as he was on my arm. Soon I was once again out on the tarmacked cycle-and-pedestrian path along the E10 highway. I wanted to show you the Lofoten Cathedral, and I'd asked you to join me for lunch in Kabelvåg.

Today there were no men dressed in black on the path. It struck me that walking along with another person is quite different to being one of three black-clad men who've never met, walking at a distance of half a kilometre from one another, each weighed down by dark mountains.

I saw it as a blessing to walk alongside you, Agnes. You'd insisted that Pelle should come along too. Now he was lying in my black knapsack, and several times you asked to speak to him, perhaps at points when our own conversation stalled. It was impossible to ignore the fact that you and Pelle had better chemistry than the two of us. Even I noticed that.

Pelle has always seen the sunny side, and I suppose I myself have, for the most part, lived in the shadows. But I've had that sunny side too. I've had Pelle.

One of the first things we talked about as the cars rushed by was Marianne and Sverre, who'd spent the previous day at the funeral of a friend from their youth.

'Who was also a friend of yours?' you asked.

I answered in the affirmative. But you didn't let it go so easily:

'Someone you really knew?'

'Yes, yes,' I insisted. 'All four of us knew each other – Marianne, Sverre, Jon-Jon and I.'

I told her that Jon-Jon was from these parts, and no sooner had I said it, than we passed a sign pointing the way down to the pier from which a ferry went out to Skrova. I said that Jon-Jon came from a fishing village out there.

From the point your cousin joined the Lundin family almost thirty years ago, you'd known that Marianne and Sverre had had a career as hippies of the most perseverant kind, and I talked a little about my impressions from the few months I myself sat in on that scene.

You, however, hadn't heard of Jon-Jon before Truls rang you the previous day. And yet you were the one to update me on the final racy detail in relation to that – again, something that had come to your cousin's attention over the course of the last few days.

A few days after Jon-Jon's death was announced in the paper, Ylva had visited her childhood home in Berg. Only Marianne was home. On an old escritoire, alongside a new death notice, there lay a couple of yellowed newspaper clippings from the end of the sixties, and one of them was a hippie picture of Marianne and Jon-Jon from the time the two of them were together.

Ylva had only cast a glance at this photograph before turning to her mother and saying: 'That's my biological father!' And she'd picked up the death notice, put her hand to her mouth and exclaimed: 'And now he's dead?'

Marianne hadn't made any attempt to refute or call into question Ylva's assertion. The two of them sat together out in the garden for a long time. When Sverre came home, Ylva had thrown her arms around his neck and cried.

Of course, you'll remember just as well as me that we talked about everything I'm relating now on our long stroll along the highway. But still, I'm including it in my story so that, should anyone else come to read it one day, they will understand it too. And in fact I still haven't decided whether I'm going to let you read anything at all. So far I haven't breathed a word of the fact that I'll soon have written a whole book about my exploits. It has occurred to me that I may well be writing as much to myself as addressing you.

As you know, we talked about a whole range of other matters I won't bring up here. And a few times we sat at the side of the road so you could have a chat with Pelle. On one occasion you frightened a whole flock of gulls into the air with one of your peals of laughter.

I showed you the Lofoten Cathedral before we crossed the road and walked to Jon-Jon's grave right up in the furthermost corner of the churchyard. The wooden cross bore only the words Johannes Skrova, along with his dates of birth and death. The flowers were still fresh.

I spoke of Jon-Jon's last message, which the priest had read after the burial. I think it really made an impression on you.

And I got Pelle out of the bag and placed him by the cross. I thought it wouldn't be fair not to let him join us. I told you about the time Jon-Jon met Pelle and had a long chat with him. It was when he was reading Gurdjieff, Koestler and Huxley, and before he was back here in Lofoten, where he finally got in touch with reality.

You asked to speak to Pelle again, and, stronger than before, I felt a stab of jealousy.

As we sat between the gravestones, I thought again of Jon-Jon, Sverre and Marianne, once a love triangle amid the greenery, just like us today, more than forty years later. Sverre betrayed his best friend and took the love of his life away from him. But Marianne also betrayed.

I would never have been able to bring this up myself, especially not as we sat there by Jon-Jon's

grave. It was Pelle who soon expressed his feelings
of shame and guilt over the fact that you openly
displayed much greater interest in him than in me.
Since it was Pelle you were talking to at that point,
you were particularly open-hearted – I could have
written ruthless – not towards Pelle, of course, but
towards me.

Pelle tried once again to bring us together: he
made an Ibsen-esque attempt to confront us like
two castaways, and his thoughtfulness was incredibly touching, but you were unmoved. It was nice to
meet Jakop again, you repeated, but you had a right
to favour Pelle. That's exactly what you said. Admittedly, you finished with a charming laugh, but those
were your very words. You didn't give me any false
hope. Neatly done.

Sometimes, an actor enters into a role that is
bolder than he is, you explained. An artwork can be
more sublime than the sum of its materials, and any
work of art can surpass its creator. But in such cases
the creator also deserves to be acknowledged.

At that point in this intimate chat between Pelle
and you, you took your eyes off him for once, and let
them settle on me for a second or two as you placed
a hand on my right knee – we were sitting after all
almost like flower children in the grass in front of
Jon-Jon's grave. Something similar had happened

when you'd talked to Pelle in Arendal. I was about to start the car and had my hand on the gearstick. For a second your hand lay on mine. I have difficulty forgetting these things.

We put Pelle back in the knapsack, walked through the churchyard to the highway and further on up the slope and down to Kabelvåg where we'd planned a late lunch. You'd slept little the previous night, because you hadn't managed to accustom yourself to the round-the-clock daylight, while I'd slept much too heavily, and we were in agreement that this extensive lunch we were now consuming would serve as both lunch and dinner. We'd already arranged with the hotel that they would make up the side room for you.

While we were walking, I thought about something I'd spent a lot of time wondering these past years. And at last I asked you, though not as directly as Pelle might have done. I asked why you'd stopped me leaving Bakkekroen. After all, that was long before you'd met Pelle.

You smiled mysteriously, and I couldn't understand why. I couldn't figure it out. But then you explained.

You told me you'd already been struck at the memorial service by my extraordinary ability to be someone other than myself, and in a way *more* than myself. You said that I'd got into the role of Grethe Cecilie's affable friend so well that I myself was taken aback by the things I was saying. It had been as though I was delirious, speaking in some kind of peculiar rapture, almost as though I was speaking in tongues. And you saw that as a parallel to the way I'd given Pelle free reign to be an independent individual. And that was the reason you'd asked me to tell you more about my walking trip with Grethe Cecilie in the car back from Arendal – to get more of that. You wanted me back in the role you'd so enjoyed at the memorial service. It was these sides of me – as Pelle, and as Grethe Cecilie's walking partner – that made you want to sit with me the whole way back to Oslo.

We talked about that for a long time. You said you stopped me leaving Bakkekroen because you wanted to get to know me a little better, or to observe me more closely, as you were disrespectful enough to express it. Because the psychotherapist in you also found it interesting to speak to me. In the car home from Arendal you wanted to make the most of the opportunity to get closer to Pelle and me. Together, we constituted an interesting 'complex'. You said that. Complex.

And there was one more thing. At the memorial

service for Andreas, you saved me from losing face, and that too was before you'd met Pelle. Just as convincingly, you assured everyone we'd come to the southern town together.

When I mentioned that, you smiled too. You said you'd come to my aid because you realised I'd backed myself into a corner. After claiming that I'd come to the funeral as your companion, you confided, you'd felt obliged to do a spot of ringing round once you were back in Oslo.

To everything there is a season, as it says in Ecclesiastes. And now it was time for a retraction.

A spot of ringing round, I thought. So, that was that.

But I thought it rather shoddy.

We took the last slopes down towards Kabelvåg. I was having a bad day, and still felt I was speaking dully, you too were worn out, you told me as much, but at this point it seemed you were as free and fluent in your speech as you were when talking to Pelle.

I tried to take in what you'd actually said. In as many words, I was just a shadow of the impressive man who'd walked down through Aurlandsdalen with your sister, and who'd so vividly depicted Grethe Cecilie and her doctoral thesis. As myself, I was both timid and repressed, not even a pale imitation of my own hand puppet.

I was no more than a prerequisite for Pelle's ability to sparkle with life and spontaneity. I could claim no more credit for Herr Skrindo than the black earth could for a rosebush. Without the soil no rose could bloom, but that was all it was good for.

As I write this, it occurs to me that I have written about roses elsewhere in this text. When I lived as a flower child, I happened to point out a rosebush and pronounce a few words from the *Upanishads*: *tat tvam asi*, I said. 'That is you!'

I've always held that Pelle and I are two separate people, and I've been careful to emphasise Pelle's autonomy. But based on the Advaita philosophy, I would also be completely within my rights if I were to pull Pelle over my arm, point at him and say that he was me. Deep down, Pelle *is* me, and I am Pelle, just as we are all the world we live in, the air we breathe and exhale. Perhaps it's difficult to process, but it necessarily follows from the Vedanta philosophy's principle of *advaita*, or 'not-two'. The fact that Pelle is not me, and that I am not Pelle, depends only on an illusion, a trick, *maya*.

I wonder if I'll ever manage to convince you

of this. Perhaps one day I'll try it, but I doubt I'll succeed.

You only see the rose, not the ground that gives the rose life. You see the puppet on the master's arm, but you have no eye for the puppet master.

We sat in the pleasant restaurant down on the main square in Kabelvåg, ordered food and wine, and only then did you tell me about your idea. It seems I'd passed an informal exam that afternoon – which was something at least.

You've worked with puppet theatre all your life. You've used puppets in a therapeutic context too. And now you wanted to take Pelle, and me of course, to a kind of puppet theatre festival in Slovakia. You'd travelled from Stamsund to talk to Pelle and me about this, and time was almost up. If anything was to come of it, we would have to travel from Oslo to Bratislava the day after tomorrow.

You asked if I spoke German. I'd drunk a few glasses of white wine, and so I threw my arms wide: '*Aber natürlich, beliebte Frau!*' That's what I said. And I think you liked the fact I was getting back on form.

You asked about Pelle. Was he also confident in German?

I laughed. I don't know if I've laughed so much for a long time. I told you Pelle was much better at German than me. He doesn't even have to stop and think, I said. Cases and conjunctives flow like a dream, it just runs right out of him.

My good mood infected you too, and I confided in you that I loved speaking German, but that I tried to avoid doing so when I had Pelle on my arm. Pelle just kept interrupting me with irritating interjections because I'd miss a dative or a conjunction.

We took a taxi back to Svolvær, and now the atmosphere was cheerful. The glasses of white wine had settled like balm on the wounds from the previous day's whisky bottle. You didn't ask for Pelle to come up from the bag again that evening.

At the hotel you went straight to bed. You've already been sleeping for many hours, and I've once again been sitting bent over my laptop, trying to finish my story.

So now it's your turn, Agnes. When you read these lines, you'll know who I am. I've decided that you'll get the chance to read the whole thing when you wake up tomorrow. The last thing I'll do before going to bed is to send this whole chronicle over to your tablet.

If, after reading it all, you still think I'm worthy, I'd be happy to come with you to Slovakia the day after tomorrow. Pelle is looking forward to the trip; you'd expect nothing less. I think he's a lucky guy. From a tombola at a country fair in Hol, all the way to Bratislava, is quite the journey for a hand puppet.

Pelle has promised to behave as well as he can. But as you've already seen, I can't promise anything on his behalf. Were that not the case, I don't suppose you'd have fallen so hard for the guy.

It's Pelle you adore, not me. I've come to accept that now. Please don't feel any guilt in this matter. I'll be rooting for the two of you.

Let Jostein Gaarder introduce you to another magical heroine in

The World According to Anna

When fifteen-year-old Anna begins receiving messages from another time, her parents take her to the doctor. But he can find nothing wrong with Anna; in fact he believes there may be some truth to what she is seeing.

Anna is haunted by visions of the desolate world of 2082. She sees her great-granddaughter, Nova, in a wasteland peopled by ragged survivors, after animals and plants have died out.

The more Anna sees, the more she realises she must act to prevent the future in her visions becoming real. But can she act quickly enough?

Haunting, gripping and magical, *The World According to Anna* is a fable for our time.

A beautifully designed 20th anniversary edition of *Sophie's World* with a new introduction by the author.

The perfect gift for anyone yet to discover this phenomenal novel, which has been translated into 60 languages and has sold over 40 million copies worldwide.

'A unique popular classic'
The Times

'It should be read by all'
Vogue

'A modern fairy tale'
Heat

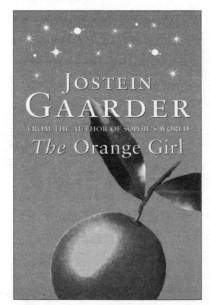

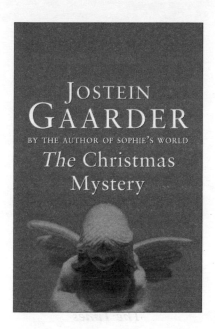

'A perfect Christmas tale'
The Times

'Anyone who enjoyed
Jostein Gaarder's
philosophical bestseller
Sophie's World will relish
The Christmas Mystery'
Sunday Times

'A masterful mixture of
fantasy and reality ...
a simply wonderful read'
She

'*The Ringmaster's Daughter*
confirms [Gaarder's] status
as one of Scandinavia's finest
literary exports and as a
novelist and storyteller of
outstanding calibre'
Herald

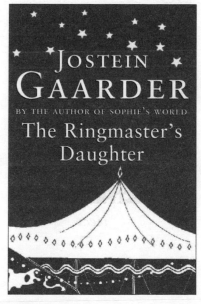

Available now in paperback and ebook